Aaron Hartzler

WHAT WE SAW

HARPER TEEN
An Imprint of HarperCollinsPublishers

HarperTeen is an imprint of HarperCollins Publishers.

What We Saw
Copyright © 2015 by HarperCollins Publishers
All rights reserved. Printed in the United States of America.
No part of this book may be used or reproduced in any manner whatsoever without written permission except in the case of brief quotations embodied in critical
articles and reviews. For information address HarperCollins Children's Books, a
division of HarperCollins Publishers, 195 Broadway, New York, NY 10007.
www.epicreads.com

Library of Congress Cataloging-in-Publication Data
Hartzler, Aaron.
    What we saw / Aaron Hartzler. — First edition.
        pages   cm
    Summary: "The story of a town torn apart by the events surrounding the
rape of a drunk girl at a house party, from the perspective of the partygoers who
witnessed it"— Provided by publisher.
    ISBN 978-0-06-233874-7 (hardback) — ISBN 978-0-06-243062-5 (int. ed.)
    [1. Rape—Fiction.   2. Witnesses—Fiction.]   I. Title.
PZ7.1.H377Wh   2015   2015005619
[Fic]—dc23   CIP
                                                                      AC

Typography by Brad Mead
15 16 17 18 19   CG/RRDH   10 9 8 7 6 5 4 3 2 1
❖
First Edition

For Rachel Parker, the first person who showed me what it meant to be both a feminist, and a writer.

For Kim Turrisi, who reminds me to #gallop.

And for every "Stacey" whose story was never told.

WHAT WE SAW

one

THIS VIDEO DOESN'T show you everything.

For instance, you can't tell that it's been raining or that the grass is still wet beneath our cleats. I'm five years old in the shaky footage, which was shot before you could make a video using your phone. I pull out Dad's old camera every once in a while and watch my first game. This tape from twelve years ago is always inside when I do. Nobody else has used this weird little machine with the flip-out screen for a long time. Back then, Dad says every gadget had a single purpose: Phones were for making calls, video cameras were for shooting videos.

Soccer games were for making friends. At least that's what Mom said to me when she French-braided my hair the morning this video was made. I was nervous because it was my first game, and I wanted to do a good job.

"I don't want to mess up," I told her.

"It's okay if you mess up," she said. "Everybody does. All you can do is try your best."

I told Mom that Ben didn't ever mess up. She asked who Ben was as she twisted an elastic onto the end of my braid.

"My friend."

You never see Dad on-screen, but his is the only voice you can hear clearly most of the time. He was holding the video camera in one hand and an umbrella in the other. You can't see Will, either, but you can hear him fussing in Mom's arms every time Dad stops shouting.

My father yelled himself hoarse that morning: "Hustle, Kate!" "Atta girl!" He cheered me on while I did what five-year-olds playing soccer tend to do: chase the ball around the field in a giant herd. All the good intentions and sideline instructions from the coach to "play your position" and "hang back" are no match for the thrill of seeing the ball bounce your way, the hope for a clear shot, the rush of true connection.

The moment when Ben breaks away from the pack with the ball still makes me smile. He was a couple inches shorter than I was back then. He didn't pass me up until the summer before seventh grade. As he taps the ball out ahead, I turn on the speed and run at his heels, just the two of us leaving the group, my braid flying behind us. Dad yells his head off behind the camera and the picture bounces wildly as he jumps up and down, then remembers he's filming this and zooms in on us.

If you look closely, you can see Ben's tongue sticking out of his mouth slightly, pressed against his lower lip, his forehead wrinkled in concentration as he exhibits the early makings of a great athlete: control, stamina, dexterity. Of course, he's only five years old. This brief glimpse of what Ben will one day be goes down in flames as the ball hits a bump in the field, bounces up against his knee, and trips him. Not a major error, but he goes down hard. His feet were in the wrong place at the wrong time.

I pause the playback at this point and wish that all of life could work the way this camera does.

Sometimes, things happen too fast.

On the screen, my five-year-old self is frozen in mid-stride, right foot raised. My body is still running as my brain attempts to adjust to the fact that Ben isn't where I saw him just a moment ago. In the next few frames, I'll scramble. I'll fight to stay upright. I push play and watch as young me tries to adjust, to not hurt Ben, attempting to keep my feet beneath me and avoid a collision.

Even now it makes my stomach drop when I see my right cleat clip Ben in the back of the head. I'll never forget that feeling, wheeling around and seeing the small stream of red trailing down the skin behind his left ear. I didn't do any major damage—just a cut near his hairline—but I didn't know that at the time. All I knew is I had kicked my friend in the head, and now he was bleeding. A couple of stitches fixed it right up. You can barely see the scar now. Unless you know where to look, you'll miss it completely.

As Dad runs toward me on the field, the sky and ground bounce back and forth across the frame. The picture goes still as he lays the camera in the grass. You can see a few blades of green and a wide patch of blue sky, the lens telescoping in and out as it attempts to focus on the goal and net beyond.

You can't see it on the tape, but Ben didn't shed a single tear. I was the one crying. "I hurt my friend. I hurt *my friend.*" I say this over and over again.

Sobbing into my father's shoulder, I felt a hand on my back. It was Ben. Suddenly, his mother was there. Coaches and team-mates surrounded us. His forehead was creased once more, but this time because he was worried about me. The camera picked up his voice. Over my sobs, you can hear him saying, "It's okay. It's going to be fine."

What you don't see is that Ben has wrapped both arms around me and is patting me on the back. What you can't learn from watching is that this was the moment when I knew for the first time what it really means to have a friend. What this tape can never show you is the instant I first felt true connection.

And in that sense, this video doesn't show you anything at all.

two

I'VE BEEN WORKING up the courage to open my eyes again.

I tried once about ten minutes ago. Stab of light. Vise on my brain. Jackhammer in my stomach. Deep breaths. *Don't throw up.*

Lately, I've been having these moments where I examine my life and think, *Kate Weston, how did you get here? How did this happen?* Sometimes it's a situation so excellent I'm convinced I did something truly selfless in a past life to gain the extreme good fortune of my present.

This is not one of those situations.

When I woke up, I was pretty sure I'd managed to park the

old pickup I inherited from Dad last year on top of my own head. A glimpse of the curtains as the room spun by confirmed I'm in my bedroom and not in the driveway. This allowed me to rule out a dinged-up Chevy Silverado as the source of my pain and work backward through the events of last night to find the true cause. I did so while holding one pillow over my head and moaning, facedown, into another. After several minutes of deliberation, I'm pleased to announce I've reached a verdict:

I blame John Doone's grandma.

If Betty Lee Troyer hadn't decided to try sushi for the first time at a mall food court in Grand Island, Nebraska, a few days before Christmas, she wouldn't have spent the last two weeks of December in the hospital. If her mother hadn't been in the hospital, Margie Doone wouldn't have postponed the family ski trip until spring break so she could rush to Grand Island. If the Doones had gone skiing over Christmas instead of spring break, John would've gone with them. Instead, he stayed home alone so he wouldn't miss the final basketball practices before the state tournament. If John hadn't had the house to himself, he never would've been allowed to throw a party that inspired its own hashtag. And if there had been no party last night, I wouldn't have lost count after three shots of tequila, and wound up lying here terrified to open my eyes again.

I waver back and forth between the fear of dying and the fear that I will not die—that instead this pain will continue indefinitely. There are a few snapshots of last night in my head— animated GIFs at the very best. No video so far. The only thing

I remember for sure is more of a feeling than a conversation.

Something about Ben.

His arm around my waist, propping me up. His hand in the pocket of my shorts, fishing for my keys. His breath on my neck as he said he wasn't letting me drive my truck home. I know we were on the sidewalk, but I can't remember what I said back to him. Maybe "thank you"?

His cheek against mine. Spring breeze. Goose bumps. That grin.

"Sure," he whispered. "What are friends for?"

I do remember one thing for certain: Ben, leaning in toward me. So close our foreheads touch. Closer than we've been in a long time.

It was different.

It was more.

More than chivalry. More than playing soccer as kids. More than just friends. The certainty of this is a laser, slicing through the thick fog of too much tequila. I replay the scene. This time I remember how close his lips were to mine.

And the hiccups.

The first one occurred at exactly that moment, his forehead resting against mine. Any other girl in any other town in any other state on any other sidewalk with any other guy—that's a sure bet, right? I mean, forehead to forehead? You just close your eyes and lean in.

Not me.

Nope, one inch from the lips of a guy who's had a few beers

on a night when Coral Sands, Iowa, is the center of the universe? Kate Weston comes through with the hiccups. Just the way I roll.

He laughed as he pulled away, taking my keys with him.

Shit. The truck.

Did Ben drive me home in *my* truck or his? This thought pulls me into a panic. My stomach rolls like a ship in heavy seas, threatening to crest my tongue and spill across the rug. If I left my truck across town, I won't have to worry about the alcohol killing me. My father will be happy to assist.

My phone chirps and flaps across the nightstand, a rooster that's been crowing for the last ten minutes. Each new alert sends a rattle through the fossils I've arranged there, little petrified skeletons, three of the specimens for geology that Ben and I collected last fall. Who knew Rocks for Jocks would get us talking again? Eyes still closed, my fingers fumble for the phone, knocking a piece of coral to the carpet. Finally, I squint at the screen. Seven texts from Rachel Henderling.

The last one is a picture of me from last night.

It isn't pretty.

I appear to be a member of the Cross-Eyed Zombie Invasion. There is a strand of my own hair stuck in the corner of my mouth, and my arm is thrown around Stacey Stallard's shoulders like she's my best friend.

We're both holding tiny glasses upside down, and there's a strange green stripe, which I can only hope is a lime, peeking out from between my lips where my teeth should be. Stacey's eyes are wild and her cheeks are flushed, but a big smile is plastered across her face. If it weren't for the bottle of Cabo Wabo tequila on the Doones' kitchen island, she might be standing at the top of a mountain after a brisk hike, a cold wind in her face.

I just look trashed.

The phone buzzes in my hand. Rachel again:

My phone rings the moment I press send.

"Good morning, sunshine!" Rachel's voice is so perky I wince.

"What the hell are you doing up so early?" I croak.

"Those preschoolers don't teach themselves Sunday school."

"Will you be teaching them to make the margaritas you mixed last night?"

Rachel giggles. "You're the one who switched to shots."

"Which I would not have done if that margarita hadn't gotten me hammered. I can't believe they let you step foot in that church."

"Please. Even Jesus turned water into wine. If I can find a guy who performs that miracle, I'll never let him leave."

A guy.

Leaving.

My truck.

Jumping out of bed, I pause only briefly to adjust myself to the fresh hell of standing upright. "Shit."

Rachel scolds me for my language on the Lord's day. I would usually retort that he is her Lord, not mine, but right now I need all potential deities on my team.

Running down the hall to Will's room, I blow past our family Wall of Fame. Fifth-grade me leers back from a gallery frame: braces, shin guards, rubbery sports glasses strapped across the wavy hair bursting from my braid in all directions. Over the past few years, my exterior has been transformed by contact lenses and a flat iron, but most days I'm still surprised not to see that little mess in the mirror.

Will's bed is empty, and I scale a mountain range of high-tops and basketball jerseys like the Von Trapps escaping over the Alps. The window in his room faces the driveway, and as I pull back the curtain, I take in the glorious vision of my truck parked at the curb.

"Yes!" I hiss this at the phone while performing an unplanned fist pump that sends an electric shock through my forehead, as my stomach reels in a hoedown of misery.

"What?" Rachel is confused.

I take a deep breath and grasp the back of the chair at Will's desk, trying to persuade my insides not to rebel. "I wasn't sure how I got home. I guess Ben drove me back here in my truck?"

"Uh, yeah. He was gone from the party for like an hour. Must've walked back."

"Wait, he went back to the party?"

"The night was still young. You were toast by ten forty-five."

"Again, your fault."

"Whatever. I left a little before midnight. Ran into Ben coming up the Doones' driveway. Oh—" She pauses.

"What?" I ask.

"Just a tweet. Looks like we aren't the only ones who had fun last night." She giggles. "And there are some Instagram pictures to prove it."

"Who is it?"

"Crap. Gotta go. I have to get there a few minutes early so I can make copies of the coloring sheets. Text you later." Rachel yells down the hall for her mom to hurry, and my phone beeps that the call has ended.

"How you feeling, rock star?"

Will is standing in the doorway. He's wearing the shiny gray basketball shorts he sleeps in and stretching, his fingers hooked onto the top of the doorframe. I am briefly dumbfounded. When did he get that tall? His hair is doing its own electromagnetic experiment, and as I take a step toward him, I trip on a pair of Nikes and collapse onto his bed with a groan.

He laughs. "That good, huh?"

Will slips into the room and closes the door behind him, gingerly sitting next to me so as not to bounce my head. A blurred memory of slipping past him in the hallway last night flashes before my eyes.

"You're not gonna tell Mom and Dad, are you?"

"Depends . . ." There's a smirk in his voice. I squint at him through my headache.

"On what?" I try to affect my imperial Katherine the Great voice. He's not buying it.

"On whether you take me with you next time."

It takes every ounce of strength I can muster to sit up, grab a pillow, and swing it at Will. He catches it easily with one hand and tosses it back at me. We both laugh, me grasping at my head and begging him to make it stop.

"You were pretty wrecked last night," he says. "I think I should chaperone next time." Ignoring him, I gingerly pick my way across the mounds of stuff between me and the door. He jumps up and clears a path. "Please?"

I stop and try to press one of his enormous cowlicks down on the side of his head. It springs back like a hydra—messier, angrier. "Let's see if I survive *this* time."

A grin spreads across his face. "That's not a no . . ."

I laugh, and give him a little push so I can get to the doorknob. "I'll think about it. Just don't tell Mom and Dad."

"What are you doing today?"

"First, Advil. Then, a shower. I haven't allowed myself to dream beyond that."

Will smiles as I step into the hall. "Brush your teeth," he whispers. "You smell like the bar at Don Chilitos."

I try to punch him in the arm, but he dodges and pulls

the door closed. Off balance, I stumble gently into the Wall of Fame, narrowly avoiding a collision with a picture of me and Ben. We are in second grade, standing in the front yard, soaking wet. I am wearing a red swimsuit with white polka dots. Ben has on little board shorts covered in cartoon monkeys. I should text him to say thank you for getting me home, but back in my bedroom my fingers pause over the screen, and I toss the phone on my bed. Something about that shot of us in the hall changes my mind. If I can rally after my shower, I'll go over to his house and offer my gratitude in person.

Still smiling about the picture, I gulp down three ibuprofen, holding my hair out of the sink and slurping straight from the tap. We were playing "rainstorm on the beach" the day that shot was taken. Mom had put the sprinkler next to the sandbox, and Ben tried to explain what it felt like when the surf boils over your toes.

Stepping into a steaming shower, I remember the question I asked him that day. *Can you see all the way to the other side?*

He answered me with wide blue eyes and awe in his voice.

There's only one side. The waves go on forever.

three

IOWA WAS ONCE an ocean.

Sounds crazy, I know, but it's true. Three hundred and seventy-five million years ago, there were no cornfields. Only a large, shallow sea filled with trilobites and mud worms and prehistoric fish, all splashing around in the soup, trying to turn their fins into legs—probably so they could walk to California before the ice age hit.

After surviving this winter, I understand that urge. Sometimes we have snow in March, but today the sun is warm on my face, and I'm glad I'm walking over to Ben's instead of driving. It'll take twenty minutes, and after this year's deep freeze, the last week of upper sixties has felt like a heat wave. It's supposed to be seventy-one degrees this afternoon—practically bikini weather. I want to soak up every ray I can. Turning the corner at the end of our block, I stare up the gentle slope of Oaklawn Avenue and try to imagine my landlocked farm town as an ancient tropical paradise.

Mr. Johnston explained all of this last fall, the very first week of geology. Rachel's hand flew up as soon as he said the words *Devonian Era*. I knew what was coming before she opened her mouth. She's my best friend, but a true forward: aggressive on the field and off. The only things Rachel loves more than scoring are the fight to get the ball, and her Lord and Savior, Jesus Christ.

"Isn't it true that this is all just a *theory*, Mr. Johnston?"

"Just a theory?"

"This whole three hundred and seventy-five million years ago thing. I mean, no one was around to see that. There's no proof."

Mr. Johnston turned thirty on the first day of school. I always forget how crystal clear his green eyes are until he pulls off his funky horn-rimmed glasses, which he did right then.

"Is that the point of science?" he asked Rachel. "Proof?"

"Well, yeah," she said. "Isn't that why we observe stuff? To prove theories are right or wrong? That's why all this evolution stuff is just a theory. Because you can't observe when the world began, so you can't prove it."

"There's no such thing as a 'proof' in science," Mr. Johnston said, and put his glasses back on. "You can have a proof in math or in logic, but not in science. Anybody tell me why?"

Lindsey Chen tucked a strand of hair behind her ear and raised her hand. She's a defender on the field, always a surprise to the opposing team. They write her off as a "little Asian girl" and are unprepared for her to be both fleet and fierce.

"Yes, Miss Chen?"

"Math and logic are closed systems. Like in algebra, there's only one possible answer to a problem. You solve for x."

Mr. Johnston nodded. "Exactly. There's no such thing as 'proving' something true or false with science. It all comes down to what we mean when we use that word *theory*."

He asked who could tell him the difference between a scientific theory and what most people mean when they say theory. Mr. Johnston pointed toward the back, and I swiveled around in surprise when I heard Ben's voice.

"I have a theory that the tacos in the cafeteria are made out of stray cats."

Mr. Johnston laughed along with the rest of us. "Yes! But is that a *scientific* theory, Mr. Cody?"

"Nope."

"Why not?"

Ben shrugged. "I don't have any observations to back it up. Just a hunch. Based on taste."

Mr. Johnston kept driving toward his point over the laughter. "And what do we call a 'hunch' in science? Anyone?" He pointed at me. "Kate?"

"A hypothesis?"

"Bingo! And how is an unproven hypothesis different from a scientific theory?"

Lindsey spoke up again. "A scientific theory is the best explanation for something based on all the evidence we have so far. You can use it to make predictions."

"Very good." Mr. Johnston smiled, mission accomplished. "Remember that words have specific meanings depending on context. When we say that evolution is a 'scientific theory' we mean it's the most likely explanation—the one strongly supported by all of our observations of the natural world."

Rachel was waving her hand like a castaway in choppy water. "Yes, Rachel?"

"But nobody was here three hundred and seventy-five million years ago to observe anything. So, how can we say that Iowa used to be an ocean if no one saw that?"

"We observe the evidence." Mr. Johnston smiled. "Even if you don't witness an event firsthand, there's always plenty of evidence to be found."

Rachel rolled her eyes. "Like what?"

Mr. Johnston passed around eighteen plastic buckets, assigned partners at random, and sent us out to look for coral fossils in a ditch behind the school—roughly twelve hundred miles from the nearest ocean.

I can hear the basketball pinging on Ben's driveway from half a block away. Pausing at the corner of the front hedge, I watch him shoot free throws. He is sweaty and shirtless.

It is unseasonably warm.

Bounce-bounce.

Bounce-bounce.

He spins the ball to his hip, then squares and shoots.

Thwfft.

Precision, timing, balance, concentration: Ben in his natural habitat.

Until that day in the ditch during Mr. Johnston's class last fall, neither of us realized we'd stopped speaking beyond a quick "hey, how's it going?"

It happened so slowly—us taking each other for granted. The ebb and flow of our separate lives became a steady current, carrying us toward different pursuits.

Ben shot up almost a foot the summer after sixth grade and traded his cleats for high-tops. The promise of Hawkeye basketball has a chokehold on this town, and any boy who crests six feet in seventh grade is drafted without mercy. The Friday night lights on the Coral Sands football field in October can't hold a candle to the ones in the gymnasium come December. Our football team has never done very well, and soccer is fine for girls, but varsity basketball? They get all the glory—and, lately, the Division 1 scouts.

Ben and I were still in classes together, but over time the familiar has a way of getting covered up by layer after layer of life, the everyday sediment of homework and practice and parties and who eats lunch where. Our moms talked a lot when his dad filed for divorce a couple years ago, but I didn't know how to bring it up with Ben. I'd wanted to tell him that I was here for him, that I missed him, but it seemed weird to walk up and say, "Heard your parents are splitting up." So, we just continued to nod at each other as we passed in the hallway.

Maybe digging around in the dirt made us remember being kids again. Whatever the reason, tromping through that culvert out behind the school last September, all of the ease I used to have with Ben came flooding back. It only took five minutes, and we were laughing like six-year-olds at soccer practice.

I read a novel last summer, and there was a scene where two people saw each other again after a long absence. The author wrote, "It was as if no time had passed at all." At the time, I wondered how that could be. There's no way to stop time from passing or people from changing. Ben's most rapid and dramatic change had been his height—practically overnight—but lots of other changes had been more subtle. In many ways, Ben had grown up right in front of me, only I hadn't been paying attention. I'd missed all the tiny changes because they'd occurred so slowly.

We learned last year in biology that the cells in our bodies are completely replaced by new ones every seven years. Ben and I are literally different people now than we were as children—fundamentally changed on a molecular level.

As we dug around that ditch, I saw how broad his shoulders had become, how his biceps stretched the sleeves of his clingy gray T-shirt. An eon's worth of natural selection had come to pass. The boy who used to be shorter than me now towered overhead at six feet, four inches. Those years between twelve and sixteen might as well have been the Paleolithic Period.

That afternoon, Ben held the bucket while I brushed off tiny bits of ancient history, but we unearthed more than a few hunks of limestone for Mr. Johnston's class. As Ben bent to grab one last piece of coral, I glimpsed the scar behind his ear, and when I saw it, a tremor fluttered through my chest.

A tiny seismic shift.

The layers inside me got all stirred up that day.

I uncovered something beautiful buried deep within my heart, and realized it had been there all along.

four

BEN DOESN'T MISS a single shot—even when I call his name. He grabs his own rebound, then turns to face me with a grin.

"She lives."

I cross my arms. "Disappointed?"

He bounces the ball in my direction. I catch it and slowly dribble in place without looking at my hands, daring him. He stands between the basket and me, smiling and nodding. "Okay, then. Show me whatcha got."

I drop back like I'm going to take the shot, then try to fake him out and drive around him.

As if.

In a single step, he's cut me off, his stance wide and low, his arms over his head, blocking my layup. It's a textbook illustration of that chant the cheerleaders do: *Hands up. Defense.*

Of course, I realize this too late. I'm already jumping toward the basket. I can't stop my forward momentum, but Ben's leg does, and in a flash I'm sailing headfirst toward the pole that holds the backboard aloft.

I close my eyes and brace for impact. Instead, my body is suddenly redirected. Ben's arm snakes around my waist and pulls me sideways into him. When I open my eyes, his face is inches from mine.

"Gotcha, hotshot."

I'm still off balance. Ben is the only thing holding me up—like it's nothing, as if I were made of pure air. His arm is solid in the small of my back, the grip of his hand at my waist steady and sure. I'm not going anywhere.

We are pressed together so tightly he must be able to feel my heart beating against his chest. Each breath I exhale bounces off his neck and back into my face. I make a mental note to thank Will for reminding me to brush my teeth.

I arch an eyebrow. "That was a foul."

Ben laughs. "Yep. On you." He gently sets me upright, and goes to grab the ball from the grass next to the driveway. "We call that charging."

I can still feel the heat where his arm roped my waist. The scent of his skin lingers in my nose—a whisper of the cologne he wore to the party last night: fresh oranges and pepper and smoke from a campfire.

"No way. You fouled me. And you almost brained me on that pole."

Ben bounces the ball between his legs as he walks. "I was in a legal defensive position."

"Oh, is that what we call 'cheating' these days?"

He's close again, spinning the ball on his index finger, a challenge in his smirk. He palms the ball and holds it over my head. I try to grab it but he is too quick. He swings it low, and high again, then whips it around his back and tosses a perfect hook shot through the net. *Thwfft*. No rim. Barely looked.

"Don't hate the player. Those are the rules. I was set and you made contact."

"I'll show you contact." I charge him with a growl.

He yelps and turns to protect his rebound as I jump on his back, throwing my arms around his neck. I try for a headlock, but I'm weightless to him. He clamps his arms over my legs and takes off. I hang on for dear life as he swings me around in circles. My stomach gets woozy again, and we laugh like crazy people.

He skids to a halt under the hulking oak tree in his front yard, both of us giggling and panting. Dizzy, I slide from my perch. As I slip down his back, my eyes find the scar behind his ear. In a flash, I am seized by the urge to brush my lips against it.

I didn't mean to feel this way about Ben. I thought it was

a fluke when it started last September—something that would fade away. Like the tan I got on Labor Day, I assumed it would be gone by October. I thought I could control it. Cover it back up like my freckles—toned down with some foundation, hidden with a little powder. I'd always planned to choose the person I fell in love with.

I didn't know it doesn't work that way.

You were once my friend.

Iowa was once an ocean.

Given enough time, everything changes.

I hover there in midair. I can't say it yet—but maybe he knows already. I reach out and lightly trace the scar with the tip of my finger, then my sneakers hit the grass, and I am back on earth.

Ben touches the place behind his ear and shakes his head. "The first time you fouled me."

"It was an accident," I protest, but his eyes snap and crackle above his smile. His laugh spills across the space between us.

He looks up into the bare branches over our heads, and when he turns back to me, his face is dead serious. "You've always had it out for me, Weston."

What are we talking about now?

He turns and walks back toward the driveway. All at once my legs have gone wobbly. "It's just that . . ." I follow him, my throat suddenly stuffed with cotton.

Ben picks up his orange T-shirt off the ground, but instead

of putting it on, he tucks the hem into the waistband of his shorts. "It's just that what?" he asks.

The air is thick between us. A system of high pressure threatens to flatten me into the driveway. I try to look anywhere but at Ben's body. There are crocuses shooting vivid leaves up through the dormant grass around the mailbox. The kids across the street and one house down hit a Wiffle ball into the neighbor's yard, then start yelling at each other—words their mothers wish they did not know.

All the words I know are jammed inside my brain trying to force themselves past my teeth. The muted trumpet of too much tequila squawks behind my eyes.

This is a first. I've never been tongue-tied around Ben Cody in the almost thirteen years I've known him. Have I always "had it out for him"? Or only since last fall? And how does he know?

The first two words that escape the logjam in my head are "Thank you."

"What?" He frowns and smiles at the same time.

I almost stutter, but I don't. I keep my eyes fixed on his. I will not embarrass myself further by staring at the place where his T-shirt hangs from his waistband. "For inviting me to the party last night. For driving me home. Thank you. You didn't have to do that."

He grins. "*Somebody* did."

"Well, I'm glad it was you."

"Wasn't gonna trust any of those other yahoos."

There's a spark in his eye when he says it. This is our short-hand. *Yahoo* is my dad's word. When Ben and I were kids, if we were making too much noise while the Hawkeyes' game was on, Dad would bellow at us from the couch: *You two stop acting like a bunch of yahoos.*

I smile. This is what Ben does for me: He makes every-thing easy. Even as I'm standing here red-faced and worried, he's reminding me of all the reasons I shouldn't be. "Yeah, Dad woulda been pissed if I'd left my truck at the Doones'. Thanks for that, too."

"What are friends for?"

Crap. I was afraid of that. Clearly, I'm stuck in the friend zone.

I wonder if he remembers saying the same thing on the sidewalk last night. Him taking my keys, leaning in, touch-ing his forehead to mine. It seemed like so much more than "friends" to me. Was I the only one who felt it? A side effect of agave and lime?

Have I invented that moment? Or has he forgotten it?

I open my mouth to say something—anything—I have no idea what. I am out of my element, trying to reach a new dimension on old machinery, pedaling toward the Galaxy of Lovers on the Rusty Ten-Speed of Friendship. I feel certain I'll never even get off the ground.

Maybe the universe acts on my behalf, or Rachel's heavenly father intervenes, but before I can utter any word I may regret forever, Mrs. Cody's old Ford Explorer roars into the driveway. She screeches to a halt a few feet from Ben's knees, and mercifully, I am saved by Adele.

"Jesus, Mom!" Ben shouts through her rolled-down window. He jumps back, pulling me with him. "Coming in hot."

Adele Cody heaves herself from the car as if flames were licking the gas tank. She is wearing a neon-green tracksuit, and sprints around to the back where she pops the hatch, and begins jerking entire flats of a purple sports drink onto the driveway. "Gotta get to Hy-Vee and hit the Right Guard special before Esther Harris cleans 'em out. Hi, Katie!"

No one has ever called me "Katie" except Ben's mom and my dad.

Ben goes tense as he watches his mother's electric mop of auburn curls, bouncing around on the spring of her Zumba-coiled body.

Divorce sometimes turns the women of Coral Sands into shapeless prisoners of depression, a doughnut in one hand and a Diet Coke in the other. It took Adele Cody in the opposite direction. The summer after eighth grade, Ben's dad, Brian, attended a week-long convention in Omaha for the pharmaceutical company he reps. Over dirty martinis in the hotel bar, he met a regional manager from Lincoln named Linda and never returned. Within a month of signing divorce papers, Adele's transformation began. She renewed her certification as a paralegal that summer, and when Ben took the bus to our first day of freshman year, his mom took a job at the law firm owned by John Doone's dad.

Adele followed up gainful employment with a membership at the LadyFit Gym. There, she met a group of women who introduced her to the thrill of Latin dancersize and the rush of extreme coupon deals. By Christmas, she'd lost twelve pounds and found that the empty space in her two-car garage was the perfect place for eight aisles of utility shelving. In the years since, hours of online coupon swaps have created a stockpile of nonperishable goods that may prove handy if the rapture Rachel speaks of ever comes to pass.

Ben squints into the sky as if deliverance from the puzzle of his mother's addiction might indeed be coming in the clouds. I touch his back lightly without looking at him. He lets out a slow sigh. "Looks like we're filling the pool with Powerade," he whispers.

"C'mon." I take his hand and pull him behind me toward the back of the car. I used to drag him around like this when we were kids. Only now, I lace my fingers through his, brazen and bold. This is my answer to his earlier question. This is what friends are for.

"Let us help you with that, Mrs. Cody."

Adele claps her palms together, holding back the tips of her bejeweled manicure. "Oh, bless your heart, Katie." She jerks her chin at Ben. "This one just thinks I'm crazy."

I wrinkle my nose. "Well, this one needs all the free deodorant you can bring home."

Adele giggles as I slide a flat of Powerade out of her Explorer and plop it into Ben's arms, then tell him to wait while I give him another one. The combined weight of forty-eight twenty-ounce bottles makes every muscle in his arms and shoulders pop while he lugs them over to the growing stack at the edge of the drive.

"Benny, do you think you can get these into the garage for me? I have to hurry."

"Mom, we don't have room for all this crap."

"I cleared some space this morning," Adele says, digging through an accordion file. It is filled with stacks of coupons thick as paperbacks clamped with binder clips. "The shelf under the ramen and over the Tapatío."

Ben frowns. "But this is Powerade. *P* comes before *R*."

Adele waves a hand as she finds the stack for her next conquest, then runs back to the driver's seat. "*S* for 'sports drink,'" she calls out. "If we land some Gatorade next week I don't want it all on different shelves."

We stand aside as she screeches out of the driveway, blowing kisses and honking. In the silence that follows, Ben contemplates the stack of Powerade. It's the size of a small mastodon.

He groans. "Guess I'll get the dolly."

I stop him as he turns toward the garage. "Might as well take a couple with you."

He frowns as I drop one flat into his arms and bend down to grab another. "Why do I have to take two?"

"Part of the Powerade workout," I say with a smile.

"What are you gonna do while I haul these around?"

I want out of the friend zone and decide to go for broke. "Enjoy the view."

I think he starts to blush. I'm not sure because he turns around pretty fast and lugs those drinks up to the garage in record time.

five

BEN OFFERS TO drive me back to my place.

"What if your mom needs help with the Right Guard?" I'm only sort of joking.

"Can't handle the shame. Have to get out of here." He says this with a grim finality. I understand what he's talking about. He doesn't mean get out of here today, right now, this afternoon.

He means *get out of here*.

Forever.

We've talked about this more than once since we started hanging out again.

It was an accident that I saw his garage last fall. I'd come over to study for a geology test and arrived a few minutes before he came home from practice. Adele greeted me at the door and asked if I wanted a Diet Coke or a Coke Zero. In her excitement to serve me the Coke Zero I requested, she pulled me down the stairs to the garage entrance off the rec room of their raised ranch. While I was standing in that doorway Ben arrived and discovered me, slack-jawed, watching his mother slide a twelve-pack off the shelf just beneath CHARMIN and right above DRĀNO.

The first time I saw those perfectly packed shelves, I was seized by the urge to grab a canvas bag and do a supermarket sweep. From ballpoint pens and batteries to Post-its and Sticky Tack, Adele gave me the grand tour, tallying the money she'd saved and pointing out which products were the best deals. Most of the time, with double coupons and deals that "stack," she actually got money back. She'd haul out a colossal pile of product for free, and because of her coupons and the way the deals worked, the store would also pay her. I stared up in wonder that first afternoon, laughing in amazement as she explained her system.

I've only seen her in action for a few months, but I now know it's no laughing matter. Adele has a coupon compulsion, no doubt about it. She can't *not* do it. The urge to get the next deal overwhelms her to the point that she's missed several of Ben's games this year—not to mention moments like this one, when it might be nice to sit on the deck out back, have some iced tea, and hang out.

Instead, she's running for the Right Guard special. It has nothing to do with deodorant. It has to do with the fix she gets from the deal, the short-lived euphoria of the score. As we watch her screech around the corner onto Oaklawn, I wonder what it was that actually caused this malfunction in Ben's mom. Had it always lurked beneath the surface? Did the divorce just uncover it, buried beneath thick layers of "normal"?

As we climb into Ben's truck, he says, "Thanks for being cool about . . . all this."

I know that "all this" means his mom and her stockpile. I know that "being cool" means taking it in stride and not telling anyone at school. I also know how hard it is for him to talk about it.

Ben puts the truck in reverse but pauses, foot on the break, hands on the wheel. He glances over at me. "You really have to get home?"

"Eventually. No rush. Did you have a pressing errand with which you require my immediate assistance?"

He smirks at me and shakes his head.

"What?" I ask, blinking with wide eyes of false innocence.

"You," he says, "and your attempts to pepper all conversation with iambic pentameter."

"From the boy who just used *iambic pentameter* in a sentence, modified by the verb *pepper*."

"Touché."

"Conversational French. Further proving my point."

"It was *my* point," he says with a laugh.

I cross my arms. "Which was to mock me?" I love giving him a hard time.

"No! Just—it's nice not to have to dumb things down. It's one of the reasons I like talking with you: Your communication skills are both scintillating and exquisite."

"Wow!" I snort-laugh, which cracks him up. "Okay, now you need to cool your jets."

"Mmmm. Ice cream sounds perfect," he says. "I'd suggest Dairy Queen, but I think I'm too smart to be served there."

"Drive, Einstein. Your secret is safe."

six

WE CARRY DIP cones and French fries across the street to the park and plop down in the grass against a big tree near the jungle gym. A group of kids shriek from a spinning tire swing. Two little boys chase each other, scooping fistfuls of wood chips off the ground and chucking them at each other. Their dad shouts from a grill near the picnic tables that they should stop it. They ignore him.

Ben has nearly finished off the hard chocolate shell on his vanilla soft-serve and starts dipping French fries into the ice cream. We sit in silence, letting the afternoon sun make us lazy. The quiet between us is different from the tongue-tied awkwardness I first felt just a half hour ago. Most of the time, I'm not frantic to invent conversation around Ben or worried about forcing words out if they won't come. I know he's cool just hanging out with our thoughts. Somehow, this makes me feel closer to him, not farther away.

I'm crunching the last bite of my ice cream cone when a group of guys start a pickup basketball game on the court by the parking lot, and I wonder aloud if Ben's heard from any scouts lately.

"Iowa and Indiana have been watching my clips online," he says. "Told Coach they're both sending people to see the tournament."

"Are you kidding? That's huge. You're only a junior."

He shrugs. "Don't know whether to feel relieved or guilty."

"Guilty?"

"About leaving her."

He's talking about Adele, and I proceed with caution, letting his remark sink in before I pursue it. "Is she collecting all that crap in case you don't get a scholarship? Stocking up now so she can spend all her money on tuition later?"

"Who knows? She's constantly afraid of not having enough cash, or enough . . . *anything*, ever since Dad took off."

I can feel the curtain fall in his voice. We never talk about his dad. Ever. It's as if Brian Cody never existed. "Ben, she *wants* you to go to college. She'll be so excited if you get a full ride."

"Just afraid I'll come home to shelves in every room. Whole damn place will be packed full of crap from Ajax to Zyrtec."

I squirt some ketchup across my fries, and wait. If he wants to tell me what that means he will. A guy on the basketball court yelps and goes down. The players gather around him as he rolls onto his back and grabs at his ankle.

"She's been hiding stuff in the house again."

I glance over at Ben, who keeps his eyes on the injured player. After a minute or two the guy's friends get him up off the ground, and he starts limping toward a bench between two buddies.

"I thought you said she agreed to keep all her bargains on the shelves in the garage."

"Oh, she did. Then the other day I walked by the guest room and the closet door was open a little. Whole thing was stacked with Rubbermaid bins packed full of tube socks and boxer briefs."

"For you?"

He sighs. "I can buy my own goddamn underwear."

A woman with a booming voice calls her kids to the picnic table. Ben chews his cheek, watching as they obey in double time. "I know I'm a total tool for feeling this way. It's just, Mom's obsessed. There's enough crap in the guest room to fill every sock drawer I own from now until I'm seventy."

"Maybe she's just trying to show you how much she cares about you."

"Maybe. But wouldn't it be better to show me she cares by sticking to our agreement? Those Rubbermaid bins aren't for me. They're for her."

"If you can nail down a scholarship do you think she'll chill out?"

He looks at me with a sad smile. "I don't think it works that way. Pretty sure I have zero power where this whole coupon-hoarding thing is concerned. It's like some bad reality show."

"I understand," I say. "Sort of. I mean, my parents have their own crazy. Dad makes bad bets in his fantasy football league with the guys on his construction crew, but he's always on my case about saving more money. Mom is always complaining about how she needs to lose ten pounds, but she'd rather try crazy diets than just eat more fruit and come running with me."

Ben smiles. "Remember when she did that grapefruit diet when we were in elementary school? Your dad told her if she didn't watch it she was gonna squirt herself in the eye every time she peed."

"She got so mad at him," I say. "And then at us because we couldn't stop laughing about it."

We both giggle at the memory. A breeze rustles the new buds on the elm branches above us and blows a strand of hair over my face. I reach up to brush it away.

"I like my mom and dad," I tell him, "but sometimes, I wish they'd admit they don't know everything."

"All parents have that thing they don't know about themselves," says Ben. "It's like a room they aren't aware exists. They don't know it's there, so they can't even look for the light switch."

Before I can agree, Ben tosses aside the DQ bag full of

empty fry boxes and ketchup packets. He stretches full length on the grass under the tree, lays his head on my leg, and closes his eyes.

The words on my tongue disappear. My first instinct is to run my fingers through his hair, but I stop my hand midair. It floats over his head for a second, before I press it against my lips, and slowly drop it back into the grass. I relax against the tree, attempting to breathe normally.

After a few minutes, my heart stops pounding. I can feel the weight of Ben's head pressed against my thigh, keeping me from floating away. The basketball game has resumed, minus one, and as I watch I realize how lucky I am that my parents and their crazy isn't so bad in comparison to Adele's. Losing fifty bucks or ten pounds isn't going to land you in a psychiatrist's office or take over your life. Still, it might be easier to relate if we could all just turn on the lights.

Of course, to them, we're just kids.

One day, they say, we'll understand.

But I wonder if maybe I'm the one who does understand.

Sometimes I get the feeling they've asked me to hold this big invisible secret for them, like a backpack full of rocks—all these things they don't want to know about themselves. I'm supposed to wear it as I hike up this trail toward my adulthood. They're already at the summit of Full Grown Mountain. They're waiting for me to get there and cheering me on, telling me I can do it, and sometimes scolding and asking why I'm not hiking any faster or why I'm not having more fun along the way. I know I'm not supposed to talk about this backpack full of their crazy, but sometimes I really wish we could all stop for a second. Maybe they could walk down the trail from the top and meet me. We could unzip that backpack, pull out all of those rocks, and leave the ones we no longer need by the side of the trail. It'd make the walk a lot easier. Maybe then my shoulders wouldn't get so tense when Dad lectures me about money or Mom starts a new diet she saw on the cover of a magazine at the grocery store.

The sun is hanging a little lower in the sky, and the guys on the basketball court haul their friend with the sprained ankle into a car as the mother at the picnic table packs up the leftovers. My leg is all pins and needles from the weight of Ben's head, and before I can talk myself out of it again, I run my fingers lightly through his hair. He stirs and opens his eyes.

"Did I go to sleep?" He rubs his eyes and yawns.

"Yeah. So did my leg."

He smiles and helps me up, grabbing our trash and tossing it in a barrel on the way back to his truck.

seven

AS WE DRIVE away from the park, Ben's phone rattles in the cup holder. The music from the playlist pauses as John Doone's picture pops up on the screen under the name "Dooney." Ben glances down and frowns.

"Want me to answer it for you?" I reach toward the phone, but Ben grabs it in a hurry and taps ignore. The music swells to full volume automatically.

"Nah—I'll call him back. Probably just woke up."

"How is he going to put his house back together before his parents come home?"

Ben smiles. "Deacon told him just to burn it down."

"Wish I could've stayed longer," I groan. "Was it fun after you dropped me off?"

Ben glances over at me, but I can't read what's behind his eyes. "Nothing's ever as fun without you there."

My stomach drops and I try to stop myself from staring at him. Too late. There is no oxygen in the cab of this truck anymore. Ben takes a big breath, then opens his mouth to speak. Only he doesn't speak. He bellows a song like one of those opera guys on PBS:

"*Yoooooooooou, light up my liiiiiiiiiife. Yoooooooooooou give me hoooooooope to carry ooooooooooooooooon—*"

I punch him in the shoulder. "Asshole."

He laughs. "No! Don't be pissed." I feel his hand on my knee and look back at him. He's smiling his Irresistible Grin. The one that made my mom sneak him an extra juice box back at age six when we had snacks after the game. *Some things never change.*

"Seriously," he says, turning onto Oaklawn. "Would've stayed at the party later if you'd been with me. Since you weren't, I walked back to get my truck and left."

"Oh. Rachel said she saw you coming in when she was headed out."

"Told Dooney bye. He and Deacon were wrecked by that point."

"Yeah, Rach sent me a picture, and—"

"Of what?"

There's an awkward pause. "Um . . . of me?"

"Oh, cool." He drums his thumbs on the steering wheel.

"It was *not* cool. I was blotto. Don't worry, I deleted it. Made Rachel delete it, too. I was doing shots with Stacey."

Ben turns up the volume and a male voice raps about girls in their bras and thongs falling at his feet like trees, "Timber." Ben taps along on the steering wheel as we pull down my street.

"Didn't remember Stacey even being there," I confess. "Until I saw the picture."

Ben shrugs and nods his head with the lyrics, *She say she won't, but I bet she will, timber.*

"I didn't know she hung out with Dooney much."

He glances over at me with a grin, turns down the music a little. "Sorry, what'd you say?"

Why am I talking about Stacey at a moment like this?

"Nothing."

Will is in our driveway shooting baskets, missing more than he's making. As we climb out of Ben's truck, I hear more rim than net—more *donk* than *thwfft*.

Ben's immediately in action, running into the drive, hands up. "Dude. I'm open."

Will tosses him the ball. Ben takes it down for a couple of through-the-leg dribbles, pivoting low as if he's being double-teamed in a tight imaginary defense. He drives to the basket and alley-oops, like he's going for a layup, but expertly hooks a pass to Will, who is caught completely off guard. My brother bobbles the ball and chases it into the grass.

"Awwww, man! Gotta be ready." Ben shakes his head. "Eyes on the ball, not on my face. I can make you think I'm headed one way with my eyes, but my hands and feet are busy doing something else."

There's a big brother friendliness about this chiding that makes Will nod and smile, and beg Ben to show him how he did that. Before long, Ben's shirt is off again, and the two of them are locked in a lopsided one-on-one—Will, losing, but triumphant. Court time with a starting junior is a rare commodity for a benchwarmer on the JV team.

Mom sits down next to me on the front porch steps. She offers me an open bag of gummy worms bearing a large green seal across the front that proclaims them to be FAT FREE!

I smile and try to look away, but she catches me and pokes me in the ribs. I jump and we both laugh. "Are you making fun of me?" she asks.

"Mom, *all* gummy worms are fat free. They always have been. Because they're made of corn syrup."

Her laugh is warm and breezy. She slides an arm around my shoulders. "Well, I'm certainly no scientist like you are, but at least they're not full of sugar *and* fat." She holds the bag toward me once more with a sly smile. "Every little bit helps, I always say."

I relent and pull out a red-and-green worm, then bite its head off. "I'm not a scientist," I say between chews. "I'm a soccer player."

"Oh yes. Yes, of course"—she gives me her mom version of side-eye—"I suppose that's why you've covered every horizontal surface in your bedroom with old rocks."

"Fossils, Mom. Those are corals."

She hands me another gummy worm, which I accept. Ice cream, French fries, and candy have helped my hangover immensely. "All I'm saying is, you can be both, you know. A soccer-playing scientist sounds fine to me."

She studies me for a moment as I watch Ben squatting low on defense. "Your powers of observation seem especially well tuned today."

I whirl to face her, and see a tiny smile and raised eyebrow. Before I can protest, she jumps up and cheers for Will, who has stolen the ball from Ben. He presses in a wide arc to the top of the driveway, trying to shake Ben, then abruptly pulls up for a jump shot. Ben is a split second late, and the ball barely clears the tips of his fingers as he leaps for the block. There is a *thwfft,* and then Will's unbridled hoot of joy.

"No way, dude!" Ben is as excited as Will. "Where the hell did that shot come from?" He holds up a hand and Will leaps to high-five him, both of them yelping. Ben turns to me. "Your bro is a freakin' pistol."

Will looks more like a balloon on the verge of exploding, his whole body puffed to the bursting point by Ben's praise. I know how much it means to him that Ben thinks he's got skills. He pushes his skinny chest out a little farther as he runs to get the ball.

"Don't brag on him too much," I warn. "His head gets any bigger, he'll float away."

Ben grabs my brother in a headlock and rubs his knuckles

across Will's hair. "Nah, we'll keep Pistol humble."

Will laughs and struggles free with a smile that's lit from within. He's in heaven. I've seen him aping what Ben and the rest of the guys on the varsity team do: haircuts, high-tops, slim shorts, baggy tank tops, Ben's side-swept bangs, a wristband pushed up by his elbow like Dooney, striped socks to his knees like Deacon. Now he's been handed the highest honor an upperclassman can bestow upon a humble frosh: the Nickname.

In an instant, I can see it all: Will's efforts to persuade me to bring him along to the next party will double. He followed me around for two weeks begging to go to Dooney's last night. Now I'll never hear the end of it. Still, there's something about the look on his face that pleases me. In this town basketball is king, and Will has just been made a squire to one of the knights at the round table.

Mom tosses me the bag of gummy worms with a grin and starts up the stairs to the front door. "Well, 'Pistol,' you can shoot right into the kitchen and help me set the table. Staying for dinner, Ben?"

"Sure."

She nods. "Nice having you around again. Put your shirt on and help Carl get the grill going."

If it were anyone else, I'd die a thousand deaths, but this is Ben and he knows my mom. She's a general in search of an army. As she disappears inside, she yells for my dad to get the charcoal out of the garage. He hollers something back, but we can only make out one word before the storm door snaps closed:

"...*yahoos*..."

Ben grins and pops his arms into his T-shirt before he whips it over his head. In that split second, I feel the comfort of his presence. It doesn't matter that he hasn't come to dinner for a long time. Now he's back—only new and improved.

It's as if no time has passed at all.

My phone buzzes as I climb into bed that night.

"Oh my god," groans Rachel. "I left you three voice mails."

I smile as I reach over and switch off the lamp. "You know I never check voice mail. You might as well write me a message, put it in a bottle, and throw it into the creek behind your house."

"Clearly," she says with a sigh. "One day, someone important is going to call you, and you're going to be sorry."

"Rachel, you *are* important. You're also the only person in the twenty-first century who still leaves voice mails."

"I sent texts and Facebook messages, too. Lindsey and Christy are on high alert."

"For what?"

"A search party."

"For whom?"

Rachel sighs. "For *you*, and your flawless pronoun usage. Where *were* you all day that you couldn't check your phone?"

While I was hanging out with Ben, I didn't think about reading texts or checking Facebook or Instagram or Twitter. Not at all. Not even once.

"I was ... busy."

Rachel knows I'm hedging. "With who?"

"Whom," I correct.

She yells *aaaaaaaaaargh* into the phone, prompting me to pull it a few inches from my face and laugh. "Lindsey says she saw you hanging out at the park with Ben."

My pulse speeds up. Who else saw us? I want to keep whatever this is between us for myself—at least until I know if we're more than friends.

"So if Lindsey saw me there, why are you calling to ask me where I was?"

Rachel is quiet for a moment. "Kate?"

"Yes?"

"Don't. Make. Me. Come. Over. There."

"What? We were just hanging out," I say matter-of-factly. "From time to time, we hang out. As is our custom. Since we were five years old."

"With his head in your lap?"

This is what we do, Rachel and I. It's why we're best friends. If it were up to her, even state secrets would be shared, thus causing disaster on a global level. If it were up to me, during said disaster we'd all die alone in the dark from lack of communication and basic resources. The simple fact of the matter is, we need each other. Still, I find a strange delight in making her pry the details out of me.

"I'm waiting," she reminds me.

"For what?"

She's all business. "Confirmation of head in lap."

"I will not stand for these wild allegations."

"Oh my god," she groans. "This isn't even the biggest story of the day, and you're making me work my butt off for it. You and Ben hanging out is like a blip on the scrolling ticker under the anchor's face on CNN."

"Fine," I relent. "I walked over to his house to say thank you for bringing me back home last night."

"Aaaaaand?"

"And we went to get ice cream and sat in the park."

"Kate, this will go faster if you just tell me all of the details at once."

I smile. "But I like hearing you beg."

"Okay," she says. "Then I have no choice. You're forcing me to do this."

"Do what?"

"If you don't spill it this instant, I will tell everyone in school that you are a National Merit Semifinalist, and then whatever this is that you have with Ben will be doomed because your secret genius will be known to all."

I start to giggle. Rachel is the only person who a) gives me ultimatums, and b) makes me laugh like a sixth-grader.

"Okay, okay! Uncle." I crack. "Ben put his head in my lap while we were talking, and then he fell asleep for a few minutes."

"That's it?" she asks.

"That's it."

"You didn't bore him to death with all your smarty-pants-ness, did you? Is that why he fell asleep?"

"No, Rach. Ben has a secret, too."

"Narcolepsy? I knew it. He could never stay awake in geometry last year."

"No." I laugh, and take a deep breath. "He's also a total brainiac."

"Get. Out. He didn't—"

"He did. Semifinalist. But don't tell anyone. I'm sure he wants to break the news to Dooney and Deacon in whatever way will cause him the least"—I struggle for the right word—"hassle."

"Dooney and Deacon?"

"Promise me you won't tell them—or anybody who knows them."

Rachel pauses. "Um, I'm pretty sure they have other stuff to worry about besides Ben Cody being too smart."

"What are you talking about?"

"Only the biggest story of today," she says.

"You mean the party?"

"I just can't with you right now," says Rachel. "You haven't looked at your phone since you walked over to Ben's, have you?"

"Just now," I admit. "You're my first contact with the media that is social."

"This is why I love you, Kate Weston."

"What's going on?"

"Nothing I can't catch you up on tomorrow," she says. "Sleep tight."

"Wait—how do you know I'm already in bed?" I ask her.

"*Are* you in bed?"

I fluff my pillow and assume my British accent. "I might be. Or I might be about to sneak out for a clandestine rendezvous with a mysterious stranger."

"Uh-huh," says Rachel. "And I might be crowned Miss Nebraska next month. See you tomorrow, Katherine the Great."

eight

"SHE WAS SO wasted."

I can hear Christy long before I see her walk around the corner with Lindsey. It's one of the things that makes her an excellent goalie: Her voice carries clear across the field. Also, she's built like a tank: solid muscle.

The four of us got lucky this year; we were assigned spots just across from the senior stairwell where the lockers of the graduating class begin. Dooney and Deacon Mills shuffle down the steps above us. Some people claim the basketball players at our school have an arrogant strut, but Ben says they're all walking that slowly because they're in pain. Coach Sanders kills them with squats in the weight room.

Today, their lope is slowed further because they've got their noses about an inch from the screen of Dooney's phone. I hope they don't break their necks text-walking on the stairs. We need them both for the state tournament.

Christy's laugh thunders over the noise in the hall as she gets closer. "Like, *blackout* drunk."

"Is she here today?" Lindsey wants to know.

I wait behind my locker door, pretending to dig through books. Are they talking about me?

"Of course not," Christy says. She tucks a corkscrew of her blond bob behind her ear, spins the combo on her locker, and pops it open as Rachel sails around the corner. "Wait, what? Who's not here today?"

I grab my geology book and turn around. "I'm here, I'm here. And, yes, I may have been the slightest bit inebriated Saturday night."

"Not you." Christy rolls her eyes. "We all knew you'd be here today. You wouldn't miss school if the building was on fire."

"So who were you talking about?" I'm confused. Also, possibly, still a little hungover.

"Stacey," says Rachel. "No way she's showing up today."

"Maybe she's just running late." Lindsey slips a sparkly barrette into her straight black hair to hold it out of her face, then checks her lip gloss in her locker mirror. She's the only varsity defender I know who bothers with lip color or hair accessories.

"'Running late'?" Christy scoffs. "Did you see that picture? I don't think she was drunk, I think she was dead."

At the mention of a picture of Stacey, my eyes go wide. Rachel sees the stricken look on my face and holds up both hands. "I deleted it, I promise. This is a different pic."

"Wait, there are more?" Christy asks. "I need to see them. Now."

"Ugh. I don't." Lindsey sighs and closes her locker.

Rachel shakes her head. "There was one of Stacey with our precious Kate here. I took it early in the evening. Upstairs. In the kitchen."

"It has been officially redacted." I grab my purse and look pointedly at Rachel. "I better not be in any others."

"I swear. You're not."

"Don't worry." Christy drapes her arm around my shoulders. "You left before the party got moved to the basement."

"The basement?"

Rachel turns the phone toward me. "I can't believe you haven't seen this yet."

Greg Watts's Instagram feed. A shot of Deacon with a girl slung over one of his shoulders. I remember my dad hauling me around like this when I was a kid, playing in the backyard. *Oh, look! I found a sack of potatoes. Mmmm! These'll be good eatin'* . . . I'd giggle and squeal as he tromped around, his arm wrapped firmly behind my knees, the blood rushing to my face.

The girl in this picture is Stacey, and she is clearly not giggling. She's only wearing a bra and her tiny black skirt, and she doesn't even look conscious. Her mouth lolls open, eyes closed, arms hang limp. She's bent at the waist, tossed over Deacon's shoulder, his chin resting on her butt, his arm clamped across her upper thighs.

Dooney is in the picture, too, squatting down behind Deacon, holding Stacey's hair out of her face, making a goofy look meant to mimic hers: tongue stuck out, eyes rolled back in his head. And over it all, Deacon's bright grin, a smile on the verge of a laugh: inviting, warm, funny—just like him, usually—but somehow that smile doesn't seem to match this picture.

"Where's her top?" I ask.

"Still in the corner of Dooney's rec room, I'm guessing," says Rachel.

"Along with her dignity," agrees Lindsey.

Rachel grabs my shoulder and turns me to face her. "Speaking of tops, is that new?"

"Oh yeah. It was a birthday present."

Grandma Clark sent it to me last month along with a card that had a unicorn on it. It's just a cotton blouse from the Gap—probably the clearance rack at the outlet near her condo. She doesn't always get it right, but this one fits perfectly, and the deep emerald green brings out the slightest hint of red in my hair.

"You saved it since your birthday?" Lindsey is incredulous. "But it's so cute."

"Totally," agrees Rachel. "Really shows off your rack. But not in a slutty sort of way."

Dooney and Deacon have their faces buried in separate phones now, thumbs tapping like mad. Above us, Ben catches my eye as he starts down the stairs. He flips his chin up once in my direction and winks. I smile back.

Lindsey catches the whole thing. "Oh, I get it," she says. "You just needed someone to wear it for."

Rachel looks over her shoulder and sees Ben at his locker. "Right? Hey, Kate, *Ben* talking to anybody lately?"

"Stop it, you guys."

Christy catches on and her eyes narrow. "Heard about your little walk in the park yesterday. Or was it a nap?"

"We are just friends."

The warning bell rings: two minutes before first period starts. Actually, I should say the "tone sounds." Over winter break, Principal Hargrove replaced the aging standard metal bells and clappers at Coral Sands High with a new system that plays a bizarre electronic beep to signal the beginning and end of each class period. Rachel says it's a perfect concert B-flat. She can tune her flute to it at the beginning of band. Regardless, it's been three months and it still makes me jump every time.

"I will never get used to that," I groan.

"Me neither," says Lindsey.

"Why can't it be a nice prerecorded voice?" Rachel demonstrates, sounding like one of those golf commentators on TV: "Ladies and gentlemen, first period will begin in two minutes. Please proceed to your homeroom."

The four of us are laughing as we walk into geology. Ben slides into the desk behind mine as the tone beeps the beginning of class.

"Hey," he whispers. "You look great."

I try not to blush, but fail. Thankfully, Ben can't see the grin spreading across my face. Rachel can, though. She tries to catch my eye, but I refuse to look at her because she'll start laughing at me, and then my cheeks will never cool down. I will die the color of a flamingo.

Mr. Johnston starts taking attendance, and I smile the whole time he's calling names, until he gets to "Stallard, Stacey." There's complete silence for a split second before Randy Coontz does a loud fake cough: *"Whore."*

The word floats across the classroom, batted aloft by a laugh here or there. I glance at Christy, who chortles once before Rachel glares at her, and she bites her lip.

"That's a detention for you, Randy." Mr. Johnston tosses a pad of pink slips onto his desk, and scribbles across the top copy. "Anybody else want to join him?"

"What? I just coughed!" Randy squeaks, trying to sound cool. His freckles are popping out on his neck. His ears, which normally stick out like jug handles seem even bigger—blazing red.

Mr. Johnston holds up a hand. "I'm not an idiot, Mr. Coontz. I was doing the cough put-down before you were born."

"But if I miss practice tonight, Coach won't let me suit up next weekend."

"Haven't ever seen you leave the bench. Don't think Coach Sanders will care."

Ben huffs a silent laugh behind me, and I steal a glance over my shoulder. He is hiding a grin, staring straight down at his desk. My smile returns. Ben is so much smarter than the average doofus on the basketball team.

Mr. Johnston flips on a projector and opens his laptop to a series of slides showing different strata of sedimentary rock found in Iowa. He is talking about how these layers are usually only visible in vertical surfaces around our state, like boulders, or road cuts where dynamite was used to blast through hillsides so a highway could be built without curves.

I start to take notes, but I can't focus on these pictures. The only image I can see is the one of Deacon with Stacey tossed over his shoulder. It's burned into my brain. I glance over at the empty desk near the window where Stacey usually sits. We don't have assigned seats in geology, but it's funny how we all settle into a routine, static and predictable. I sit in the same desk almost every day in this class. Since September, Ben has sat behind me. Lindsey on my left, Rachel to my right, and Christy in front of her.

Stacey sits over by the window and usually spends the class period staring into the trees at the back edge of the parking lot. The light from the window makes her a silhouette, a shadow of the girl I used to know. Sometimes Mr. Johnston calls on us at random to answer a question—to see if we're following along. Each time he calls on Stacey, she startles and gives him a blank stare from eyes ringed in too much black liner.

Is that a cliché? Too much eyeliner on the girl who isn't paying attention in class?

This is just a thing we do, I guess—determine who people are by what they look like. A smoky eye means you're mysterious and dangerous and a little wild, right? Too sexy to care about geology.

Don't judge a book by its cover. Mom is always saying that, but most of the time, I think that's exactly what people are asking us to do: Please. Judge me by my cover. Judge me by exactly what I've worked so hard to show you.

Stacey used to play soccer with us, back in junior high. Now she's on the drill team with the rest of the girls whose nails are long and bright and covered in sequins. Most of the girls on drill are dancers—or wanted to be when they were little.

When we were in first grade, there was a big flood, and Miss Candy's School of Dance was nearly washed away. So was the factory where Candy's husband, Jim, worked with my dad, making lightbulb sockets for the glove compartments of every GM car built in North America.

The factory owners decided not to rebuild and moved the plant to India to be near cheap labor. Miss Candy decided not to rebuild and moved Jim to Gary, Indiana, to be near her sick father. The ballet girls eventually found that their last dance option in Coral Sands was the drill team.

They all wear a lot of eyeliner during performances, but most of them wash it off afterward. Stacey doesn't wash hers off. She has no problem attracting guys—any guys. All the guys. Jocks, preps, burnouts. Sometimes, it seems as though she's dated half the junior class. But mostly Stacey likes the guys with long hair and trench coats. They've got the weed, after all.

I know that Dooney loves to smoke out. Maybe that's how the party got moved to the basement after I left. Stacey had weed and Dooney wanted to smoke, so everybody went downstairs. There have been plenty of rumors that Stacey and Dooney have been talking to each other, even though Phoebe has been Dooney's girlfriend since last summer.

Having a girlfriend has never stopped Dooney from flirting with other girls. A random kiss at a couple parties, an ass grab in the hallway; then Dooney and Phoebe fight and get back together a week later. I don't know how Stacey ended up in that picture with Dooney and Deacon, but I have a hunch that her access to the best pot in Coral Sands was a factor.

I glance over at Lindsey's desk. A page in her binder is already covered with notes I'll have to borrow later. As I tune back in, Mr. Johnston clicks through some slides on his laptop.

"We'll be taking a field trip to the Devonian Fossil Gorge in a couple weeks," he announces. There are groans and moans as he holds up his hands and waits for things to quiet down, pausing at a shot of the reservoir spillway just outside of Iowa City.

"The floods of 1993 and 2008 stripped away fifteen feet of sediment left by glaciers in the last ice age," he explains. "I know you all find this thrilling, but it finally gave us a horizontal plane where we could observe fossils. It's actually pretty cool. I'll have permission slips for you on Friday."

He clicks to a close-up of the bare limestone at the base of the reservoir. I catch my breath as the outlines of a hundred different fossilized organisms pop into sharp focus on the screen. It's beautiful. The floodwaters that carried away Miss Candy's studio and my dad's job left behind the outline of an ancient world, evidence of the way things used to be.

"Remember," Mr. Johnston says, "nothing is exactly as it appears. The closer you look, the more you see."

There are still ten minutes of class to go, but something outside the window catches my eye. A hawk circles the trees at the back of the parking lot. She soars out of sight over the school, then appears again and perches on a nest lodged at the highest branches of the tallest oak. Is this what Stacey is always staring at?

Nothing is exactly as it appears.

The closer you look, the more you see.

nine

IT WOULD SEEM there's an epidemic in our cafeteria today, and its only cure is interaction with a smartphone. Everyone is staring at their screens, strangely muted, eyes open, mouths closed, like the whole student populace decided it was a good idea to take it down a few decibels.

Usually this place requires earplugs, especially at the farthest tables by the big glass doors where the Buccaneers gather to graze. Leave it to our landlocked alumni association to come up with a pirate-themed mascot. Maybe it was a subconscious connection to our ancient history—the same reason our French class got such a kick out of conjugating all of the verbs *a la plage* ("to the beach") with Ms. Speck last year:

Iowa was once an ocean.

Most days the varsity Buccaneers live up to their name—swashbuckling through lunch at full volume, but there's an eerie, quiet urgency about their table today. Dooney and Deacon exchange terse whispers with Greg Watts. Randy Coontz is trying to convince them all of something, but seems to be failing.

I leave the food line with a tray but before I walk down the three stairs to the level with the tables, I pause to scan the decks from this crow's-nest view. Not too long—or everyone might stare at me—but enough time to chart my course.

Lately, I've been hoping I'll catch Ben's eye from this top step and see that he has saved a seat for me right next to him, across from Phoebe and Dooney. This hasn't happened yet. It's one thing to talk to somebody. It's another thing to eat lunch with them. The basketball Buccs keep tight ranks.

Today, I don't see Ben at all—or Phoebe for that matter. Ben may have snuck off campus with a couple of the seniors. Juniors aren't supposed to leave for lunch, but the varsity players get a free pass on most of the little rules like that.

Christy waves me down toward our usual table with Lindsey and Rachel. I am about to join them when I see a flash of long dark hair and bright red nails at the Coke machine. Something loosens in my chest—a knot I hadn't realized was there. Stacey is here after all. I turn toward her as she grabs her Diet Coke and spins around—but it isn't her after all. It's a freshman I remember from JV tryouts when I helped Coach Hendrix time the hundred-meter dash. She was fast, but afraid of getting kicked. I knew she didn't stand a chance once scrimmages began. There are two types of team hopefuls: those who pull up short, close their eyes, and brace for impact, and those who race toward the ball almost longing for the possible pain of a collision. Only the latter makes a good soccer player.

I walk down the stairs with my taco salad and sit across from Christy, who is finishing off everyone's fruit cup. I hand her mine without a word and begin fishing the tortilla strips out of the lettuce. Every other Monday, I ask them to put the tortilla chip strips on the side. Every other Monday, I am ignored. As quickly as I pick them out, Christy crunches them down. This is our system.

Lindsey and Rachel are both staring at their phones. We only have these scant twenty minutes to tap and tweet and text before fifth period begins and our blinking handheld portals to Anywhere But Here must be switched to silent in our lockers for another fifty minutes.

"What's with everyone today?" I ask Christy.

She shrugs, chewing. "Whadayamean?"

I point my fork toward Lindsey and Rachel. "Everybody with their faces buried in their screens. Are they looking for clues to find the horcrux? What's so interesting?"

"Just catching up on Dooney's party," says Rachel, without looking up. "Hashtag 'doonestown.' Some crazy pictures."

"As long as none of them are of me."

Rachel laughs it off, but it makes me nervous.

"Hey—what's this hashtag?" Lindsey holds her phone out to Christy, who takes it from her and shows me. The picture of Stacey passed out is somehow worse now that I know she's not at school today. There are three hashtags: #doonestown #buccs #r&p. I shrug and keep taking bites of my salad, but the ground beef is tough. I think of Ben's contention that the tacos are made of cats and smile to myself.

"What's so funny?" Lindsey misses nothing.

"Huh? Oh—nothing. Just . . . thinking about something . . ."

All three of them start in at once:

"Oh, I'll bet you are."

"You mean some*one*."

"I won't tell you his full name, but his initials are B-E-N-C-O-D-Y."

I am laughing because what else can you do when your friends torment you, and they're right? My phone buzzes in my purse. I fish it out and see a text

Can u talk? Sr. stairs.

Lindsey sees the name before I can shield the screen. "It's from Ben!"

The volume from Christy only goes one way in these situations: up. As quickly as I can, I drop my phone into my purse and pick up my tray. Rachel squeezes my arm and raises her eyebrows in excitement as I slip away from the table. The catcalls from Christy follow me, and are met with a general wave of noise from the rest of the cafeteria—as the corn syrup of every Coke and cookie ingested hits the collective bloodstream of Coral Sands High. The strange hush is over. The tipping point toward bedlam has been achieved.

The tone will pulse to end lunch in exactly four minutes. It will take me one minute to drop off my tray and walk to the senior stairwell. There will be three minutes of relative quiet before the wave crests and tears through the halls.

I walk as quickly as I can. I see him as I pass beneath the stairwell and pause in the shadow. He is leaning against my locker, staring at his phone. Is he swiping through the same hashtags Lindsey is patrolling? Or is he waiting for a text from me?

The straps of his backpack frame his chest in a way that makes my knees weak. *Better keep walking or you might fall down.*

He glances up as I approach and slips into an easy smile that warms me from the inside out. Once more, I'm reminded why all the guys on the team look up to him—even the seniors.

"There you are."

Was there ever a more perfect greeting? Not a grunted "hey" or a "where've you been?" but *There you are.*

As if he couldn't go on until I arrived.

As if he'd have waited forever, but is so happy he won't have to.

"In the flesh." I smile back, and what possesses me I cannot say, but right there, four feet away from him and closing in, I spin on the toe of my flats. Just once.

I am not a girl for cutesy. I am not a girl for foundation on school days or mascara on weekends or fingernails that hamper typing. But here, in the hallway, this guy who leans on my locker like he owns that space—like he belongs in my world—has inspired me to whimsy.

He laughs at my twirl, his head thrown back slightly, a strand of his bangs falling down into his eyes. I reach up before my brain can stop my arm and tuck it back into the pile.

"You needed to see me?"

He nods, and exhales like he's got something important to say—something he's worried about. "Wanted to ask you a question," he says, then bites his lip.

"Shoot."

He glances over my head with a little boy's shy smile and a squirm I remember seeing a long time ago.

"I don't wanna mess anything up," he says softly.

When I hear those words, I know for certain that things have been different since September. It wasn't a figment of my imagination. My fingers tremble just a little as I rest my hand on his chest. "You can't mess up what's already changed."

His whole body relaxes and he wraps his hand around mine, holding it there over his heart. I recognize this feeling. It's the same one from the other night, when he leaned his forehead against mine. The air is ripe with possibility.

Finally, he breaks the silence. "Will you go to Spring Fling with me?"

"As . . . friends?"

He shakes his head. "As more than friends."

I squeeze his hand harder—partially from excitement, partially to stay upright.

"Wanted to ask you at Dooney's party," he says, "but I chickened out."

I nod without taking my eyes from his. I didn't just imagine that moment. He felt it, too. "Probably better this way, 'cause, you know, now I'm not . . . wasted."

He laughs, that easy, quiet huff from earlier in geology, a laugh that you only notice if you're watching. "Yeah. I didn't know if you really felt this way or if . . . you know—"

"It was the Cabo Wabo?"

He nods.

Without moving my hand from his, I straighten up, shoulders back, all business. "Ben Cody, I, Kate Weston, being stone-cold sober, will hereby accompany you to Spring Fling." I move my other hand up to his cheek, and whisper, "And anywhere else you want to go."

When you have an unexpected crush on your childhood best friend, you spend a lot of time imagining the way you might kiss him one day. The fantasies I entertained of this moment were ridiculous clichés, based on movies and TV shows and the romance novels I used to find in the pool clubhouse at Grandma Clark's condo. These scenarios often involved a helicopter over the Grand Canyon, a ski lift in Colorado, the top of the Eiffel Tower amid fireworks, or an unspecified beach in California.

But then it happens.

Right here in the hallway at Coral Sands High School, next to the senior staircase, in front of my locker. He wraps an arm around my waist, pulling me into him like it's the most natural, least preposterous thing ever.

Then he's kissing me. And I'm kissing him back.

I forget to be concerned about being good at it, or what I should do with my hands—or my lips. It all seems to happen on its own. I don't worry for an instant that there aren't fireworks over our heads or waves crashing across our feet. The *where* doesn't really matter at all. Turns out any ordinary place can be made extraordinary by the presence of the right person.

We're still kissing when that god-awful tone sounds, only this time I don't jump out of my skin. It doesn't faze me at all. In fact, neither one of us seems to hear it. With that blaring of the concert B-flat, a wave of students crashes down the hall. At some point, a gasp from Rachel filters through, then a shouted laugh from Christy. I become aware of male voices across the hallway chanting *bros before hoes* but we keep right on kissing.

All of the games and pretense, all of the manners and posturing are swept away. The truth of Ben and me is out there for everyone to see, laid bare in front of a bunch of hooting Neanderthals.

And we don't care, because we have each other.

Greg and Randy start chanting along with Dooney and Deacon. It reaches a fevered pitch and makes Ben and me start to laugh. We're both blushing as we take a step back.

He squeezes my hand.

He promises to call me later, even though he doesn't need to. I already know he will.

Lindsey lets out a tiny squeal and four italicized rapid-fire questions. "Where did *that* come from? What is *happening*? Are you *official*? Tell me *everything*." Christy is making gagging noises as she digs around in her locker for her books. Lindsey punches her in the shoulder. "I thought it was sweet."

Rachel slowly shakes her head and stares at me. "You know how to pick 'em, Weston. Hashtag: total package."

ten

ON TUESDAY MORNING, I forget it's St. Patrick's day, and spend the walk to geology dodging pinches from Rachel and Christy because I wore my green yesterday.

For the second day in a row, there is no reply when Mr. Johnston calls "Stallard, Stacey."

For the second day in a row, there is also a six-foot-four guy leaning against my locker at lunchtime.

For the first time, however, John Doone is there, too, waiting with Ben as the hall empties in the general direction of the cafeteria.

Dooney is looking at Ben's phone as I walk up. "You sure it's gone?"

Ben says, "Yep," and flicks his thumb across the screen. "See?"

"Thanks, man." Dooney glances up at me, appraising me—as if he's never seen me before; as if we haven't been in the same class at school since fifth grade. He's looking at me through the new girl-Ben-thinks-is-hot glasses he got yesterday. He's smiling in a way that isn't a dare. This isn't the leering challenge he fixes on the cheerleaders or the taunting smirk he reserves for girls he'd never give a second thought. It's as close as John Doone gets to kindness. Still, something about it makes my skin crawl.

"Hey," he says. "Come eat with us."

I've anticipated this. Last night on the phone, Ben mentioned maybe we could eat together today. I am prepared.

"Can't ditch my girls," I say. "I'd never hear the end of it."

Dooney nods slowly without smiling, as if I've passed a test. "Loyal. I like that." He pauses, weighing the evidence, then gives a quick nod. "Bring 'em. Rachel and Lindsey are hot, and that Christy chick is funny as hell. Besides, we're all Buccs." He walks toward the cafeteria. "I'll save you some seats."

Ben watches as Dooney turns the corner. "Congratulations, Kate Weston," he deadpans. "You've been granted special access to eat lunch in the promised land."

"*And* to bring guests."

"Oh yes," Ben says. "Dooney the Merciful is gracious to all who wear the uniform of blue and gold."

I laugh and push him out of the way so I can dump my calculus book.

"Dang, you soccer girls are rough."

"Only when we need to be."

As I close my locker, Ben gently flips me around and presses me against it with a kiss I am not quite expecting. The very best things surprise you in all the right ways. How long do we kiss like this at the end of the deserted hallway?

Ten seconds?

Ten minutes?

I only realize I've lost track of time when the police arrive.

The thing about living in a town of roughly sixteen thousand residents is that you tend to know everybody. I don't mean that you know their name, exactly, or have had a conversation with them. I mean that you see the same people at Target a lot. You "know" the woman who slices up a pound of smoked turkey for your mother at the deli counter every week. You "know" who Barry Jennings is because your dad used to work at the glove compartment lightbulb factory with him. His son, Wyatt, is in your class at school and has the lead in the spring musical. Now your dad runs a construction crew for a developer, and Mr. Jennings is a deputy for the county sheriff's department.

So, when Deputy Jennings marches down the hall with Principal Hargrove, it isn't odd that he nods in recognition and says, "Kate," before rounding the corner to the cafeteria. You "know" him. It's only odd that he's here in your school, in the middle of the day, wearing a gun, followed by his partner, an African American man whom, incidentally, you also "know."

Not his name, actually, but his second-grade son, Frank, who attended the soccer camp you and your friends helped run last July to earn money for the new uniforms you'll be wearing this season.

So, here are all these people that you "know" without really *knowing*, but you are familiar with them—only not here. Not in this context. Not with their clenched jaws and their gleaming badges and their guns.

The last thing you see as they round the corner under the senior stairwell is Deputy Jennings reach back to tap at the handcuffs tucked into a little holder strapped to his belt. It's a gesture that seems to reassure him he's got everything he needs, like he's mentally ticking the checklist in his head, getting prepared for whatever happens next.

That's when you feel the hand of the guy you were kissing moments ago sliding into yours, and without a word, you follow the police and the principal into the cafeteria.

"John Doone?"

Dooney looks up when Deputy Jennings says his name and does the exact opposite of what I would do in that same situation.

He smiles.

This is a shit-eating grin. A cold-as-ice, what-you-gonna-do-about-it type of grin. He leans back in his seat and folds his arms, then flips up his chin in acknowledgment.

"Hey, Barry."

"Gonna need you to come with us, son."

Mr. Jennings's partner steps up to the table. I am close enough now to read that his badge says TRUMBLE. "You, too, Deacon. Also, Greg Watts?" He scans the table. Greg glances at Dooney, then Deacon. Neither one of them meets his eyes, but it's enough for Officer Trumble to ID him. "And Randy Coontz?"

Randy looks like he might throw up when they say his name. He raises his hand slowly. "Here, sir."

Deputy Jennings takes a step back from the table indicating they should all get up.

"Dad?" Wyatt has appeared next to us, at his father's elbow. He looks panicked. "Dad, what's going on?"

Jennings doesn't hear Wyatt, or ignores him. He waves his hand in a tight circle, index finger out: *Wrap it up.* "Bring your things, fellas. Follow me." Greg and Randy slowly scoot their chairs back and begin to rise. Trumble places his hand on Deacon's shoulder.

"Aw, c'mon, Dippity-do!" Dooney shouts at Deputy Jennings. Whatever noise is still echoing off lunch trays dies instantly. Those who didn't see the police upon entry certainly register their presence now, stretching and craning for a glimpse.

It's so quiet I can hear the rattle of pans being washed in the dish room behind the kitchen. The smell of spaghetti wafts up in all directions, but there is no air to breathe. All eyes are here. All ears are pricked up. Nobody moves—even to lift a fork. The entire room seems ready to implode as Deputy Jennings places both hands on the table and leans across to level his gaze at Dooney.

"We can do this right here in front of everybody, or we can do it in the office. You have three seconds to choose." His voice is low and calm. There is power in his words. I see Dooney's jaw twitch as he grits his teeth in defiance.

A tiny seismic shift.

Deacon moves first, standing slowly.

"Don't, man," Dooney warns him.

Deacon shakes his head and runs a hand across his close-cropped fade. He glances down at Trumble—nearly a foot shorter now that Deacon is standing. "Where to?" he asks.

The officer steers Deacon toward the door by the elbow, jerking his head at Greg and Randy, who follow, leaving behind the remains of their lunches.

"Either you're walking or I'm dragging." Jennings's eyes don't leave Dooney's for a moment. Dooney stares back without a word, but slowly folds his arms across his chest.

Deputy Jennings walks around the table and jerks Dooney's chair, grabbing the back of his shirt and hauling him forward, scattering lunch trays as one hand reaches for the cuffs on his belt.

"John Doone, you are under arrest for the sexual assault of a minor and dissemination of child pornography." Right arm back. "You have the right to remain silent. Anything you say can and will be used against you in a court of law. You have the right to an attorney." Left arm back. "If you cannot afford an attorney one will be provided for you. Do you understand the rights I have just read to you?"

Jennings snaps the cuffs.

"My dad's gonna have your badge," Dooney growls, eyes blazing.

The deputy pulls Dooney up and pushes him toward the door. "After today? He's welcome to it."

Dooney's walk between the rows of tables seems endless. Principal Hargrove turns on the top step as Jennings wrestles Dooney into the hall. He stops near the salad bar and raises his hands as if to call for silence, only there is no sound. Even the dishwasher has somehow gone quiet. "We'll have an assembly. Seventh period. Get to class."

He turns to leave, but I do not see him go. All I see is an ocean in Iowa. A sea of screens. Camera phones—at least one at every table—recording each moment, with a silent, watchful eye that will never forget.

As the principal disappears down the hall, the held breath of five hundred students is released in a single question:

What the hell just happened?

Ben stares at the door where Dooney was hauled away in handcuffs. His jaw is slack. Rachel, Lindsey, and Christy descend on us. Each shouts three questions at once. Now Will is here, too, pulling on my sleeve, asking what I know, asking what Ben knows. In unison, they all aim their questions at him:

Do you know do you know do you know?

"Do I know *what*?"

Ben sinks into a chair at the corner of an empty table, stunned. A migration is occurring into the hallway, and beyond.

I sit down next to him. My hand finds his shoulder. At my touch, his face snaps toward me, as if he's forgotten I am here.

"What is going on?" Christy is almost shouting.

"Did they say 'child pornography'?" Rachel asks, her voice trembling.

"Oh my god, you guys, Phoebe is a wreck." Lindsey points a couple tables over where Dooney's girlfriend is sobbing, two seniors, both named Tracy (one spelled "Tracie"), have an arm around her.

"Sexual assault?" Christy is still badgering Ben with questions. "What do they mean? Like rape?"

"What?" Ben holds up both hands, surrendering. "Look, I have no idea what this is about."

The electronic tone sounds, announcing lunch is at an end. We have five minutes to make it to fifth period. Christy and Lindsey scatter to collect their books. Will raises a tentative hand in farewell. Ben manages to nod at him. "Later, Pistol."

"You guys coming?" Rachel asks.

I nod. "Right behind you."

But I don't move. Instead, I sit with Ben in silence for a few more minutes as two women in hairnets and rubber gloves point an old boom box in our direction. Mariachis sing as they begin to wipe down tables with sponges in little buckets full of warm water and bleach. I don't get up until Ben does.

"You okay?" I slip my hand into his as we walk back toward our lockers.

He brings my fingers to his lips, kissing them lightly,

absently. His mind is in another place.

The second tone sounds. True, we'll both get tardy slips, but this time the weird electronic beep holds another message, too. Its unsettling pitch lodges deep in my stomach, a warning I can't quite make out. As it echoes through the hallways, Ben drops my hand and walks to his next class without looking back.

eleven

WE ASSEMBLE IN the gymnasium.

Rachel's face is buried in her phone. She and Christy point and gasp at their screens. A hashtag has sprung up with pictures and videos of the lunchroom arrest two hours ago: #buccsincuffs on most, the tag #r&p on some. No one can figure out what that means. I am turning my phone in my hands as we wait, but do not swipe to see. Something in me doesn't want to know.

Lindsey joins us, sliding onto the bleacher next to me. I left enough space for two people between me and the aisle, knowing she'd join us, and hoping Ben will, too.

"Are you okay?" Lindsey's eyes narrow. I nod and she follows my gaze to the stage where Wyatt Jennings and Shauna Waring from the drama club ready a microphone and podium. Behind them is the set for the musical that began taking shape last week during spring break. Rydell High is almost fully formed with flats painted to look like hot-pink versions of the lockers we have in the hallway. *Grease!* opens Saturday night, and runs for a week. The stage is now a school within a school, a hyper-colored backdrop for our drama in real life.

Rachel watches as Shauna uncoils a mic cable. "She's playing Sandy."

Christy glances up from her phone. "Wyatt'll look great in a poodle skirt." She snorts with laughter at her own joke as Wyatt plugs in the mic and steps to the podium. "Testing, testing, one-two-three." He gives Principal Hargrove a thumbs-up.

There is a loud whistle—a catcall from behind us. A group of the varsity Buccaneers is filing into the bleachers. Reggie Grant shouts up at Wyatt to "Shake it, baby." There are jeers and cheers, groans and shouts, taunts of "fag" and "fabulous."

"Seriously?" Christy snickers. "We're supposed to believe that he's in love with Sandy? Wyatt would run off with one of the other T-Birds the first chance he got."

"Uh-huh, 'cause John Travolta's just as straight as they come," says Rachel.

"What?" Christy doesn't get it.

"Do a search on TMZ," says Lindsey. "We'll wait."

"Look," says Christy, "I'm just saying that Danny Zuko in that movie was way more butch than Wyatt will ever be."

"Jesus, Christy," I say, sighing. "You're way more butch than Wyatt will ever be." Her arm shoots across Rachel's lap, and I narrowly avoid the punch she aims at my shoulder.

"Take that back!"

"If the shoe fits . . ." Rachel giggles.

". . . buy it." Lindsey finishes for her.

"This seat taken?" Ben is pointing at the space next to Lindsey.

I shake my head. "All yours."

Lindsey stands and switches places with me. I don't even have to ask her. This, I believe, is the true meaning of friendship. Ben puts his arm around me as he sits down and pulls us a little closer as Principal Hargrove takes the stage. Ms. Speck stands next to him.

"We wanted to let you know the facts about what happened today in the cafeteria." Principal Hargrove is wearing a burgundy blazer made of a fabric that does not contain a single natural fiber. There is enough polyester in this jacket to make it shine beneath the stage lights. The rumor is he bought it in 1991 and has kept it in his office ever since for the sole purpose of these assemblies and impromptu parent meetings. He pauses and runs a hand across his forehead as if patting his bangs into place. He's bald, but he didn't used to be, I suppose.

Given enough time, everything changes.

"It is important that when events like this one occur, you get your information directly from the source." He says this as if it were every day that two policemen storm the cafeteria and arrest four basketball players the week before the state tournament.

"These are the facts: Today, four students were taken into custody by the county sheriff for the alleged sexual assault and rape of a female student." A buzz rips through the assembly. Shouts and murmurs of "who was it" and "that's bullshit" rise and fall. Principal Hargrove holds up his hands and waits for things to settle down.

"It's important to remember that all students are innocent until proven guilty by a court of law. And it is up to me to remind you that the one and only place for that trial to be held is in a courthouse, and not on a blog or a website or in these hallways. We are under strict instructions to protect the victim's anonymity—"

"Too late," mutters Christy.

Rachel shushes her as Principal Hargrove brings Ms. Speck to the microphone. She's more stylish than most of our other teachers, her crisp white blouse tucked into charcoal gabardine slacks. A sweater the color of a Granny Smith apple is draped across her shoulders, and her dark hair falls to her chin, all one length, a silver streak at her forehead. When her husband left her in New York, Ms. Speck moved to Paris with her son. When her son left for college, she moved back here to Iowa to care for her sick mother. When her mother left us all two years ago, Ms. Speck stayed. I guess when you've already lived in New York and Paris, there's no point in trying anywhere else.

"I'd like to remind you," Ms. Speck begins, "that as the guidance counselor here at Coral Sands High, I am always available to speak with you about anything, and our conversations are absolutely confidential. Sexual violence of any kind can be frightening and unsettling, also confusing. I encourage you to talk about any concerns or feelings you may have with your parents or with me or one of the other teachers here. You can use the school website to sign up for an appointment with me, or stop by the French room. My email and contact information are on the bulletin board."

Principal Hargrove comes back to the mic to say one more thing. "Remember that this is an ongoing investigation. We will be cooperating with the police, and some of you may be asked to surrender your phones and tablets. Apparently, there were pictures and videos circulating of the event in question. If you have any evidence at all, we urge you to come forward. We will help you make a report to the proper authorities."

This final announcement bounces across the gym like a stick of dynamite, which rolls to a stop beneath the bleachers. The Coral Sands basketball elite are seated all around me. Every single person I can see was at Dooney's party, and each one of them had their phone out that night at one point or another.

Rachel and Christy tap at their screens like mad. The principal's words, "surrender your phone or tablet" have ignited a fuse, and whispers erupt all over the gym.

Bullshit.

Nobody's taking my phone, I'll guarantee you that.

Homes, you fucking crazy.

Fascists. They can't treat us like that.

Who they think is about to win 'em the state tourney?

"Wow," Lindsey says. "Have you seen this?" She is scrolling through her phone, and I pick mine up to open Twitter.

I immediately regret it:

> **@B1gBlue32: Wait, the police can take my phone cause U R A SLUT? #buccsincuffs**
>
> **@BuccsRock: Gonna rape her good for SURE now. #r&p #buccsincuffs**
>
> **@Pheebus17: White trash ho was so drunk she couldn't tell a dick from a donut. #buccsincuffs**
>
> **@j#mpsh0t: JAIL: what u get for inviting a TRAMP to the party #buccsincuffs**
>
> **@fr0nt&center: If we lose state cause of this whore she's gonna get more than raped. #r&p #buccsincuffs**

A sudden sickness wells up in my throat. The picture of Stacey draped over Deacon's shoulder is attached to several tweets, and I realize that she's the target of every vile word I'm reading. I know we're not close anymore, but I can't help picturing the girl who used to play soccer with us. Long before the Stacey with the dark eyeliner, the long bright nails, and the pot hookup, she was just this other girl on the team.

She was our friend.

Stacey came over to my house a couple times back in seventh grade after Saturday morning games. Her mom was waiting tables and wouldn't be off until later in the afternoon.

We were trying to study for a vocabulary quiz one time, and Stacey kept looking out my window at the birdbath, naming the birds. I saw that her vocab worksheet was covered in doodles. A flock of tiny sparrows and blue jays hovered in the margins and corners. She had an old leather-bound field guide in her backpack. She said it was from the Audubon Society and that she wanted to be an ornithologist. I didn't even know what that meant.

"It's a person who studies birds," she told me.

"Why do you like birds so much?" I asked.

A look of pity flitted over her face, followed by a smile. "Because they can fly, silly."

I give my head a little shake, trying to clear the images in my mind and the heaviness in my chest, but the picture of Stacey tossed so carelessly over Deacon's shoulder still glows up from the screen in my hand. I can't tear my eyes away, even as Principal Hargrove announces the assembly is over and dismisses us to return to class.

Ben pulls me closer, back to this moment. His hand closes over my phone. He gently takes it from me, holds down the power button, and swipes it off.

"Not worth reading that crap. C'mon. Let's get back to class."

I know he's right, but it's too late. I can never un-see that picture or those words. My stomach jumps and twists like Phoebe Crane flying over the top of a pyramid during a halftime routine. As if summoned by my thoughts, she descends on me and Ben with the Tracies in tow. She is crying and furious.

"You know this is bullshit, right?"

Ben stands up and steps into the packed bleacher stairs leading down to the gym floor. The entire student body is bottlenecked at the doors to the hallway. "It'll all be . . . okay." He searches for the words and I see his eyes dart in both directions over Phoebe's head looking for an alternate escape route. I don't blame him. If he finds one, I'm following.

"Stacey Stallard is going to ruin Dooney's entire future." Phoebe's words sizzle, water dropped on the hot oil of her anger.

"Wait, so it is Stacey? You know for sure?" I ask.

Phoebe looks at me like I've grown a purple horn in the middle of my forehead, as if she simply can't be bothered with someone of my enormous stupidity.

"Duke is coming to the games next weekend. He's given them a verbal commitment. It's a full ride. And now, what? He misses practice today, and Coach won't let him play?" She is almost yelling in frustration. "We're supposed to go to Duke together."

"What am I supposed to do?" Ben's voice is firm and calm. "Listen, I bet Coach lets him suit up. This is all crazy."

"Besides," says Lindsey. "We don't know for sure it's Stacey who brought the charges."

Phoebe's eyes narrow to slits and she hisses through clenched teeth. "Let me tell you what I know for sure. That dumb white-trash bitch has found a way out of the trailer park. Her mom has been out turning tricks at the Flying J truck stop since we were all in grade school."

"What?" I can't believe my ears. "She's a waitress—"

Phoebe turns on me. "And what kind of pie do you think she's serving those truckers between shifts? When LeeAnne Stallard heard her baby gave it up to a black boy and that he was Dooney's best friend? Bitch smelled a payday. End of story."

"Dooney's dad is loaded," agrees Christy. "He's a lawyer."

I'm too shocked to even respond. The bleachers are mainly empty now. Phoebe is about to say more, but Ben sees his opening and takes it. I follow him, walking down the bleacher seats instead of the stairs, stepping into the hallway just as a loud slam reverberates off the opposite wall. The noise comes from Wyatt Jennings's body hitting the lockers. Two of Deacon's friends—LeRon, a sophomore benchwarmer, and Kyle, the starting center—lift Wyatt off the ground and hold him there.

"Whatcha gonna do, faggot?" Kyle sneers at him. "Have your daddy arrest us?"

"We're the law around here, sweetheart." LeRon shoves a shoulder into Wyatt's ribs. "You want Deputy Dad to take our phones so you can see if we got dick pics. Ain't that right?"

Ben moves so fast I don't realize he's gone until I see him knock Kyle sideways with a shoulder and push LeRon backward into the crowd with both hands.

"What the hell?" Kyle tries to lunge at Ben, but Ben catches him by the shirt and spins him up against the lockers, hard.

"Chill out, dude." Ben's voice echoes over the din in the hall.

Mr. Johnston wades through the crowd. "Everything okay here, gentlemen?"

"We're cool, Mr. J." Ben shoots a glare at LeRon and Kyle, who clearly want to throttle him but think better of it.

"Get to class everybody. Go! Now!" Mr. Johnston assumes the stance of a traffic cop in the middle of the hallway, hurrying stragglers along.

"You good, man?" Ben squats next to Wyatt to help pick up his books.

Wyatt gives a short nod, then jumps up and turns to flee. "Thanks." He mumbles the word and disappears around the corner.

"That was really cool of you." Lindsey looks a little surprised.

"Freakin' Superman," says Rachel.

Christy laughs, pointing down the hall after Wyatt. "Lois Lane seemed grateful."

Ben frowns at her. "Can't afford to have those jerks suspended for fighting. Gonna need every warm body on the bench next weekend—if we even have a chance now."

With those words, a cold blade of truth cuts through my confusion about what went on at Dooney's party. Whatever happened, Ben doesn't think Dooney and Deacon will be playing next weekend.

He kisses me lightly when we go our separate ways. I am

easily carried toward my study hall in the stream of students leaving the assembly, unable to shake the feeling that our being called together is the start of everything we know beginning to fall apart.

twelve

ANOTHER THING ABOUT living in a small town is that there isn't a big law enforcement presence—especially not at school. I've seen TV shows where high school students in New York and Los Angeles walk through metal detectors flanked by security guards on the way into the building, but it's like watching science fiction.

Also, nobody on those shows seems to have a mother. Or if they do, she's away in rehab, or too busy running a fashion magazine from a skyscraper in Manhattan, or acting in a soap opera on a soundstage in Burbank to notice that the police showed up at one's high school.

Mine is not one of these mothers.

She and Dad always arrive home within a half hour of each other. I hear the water running in the bathroom off my parents' room while he takes a shower. Then the crack of a beer and the sound of the five-thirty local news. *As Seen on Thirteen!* Central Iowa's news leader is doing a pet adoption and a profile on one of the teams with a good seed in the high school state tournament next weekend. I'm almost done with my homework when I hear the garage door open again and Mom calls Will and me downstairs to help her set the table. I start unloading the dishwasher, handing Will silverware while Mom rolls chicken into tortillas.

"No-guilt enchiladas tonight," she announces, drenching the first layer in a dirt-red sauce from a jar.

"Why would anyone feel guilty about eating enchiladas?" Will steals some of the cheese she's sprinkling over the casserole dish and she smacks his hand away.

"All that fat," she says, holding up the giant bag of fat-free cheddar she gets on her once-a-month pilgrimage to the Sam's Club near Iowa City. "Ran into Adele at Hy-Vee this afternoon. She handed me a coupon—then told me the police showed up at your school today?" Mom leans over the island. "Anything on the news about it, Carl?"

"Anything on the news about what?" Dad wanders in from the living room. A commercial for Crazy Al's Discount Furniture screams at us from the television.

Will pulls plates out of the cabinet. "It was wild," he says. "We're all just eating lunch, and then *boom*: Mr. Jennings was cuffing Dooney over the table."

"Cuffing him?" Dad frowns as he tosses his can in the trash.

"Recycling, Carl," Mom scolds, moving the can into a paper grocery bag under the sink. "They dragged that poor boy out in handcuffs?"

Will is bouncing around the table folding paper napkins in half and sliding them underneath the forks. "Yeah. Deacon, Greg, and Randy all walked out on their own, but not Dooney. He was pissed."

Dad gets another beer out of the fridge. He leans over the island and grabs a tortilla chip as Mom pours them into a bowl. "These chips are *gluten free*." Mom announces this with great pride as she hands me the bowl to put on the table.

"Aren't all corn chips gluten free?" I ask. "I mean, they're made from corn."

Mom ignores my question and frowns as she pops the casserole dish into the oven. "Why on earth would they put John Doone in handcuffs?"

"Ask Kate," says Will enthusiastically. "She and her boyfriend were standing right there when it happened."

Mom turns around as I put coffee mugs into the cabinet. "Boyfriend?" she asks. "Kate, are you blushing?"

I take a deep breath. "What? No, I just—"

"What's gluten, anyway?" Dad asks, grinning as he crunches on another chip. I smile back at him. He knows I don't want to talk about this. It's one of the things I love about Dad: his belief that silence is golden.

"Carl, please! Don't change the subject. Your daughter has a boyfriend."

"And if she wanted to tell you about him she would."

"It's fine," I say. "He's not . . . we're just . . ." I close the dishwasher. "Ben asked me to Spring Fling."

"Oh, honey!" Mom almost knocks me down with a hug. "Isn't that wonderful, Carl?"

"What the hell is a Spring Fling?" he asks.

"It's this really cool dance," says Will. "Everybody wears clothes they buy at the thrift store or garage sales. Tyler told me his brother found this hilarious suit from the seventies made out of denim."

Mom's face lights up. "Sounds like we'll have to go shopping."

I hold up both hands. "It's really not that big a deal. Rachel and I are going to look around after school tomorrow." Mom looks deflated and turns back to the enchiladas. "Seriously, Mom. It isn't Junior-Senior or anything." The minute the words leave my mouth, I realize I've made a mistake.

Mom's hand goes to her neck, clutching imaginary pearls. "Do you think he'll ask you to prom?"

Dad shakes his head. "Sue, let the poor girl deal with one dance at a time." He takes a handful of chips and heads back to the living room with his beer, an eyebrow raised in my direction. "If that Cody boy gets outta hand, just kick him in the head like you did the first time."

***

Dad gets all the way through the *NBC Nightly News* and half of the local news at six before the timer goes off on the oven. Mom is setting the no-guilt enchiladas on the table and telling Dad to turn off the TV and come eat when I hear the words "several arrests at Coral Sands High School," and now all four of us are staring at the screen.

A blond woman with a microphone is standing in front of the school—our school—giving the studio anchors in Des Moines a preview of the story she'll do on the ten o'clock news. Her name floats beneath her chin: Sloane Keating. Her hair falls in golden waves that frame her face. Her makeup is perfect, and her navy jacket clings in all the right places, but she doesn't look much older than I am.

> *The county sheriff's department has confirmed that four young men were taken into custody, though no names have been released as of yet. Apparently, two of the high school students are minors, and two are eighteen. The charges stem from a party that was held Saturday night at the home of a star Coral Sands basketball player, and include sexual assault, rape, and distribution of child pornography. I'll have a full report at ten. . . .*

Dad clicks off the television, and we all stare at the dark screen in silence for a moment before Mom quietly says, "Let's eat."

The enchiladas are delicious, but there is guilt in the air, and

I can hardly swallow. Why do I feel like I did something wrong? Dad is silent as Mom peppers me with questions.

Is that the party you were at?

John Doone's party?

Ben was there with you?

Did you see anything?

Did you hear anything?

Were his parents home?

Will keeps piping up with rumors his friend Tyler has heard. "Everybody knows Stacey filed the charges."

"Stacey?" Mom turns to me. "Do you know her?"

I nod, miserable. "You do, too."

"You don't mean . . ." Mom puts her fork down. "Stacey *Stallard*?"

"Isn't it crazy?" Will is close to whiplash from all of the rubbernecking. "Nothing like this ever happens around here. I mean, we're on the news and—"

"That's enough." Dad wipes his mouth and tosses his napkin onto his plate. I jump at the sharp sound of his voice. "This is nothing to gawk at, Will."

"I'm not gawk—" He falls silent as Dad fixes him with the what-did-I-just-say? look. Our father can communicate a great deal without speaking, so when he raises his voice it usually means we should pay attention.

Dad turns his gaze to me. "Were people drinking at this party?"

"Yes, sir." I can feel my cheeks go hot.

"Were *you* drinking at this party?"

My heart pounds, but I know better than to lie. I'm bad at it. I nod. His stare bores right through me.

"Ben drove me home. Early." I blurt it out. "He wouldn't let me drive my truck."

Dad nods slowly. "That was a wise choice, young lady. If I ever catch wind that you got behind the wheel after drinking, you'll be walking to college and paying for it yourself."

I stare at my plate for what feels like an eternity.

"Kate?" Finally, Dad says my name and I look up at him. There is no anger behind his eyes. "You keep your head down, understand? You do not want to get caught up in this mess. People's lives will be ruined whether there's an ounce of truth to this or not. Steer clear. As far as this family is concerned, you don't even know where that Doone boy lives."

After another moment of silence, Mom asks who wants ice cream for dessert.

Tonight, for the first time in the history of the Westons, there are no takers.

thirteen

FOUR ARRESTED IN CORAL SANDS RAPE INVESTIGATION

By Sloane Keating
Published: March 18

CORAL SANDS, Iowa—Four arrests rocked the south-central Iowa town of Coral Sands yesterday. Charges filed with the county sheriff's office allege that a 17-year-old high school junior was raped during a party held at the home of Coral Sands Buccaneers star John Doone, 18.

Doone and teammate Deacon Mills, also 18, have been

formally charged with one count each of sexual assault, and one count of rape. Doone is also charged with one count of distributing child pornography. Pictures and videos taken before and during the alleged incident, as well as during the arrest of the players, were widely circulated among partygoers and other students via social media. Under Iowa statute, any distribution of images featuring a minor in a state of undress or participating in sexual activity is considered child pornography, regardless of the age of those distributing.

Two other students taken into custody are also members of the top-ranked high school basketball team, but their names have not yet been released as both are minors.

Coral Sands principal Wendall Hargrove said late Tuesday night that he and the school's administration take the allegations very seriously. However, in a statement released this morning, Hargrove urged the community to exercise caution in their rush to judgment:

"These young men are innocent until proven guilty. It is important to understand that we are dealing with allegations against four students who have been examples of fine sportsmanship; young men who have rallied our community, despite a difficult economy, as members of our most winning basketball team in recent history. We owe them the respect and privacy they deserve as we get to the truth behind these charges."

The name of the alleged victim has not been released, but several sources close to the investigation say that there have been "troubling" reports of her behavior. Initial accounts indicate that the young woman was very drunk at the time of the alleged incident, and had refused to leave the party earlier with friends. One source, who spoke on condition of anonymity, stated, "It would appear, in our preliminary investigation, that the student making these charges wanted to be where she was and remained at the party of her own volition."

Further complicating the issue, images and messages circulated on social media suggest that some in attendance deemed the young woman's attire to be provocative. Additional online comments seem to indicate she may have been dating one or more of the young men involved.

Deputy Barry Jennings, the arresting officer, refused to comment on an ongoing investigation, saying only, "The allegations are serious and could plague these boys for the rest of their lives."

Scholarship opportunities for two of the players have already been called into question. University of Iowa, which has a signed commitment from Deacon Mills in advance of the Buccaneers' top seed in next week's state tournament, is said to be "reviewing the situation." Representatives for Duke University, said to be seriously courting John Doone, could not be reached for comment.

The four young men are still currently in custody, pending arraignment and bail hearings, set for later today.

fourteen

IF SLOANE KEATING'S live coverage last night was scant on quotes and details, no one seemed to notice. There was nothing live to cover, really, just an empty parking lot. Still, the fact that she was there, reporting from our high school, had the entire town in rapt attention. Will was texting all night, and Mom left Margie Doone three different messages before we all found ourselves in the living room to watch the ten o'clock news together for the first time in . . . well, maybe ever.

The wind had picked up, and the chilly breeze gave Sloane's report the effect of a bizarre newscaster music video, her blond hair whipping about lightly, her lips perfectly lined, her eyes huge and gleaming white, like alien dinner plates. She was a

Pixar princess in shoulder pads.

Overnight, however, she'd managed to gather more information, and though her blog post this morning on the regional page of the *Des Moines Register* lacked live video, what it did have were a couple of cold, hard facts and the scent of scandal. Just before fourth period, Lindsey pointed out that Reuters had picked it up.

The news vans in the parking lot sent a strong gust of wind across the lit embers of everyone's imagination. In the cafeteria, you could almost see heat waves rippling the air over the three tables of Buccaneers. The guys on the team were talking about last night's practice. Coach Sanders had gotten choked up, and told them that if there was ever a time to come together as a team, this was it—both on and off the court. He swore he was doing everything in his power to get Dooney and Deacon to the tournament next weekend.

Kyle kept drumming on Stacey: *liar, slut, liar, slut.* Phoebe and the Tracies were there, too, nodding and tapping their nails on the table: *Bitch'll be sorry. Bitch'll be sorry.*

Ben was quiet, just listening. Lindsey picked at her food, then said she had to finish some homework before next period. We all made plans to hit the thrift store after school and get outfits for Spring Fling. When Ben heard this, he smiled for the first time all day.

In two minutes, the tone will sound to end my journalism class and the school day. Mr. Jessup shot down any discussion of the events at hand, insisting instead that we spend the hour working on next week's blog posts for our online student news site. I wanted to tell him that there was actual journalism going on in the parking lot, but decided against it. Sometimes it's easier just to go with the flow. From my seat by the window, I can see two more news vans have now joined Sloane's team (*Thirteen's on the Scene!*) from Des Moines at the edge of the parking lot: one from Cedar Rapids and one from Sioux City.

When class is over, I stand by the window for a moment, watching as the cameraman from Cedar Rapids frames up a shot. He centers squarely on the fifteen-foot-tall Buccaneer plastered across the side of the gymnasium. It was painted by the Buccaneer Boosters last year with materials donated by Christy's dad, who owns Hank's Hardware and Lumber. This single act of goodwill by her father (whose name, surprisingly, is Harold, not Hank) started a campaign called Buccs Buy Local! Instead of driving out to Ottumwa and shopping at Home Depot, people started coming back to Hank's and asking Harold for help finding stuff in his cramped storefront on Second Avenue. Christy says it saved the business, which had all but dried up. This town loves its basketball team. I remember Dooney's face in the hallway on Monday. *Loyal. I like that.*

I take a deep breath and gather up my stuff.

Christy and Lindsey are coming from yearbook and fall in next to me. Rachel meets us at the stairs with her flute case, fresh from band.

"This time next week, we'll be headed to the field to run drills," Rachel moans.

"Bring on the pain!" Christy shouts and pounds on her locker like she's King Kong.

Lindsey laughs. "I'm going to remind you of that when you're puking next week."

"How long did you make it during first practice last year? Must've been at least a quarter mile." I poke Christy in the ribs, and she jumps, then tries to scramble after me. I spin around in the hall, and run smack into a six-foot-four tower of human. It's Ben.

"Hi," he says.

I smile up at him. "Oh. Hi."

He leans down and pecks me on the lips. Christy immediately makes a barfing sound and starts tossing loose papers over our heads from the landfill that is her locker. Rachel whistles with her fingers in her mouth. I hear LeRon down the hall holler, "Get a room." It's been like this all day—everyone is wound up.

It's overcast as we head into the parking lot. Ben holds my hand and explains that he swapped trucks with his mom today. "I can drive and drop everyone off back here," he offers. "That cool with you?"

I nod. "How come you have your mom's car?"

Ben glances around for half a second, taking stock of who's within earshot. Christy is grabbing an umbrella from her trunk and dumping her backpack. Rachel is laughing with Lindsey about finding a tie-dyed dress for the dance. I hold up a hand to stem the tide of his explanation.

I get it. No words needed.

There is relief in his eyes as he opens the back door of his mom's Explorer for Lindsey and heaves a laundry basket over the headrests into the space behind the seats. It's filled with unopened packages of tube socks. The whole team wore those awful black socks pulled up to their knees during the last three regular games of the season. A show of solidarity. Sock-erstition. At the time, I wondered where they'd come from. Now I know: Adele's shopping habit strikes again.

Will calls my name, and I see him walking up with Tyler as Christy, Rachel, and Lindsey pile into Ben's backseat. "Where you going?" he asks me. "I thought you were gonna drive me home."

"'Sup, Pistol?" Ben holds out a fist and Will grins as he bumps back, glancing at Tyler to make sure he caught the exchange. Tyler is appropriately impressed.

"Meant to text you," I say. "We're going to the thrift store. Can you get a ride home with Tyler?"

"He wanted a ride home with us."

I turn to Ben. "Sorry. Looks like I have to run carpool first. Meet you there?"

"We've got room." Ben jerks his head for Tyler and Will to follow him and pops open the hatch behind the backseat. "Just don't flip off any cops or anything. Everybody's supposed to have a seat belt."

Tyler just stands there, staring. "Dude . . ."

"C'mon, man." Will elbows him and jumps in. *Hurry up. We*

may never get another opportunity to ride in a varsity player's way-back ever again.

Will sits down on the laundry basket and Tyler crouches across from him. "Are these all the leftover rally socks?" Will's voice contains the hushed awe of the first man to see Niagara.

"All yours," says Ben.

"Really? Won't you guys need 'em for the tournament?"

Ben shakes his head once. "Plenty more where those came from. Trust me."

fifteen

CONNIE BONINE BARELY looks up from the TV when the bell jangles over the door at Second Sands Treasures. Her husband, Willie, had three storage units packed with crap when he died in the First Gulf War. His jeep got smacked by an armored Humvee in a freak accident on a base in Afghanistan, and in a town without a Goodwill at a time before eBay, Connie smelled a goldmine.

Using Willie's pension, she leased an empty storefront to sell off his junk, and though she never cashed in on much of her late husband's stuff, she has successfully cornered the market on the old clothes of anyone who's passed on since 1992. Now most funeral arrangements include an appointment with

Connie the week after the graveside service or internment. Her rusty old delivery van will show up anywhere in town to cart away the belongings of your deceased friend or loved one, free of charge. For those too overwhelmed with grief to do the job themselves, the fact that Connie will sell everything off at a small profit seems to be a fair trade.

The people who left this stuff behind may be dead, but the smell of Connie's store is a living thing. Mothballs from your grandma's basement mixed with old rubber shoe soles, and long velvet drapery panels filled with cigarette smoke that can stand up on their own. It's the scent of trash that never became treasures, left to molder for a couple decades.

Mrs. Bonine's hair is a bomb blast of wiry gray curls that would spill down her back if she didn't have it all tucked up into a bright blue Buccaneers bandanna. This grooming annoys my mother. Once a year or so when Mom manages to wrestle away from Will the shoes he's destroyed and jeans he's outgrown, she drops off a bag of donations and huffs about why *Connie won't cut that mess* once we're out of earshot. *Or at least color it, for heaven's sake.*

Behind the counter, an old thirteen-inch black-and-white TV pulls in a grainy signal. It looks like Mrs. Bonine's watching the news on a microwave. I imagine saliva pooling inside her down-turned mouth as she waits for the *beep* and am jolted back to reality by a voice I recognize. Sloane Keating gives a preview of her "full report at five" on the "Coral Sands Rape Case." Something about those words—lined up all in a row like dominos—stops me in my tracks.

Rachel and Christy are already picking through the racks of ancient dresses. Will and Tyler have found an old drum set. Mrs. Bonine glances over as Ben and Lindsey lean in on either side of me to hear the news. Her lips stretch and roll like a lazy cat in a sunny spot, a smile lighting up her face and lifting her off the stool behind the counter.

"I have a Buccaneer in my store! Wait!" She holds up her hand, palm out. "Don't tell me." She squints and chews her cheek. "Starting forward. Jersey is . . . seven . . . ?" (She squints one eye open.) "No! Seventeen. Cody! Is it . . . Barry? No! Don't tell me . . . Ben!"

Ben smiles and nods.

Connie Bonine beams at us in victory, then remembers the TV and grabs a pair of pliers, jamming them into a small hole next to the screen where a knob apparently used to be. She gives a sharp twist and Sloane flashes once, then flattens into a glowing line that shrinks to a tiny pinprick of light. *Going . . . going . . . gone.*

"Terrible news. Those boys must be friends of yours?"

Ben nods slowly.

"Well, I just think it's awful what that Stallard girl is doing to them. Dragging their good names through the mud. If you ask me, they oughta arrest her mother and put that poor girl in a good Christian home."

"Did they say her name on TV?" Lindsey stops Mrs. Bonine with a question.

"What?" She turns back to the TV as if to check. "Oh no. No, no. They won't release her name. Not that they have to around here. LeeAnne comes by looking for white shirts to wait tables in all the time. Used to hold the good ones back for her, but I can assure you that won't be happening any longer. That little girl of hers was in here, too, just the other day—Saturday, in fact. Day of this party everybody's so worked up about. Whining at her mama about having to buy other people's old clothes. Well, beggars can't be choosers, I say, but they can at least cover up their butt cheeks, for Chrissake's."

Connie stops and eyes Ben, feet to forehead. "You're here for the Spring Fling, huh?"

"How'd you know?" Ben grins. I can tell he's enjoying the VIP treatment. It's like this pretty much everywhere in town. People might not know who represents them in Congress, but they can pull up a varsity Bucc's jersey number on sight.

Ben's arm slides around my waist, and Mrs. Bonine smiles. "Oh my. Is this pretty little thing here your girlfriend? Now that's the kind of girl to date." She grabs Ben's arm, then winks at me. "I'm gonna borrow him for just a second, sweetheart." She steers Ben toward the back of the store like she's a bulldozer in tennis shoes. "C'mon with me. You're a couple feet longer than most of my customers, but I keep a stash of big-and-tall things in the back."

The point of Spring Fling is to look ridiculous without crossing the line into absurdity. As we pick through Connie's treasure trove of ancient fashions, Christy holds a flash of jade against my chest, the hanger under my chin. "Look familiar?"

"Should it?" Rachel asks.

Christy blinks from Rachel to me. "Oh, man. You two were drunk Saturday night. Stacey was wearing a red top cut almost exactly like this one."

Stacey's outfit surfaces through the fog that surrounds my Saturday memory. Red halter top, tiny black miniskirt. Spinning around Dooney's kitchen, throwing her arm over my shoulder. *You're empty, Kate. Time for some shots!* Her tipsy whoop as Dooney pours tequila. Rachel's laugh as she licks the back of her hand so the salt from the shaker Stacey is holding will stick. The burn of the liquid. The bite of the lime. Stacey turns away, but I reach out and grab her arm. *No, wait! One more shot! Don't be a quitter!*

"Don't you remember?" Christy pulls the sides of the flimsy top across my body. The fabric doesn't quite make it under my arm. She laughs. "More side boob than the law allows."

"I remember," I mumble.

"Sort of wish I didn't," says Rachel.

"Oh, c'mon. Where's your sense of humor?" Christy tosses the halter top back onto the rack and flips through more hangers, draping every other garment over her arm, and grinning as she hunts for the perfect outfit. She doesn't seem fazed by the arrests or the accusations. I've always envied her ability to let bad news roll off her back. She could lead a pep rally on the deck of the *Titanic*.

"This whole thing is making my stomach hurt," I say.

Christy shrugs a *whatever* my way and barrels into one of two makeshift dressing rooms. She tosses a rainbow of polyester pantsuits on the stool by the mirror and jerks the curtain closed. Christy shops like she plays goalie: Divide and conquer.

Rachel sighs and shakes her head. For perhaps the first time in our friendship, she's fine with not talking about something. I'd rather not discuss it either, but this isn't a comfortable silence. It's like someone has poured itching powder all over us, only we're pretending nothing's wrong and trying not to scratch ourselves. I can hear Christy pulling clothes off and on, laughing and groaning at the results.

"Find anything good?" I ask Lindsey.

She shrugs. "Feels weird shopping for a dance when all this is happening."

"Well, we don't really know for sure what's going on," Rachel says, pulling a dress off a rounder behind me.

"Yeah." A funny sensation crosses my tongue as I say that word. My agreement tastes sour. Don't we have a pretty clear picture of what went on? I smile at Rachel and keep looking for something to wear. I've flipped through a whole rack, but wasn't really paying attention. I keep seeing Stacey in that halter top.

Christy sweeps open the curtain to her dressing room. "Boom. Mic drop." She struts out in a powder-blue pantsuit that looks like a costume from an old disco movie, dancing over to us, bell-bottoms swaying. The rest of us laugh so hard we can't speak.

Lindsey regains composure first and shakes her head in amazement. "It's perfect."

"Right?" Christy is as pleased as we are. "I'll tell you one thing, Stacey woulda been just fine if she'd worn this to Dooney's."

Letting things go is not Christy's strong suit. I hold my breath for a second hoping that Rachel will allow the moment to pass, but she doesn't.

"Wait—what?" Rachel cocks her head to the side.

Christy sorts through a bin of platform shoes. "C'mon, Rach. Stacey went to that party looking for trouble."

Lindsey frowns as Rachel turns back to us, her wide eyes encouraging me to jump in at any time. Instead, I stay silent. *Please let's not talk about this here.* I try to beam the words into Rachel's brain, but she misses my mental text message.

"I think she went to that party for the same reason we all did," Rachel tells Christy. "To have some fun."

"And how do we know she didn't have fun?" Christy asks. "Maybe she had too much fun and regretted it in the morning. So she freaked out."

"It doesn't look like she's having much fun in that picture," Rachel says.

"It was one snapshot," groans Christy. "For all we know, Stacey *posed* for that."

"And then filed charges?" asks Rachel.

Christy seems to ignore this and keeps digging through shoes. As I turn to ask Rachel's opinion of a butter-yellow princess dress, Lindsey pipes up. "I'm just really confused."

"It all seems pretty obvious to me," says Christy. "Stacey's been trying to get with Dooney all year. Probably threw herself at all those guys when they went downstairs, then changed her mind after she got what she wanted."

Lindsey frowns, running her finger across the sherbet-colored marabou on the dress draped over her arm. "I don't think that makes sense."

"Me neither," says Rachel. "How do we know those guys didn't make a pass at her?"

"Whose side are you on?" Chirsty asks. "I mean, Dooney and Deacon are morons, sure. But they're *our* morons. They're not animals."

"I know, I know," Rachel says. "It's just . . . why are we automatically assuming *the guys* are the ones telling the truth?"

Christy's eyes go wide. "Excuse me? Did you see the skirt Stacey was wearing at that party? I have washcloths made of more fabric."

Rachel nods as she heads into the dressing room with a few selections, but her face looks like she caught a whiff of rotten eggs. "Stacey's clothes were pretty revealing," she says through the curtain. "My mom wouldn't have let me walk to the kitchen in that outfit she was wearing."

"Wait," Lindsey says. "Just because she's wearing skimpy clothes means that she's lying about those guys forcing themselves on her?"

"Whoa, whoa, whoa," says Christy. "It's Stacey's word

against theirs. She's accusing them." Christy settles on a pair of platform shoes and turns to address me and Lindsey. "Look, this is not rocket science. It's common sense. If you don't want to work a guy into a lather, keep your cooch covered up."

I laugh in spite of myself because of the way Christy says "cooch." Rachel giggles from behind the curtain.

Lindsey smiles, but she's not letting it drop, and part of me wants to run over and put my hands over her mouth. *Please don't egg Christy on.*

"I dunno." Lindsey sounds unconvinced. "Look at Beyoncé and Miley. They dress like that. Sometimes they wear way less than Stacey was wearing. Does that mean they want guys to have sex with them even if they say no?"

Rachel whips open the curtain. "Everyone! Shut up and look at me."

She poses, like a print model, her hands tangled in her hair, holding it up from her shoulders. The dress is a crimson eighties number with an asymmetrical neckline. The short, shiny red skirt fits her perfectly. The triangular top bares her shoulders and seems to be supported from within to keep its shape. The whole thing is finished off by a bow at the waist with a giant rhinestone center. She looks like a character in this old movie Will and I watched the other night on cable called *Heathers*.

"How *very*," I say.

"That's the one," Lindsey agrees.

Rachel walks out and steps into a pair of the highest heels I have ever seen. There are bows across both toes, and she immediately grabs my shoulder for balance. "Oh my god!" She laughs, struggling to stay upright. "And I'm not even drunk."

Christy takes Rachel's other hand to steady her.

"It's just so scary," Rachel says.

"Walking in those shoes?" I ask, hoping to avoid a return to the subject at hand.

Rachel takes a few halting steps forward. "No. I mean, this whole thing at the party." She stumbles back toward me and steps out of the shoes. "I don't know Stacey that well anymore. I only know that when you wear sexy clothes, guys get all turned on, and if you're drunk and they're drunk, you have to be really careful."

"Do you?" Lindsey frowns. "There were plenty of girls wearing sexy clothes and drinking that night."

Rachel glances at me and I can tell she is thinking the same thing I am: We were both drunk, too. This unspoken thought hangs there between us like the funk wafting up from all of these dead people's clothes. Is the ghost of somebody's grandma shocked and appalled that we're discussing this in public? Part of me is.

"I just don't believe Dooney and Deacon would have sex with a girl who told them no," Christy says. "They could be with any girl they want. They're not that stupid."

"What if she didn't tell them no because she couldn't?" Lindsey asks quietly. "What if she was too drunk to say anything?"

Christy shrugs. "And whose fault is that?"

Lindsey opens her mouth to say something else, but before she can, Connie Bonine rushes up behind her, dragging Ben along by the hand.

"Get a load of this!" she brays.

"Whatcha think?" Ben flashes one side of his suit jacket open. He's wearing a plaid sports coat in a shade of lime green so shocking I briefly see spots float before my eyes. The satin lapels are enormous. They cover nearly the entire chest of the jacket.

"Oh, hell yes." Christy whoops and leans in for a high five. Rachel and Lindsey are both laughing.

I slide one hand up a slick lapel and he pulls me toward him, dipping me between the rounders, then spinning me up and out. "Gonna get our dance on."

"Thank god you showed up." Rachel grabs the selections I've made and hangs them in the dressing room. She holds open the curtain, and waves me in. "She hasn't even tried anything on yet."

I settle on a vintage ivory silk tube. The dress is sleeveless and goes straight to the floor with a high waist and two layers of a sheer organza overlay that flutter slightly when I walk. A band of the same see-through fabric covers each shoulder, then flows down my back in a streamer. I feel like Audrey Hepburn in *Breakfast at Tiffany's*—and sort of silly for loving it, but I do. When I come out of the dressing room, Rachel catches her breath and squeals like I've tried on my wedding dress. I decide not to tell her about a couple of spots of what may be ancient spaghetti sauce near the hem at the back. I'm guessing Mom can help me scrub those out before the dance.

"You're a vision." Connie Bonine's voice is full of gravel and warmth. "I'm giving all of you half off today. We Buccaneers have to stick together!"

Connie is the benevolent grand marshal of a parade back to the cash register where we all take turns paying. Even with the discount my dress still comes to exactly the thirty dollars I had budgeted to spend. I realize there aren't any price tags on anything, only colored dots, and wonder if perhaps Connie is making up the prices as she goes along. Common sense tells me sixty seems a little steep for this dress, but she gives Ben his jacket for free.

"And yours is on the house, big man."

This is Connie Bonine's grand gesture of the day, greeted with smiles all around, and Ben insisting that he pay. Connie shakes her head and pushes Ben's wallet hand away. "Gotta take care of my Buccs."

Ben thanks her and as we leave, she grabs the pliers and cranks the TV back to life. "Don't you let the news get you down, now," Connie says. "None of this may even be true."

Ben shrugs. "Might not matter. Deacon may lose his scholarship anyway."

"No way!" Will yelps.

"Terrible shame," says Connie. "Over a dumb rumor. Well, check the source, I always say." She pats Ben's arm. "Don't you worry. Just keep your head down and keep sinking those threes.

Gonna need every one of 'em next weekend."

Ben thanks her, and as we file out the door, she fiddles with the stiff silver antenna coming out of the top of her ancient television. I think about Dad's camera with the flip-out screen and wonder how long it'll be before that little device winds up in this lair of forgotten things.

As we climb into Adele's Explorer, I glance back at the front window of the thrift store. Connie Bonine is staring at the tiny screen, and I can just make out Sloane Keating, serving up the main course.

sixteen

BEN TAKES THE back entrance into the school parking lot, driving past the football field and pulling around the side of the gym to get as close to our cars as possible while avoiding the three news vans at the main entrance. Tyler's mom is texting him as we all pile out with our purchases. I have to get him home, but I want a second to myself with Ben. I toss Will the keys. "Start it up," I say. "I'll be there in a sec."

Lindsey pecks me on the cheek. "We're gonna have so much fun this weekend. Your dress is *gorg.*"

Christy holds up a fist for me to bump, then she and Lindsey head for their cars. Rachel hangs back, staring at the satellite trucks. The bright lights are switched off now, downtime until the six o'clock report. A couple of guys from different crews lean against the grill of the Channel Thirteen van, smoking. Their laughter floats over our heads into the trees, and I remember Stacey's hawk. I look up, but we're too close to the edge of the lot, and I can't see the nest from this angle.

"How long do you think they'll hang out here?" Rachel asks.

Ben follows her gaze. "At least until this blows over."

"What if it doesn't?"

Both of them turn to look at me. I realize I let these words slip out instead of just thinking them.

Ben stares back at the vans. "Dooney's dad'll make it go away."

He says this with a certainty I find reassuring and chilling at the same time. As much as I wish none of this were happening, there is a nagging thrum in my head, the drone of a distant housefly buzzing behind the windows of my eyes. It lies still for a few minutes, then whips into a frenzy at moments like this.

What if it's all true?

What if this doesn't go away because it happened?

What if it goes away even though it did happen?

Rachel glances up at me, then gives voice to my thoughts. "The police came," she says quietly. "They put people in handcuffs."

"That's what police do," says Ben.

"Not usually," I blurt out. The pressure created by my silence in the thrift store has reached critical mass. I have to speak or my chest might blow open—all my layers exposed in a bloody mess right here, sprayed across the parking lot.

Is that concern I see in Ben's eyes, or confusion? I can't explain it. Maybe I'm as wound up from the weirdness of this day as everyone else, but I press on in spite of how much I want to talk about something else. Anything else.

"I was really wasted Saturday night, too."

"So?" Rachel asks. "You're not like Stacey, Kate. We are nothing like her."

"But we *are* like her. We go to this school. We're in the same classes. We're the same age. I was just as drunk as she was—"

"No." Rachel looks pale and starts shaking her head. "No, you weren't. She was practically passed out in those trashy clothes."

Ben has gone so silent that I have to glance over to make sure he's still standing there. Rachel's eyes are usually bright and sharp, but right now they seem wild with fear. I want to tell her it's going to be okay, but the compass inside me is pointing in the opposite direction.

"I just can't shake it—" I begin. There's more to say, but the next words get stuck in my throat.

"Can't shake what?" Ben asks.

I take a deep breath. "The idea that this isn't a rumor. That maybe something really bad happened."

"Nah," says Ben. He pulls me in, an arm around my waist— an *it's all right* in his sideways embrace. "It's all blown out of proportion. There's just that pic on Instagram. Makes it look worse than it is."

"Police don't haul teenagers into jail over one picture," I say.

Ben frowns—not in an angry way. Maybe it's thoughtful? "What do you mean?"

"There must be something more we don't know about. The police don't just go around arresting people if there's not some sort of truth to the story. They have to get a warrant."

Ben smiles and shakes his head. "Not sure if Stacey Stallard is the first person I'd turn to if you're looking for the whole truth and nothing but. Especially if we're talking about that party."

"Stop. Both of you. None of us know what really happened." When Rachel says this it sounds to me like she's trying to reassure herself, not us. "None of us were actually there."

Ben smiles at me. "I'm sorta glad you got messed up early so we didn't get tangled in any of this. Sounds to me like Stacey just did something she regretted in the morning."

"Yeah," says Rachel, nodding emphatically. "That's gotta be it."

I want to ask how they can be so sure. I want to say that I doubt Stacey is a good-enough actress to pull one over on the police. Instead, I smile at Rachel and squeeze her shoulder. "See you tomorrow?"

She nods, but she doesn't smile, and as she walks to her car, Will starts honking at me from my truck. He's sitting behind the wheel with the windows rolled down. Tyler has the crappy stereo booming a baseline.

She can be my sleeping beauty, I'm gon' put her in a coma . . .

"Gotta go," I say. "The natives are restless."

Ben laughs and pulls me closer for a kiss. The tenderness

of his lips against mine finally silences the questions rocketing around my brain. I relax into his arms. After a minute, he rests his chin on my shoulder.

"Better?"

I nod. "Just confused, I guess."

"About me?"

"About everything *but* you, Mr. Cody."

"Excellent, Miss Weston." He smiles. "My work here is done."

seventeen

THURSDAY MORNING, ANNOUNCEMENTS are made—both official, and unofficial.

On the TV in the kitchen, Sloane reports that a judge officially released Dooney, Deacon, Randy, and Greg late last night. Mom hands me a mug of coffee and we lean against the counter, taking in the news that Dooney and Deacon both pleaded "not guilty" to all charges, and posted bail. Randy and Greg were released to their parents while the judge decides whether they'll be tried as adults, or remanded to the juvenile court.

The hallway at school before first period is full of unofficial reports that Greg and his family were seen at Sizzler for burgers just before closing last night; that members of the school board are fighting over whether to suspend the guys or not; that Dooney's dad is representing Deacon, Greg, and Randy free of charge; that all of their phones have been retained by the police as evidence; that they'll all be back in school after lunch.

As first period begins, I notice the cheerleaders in their uniforms, and after the tone sounds, Principal Hargrove announces a pep rally for this afternoon. The state tournament isn't until next weekend, but the sophomores are decorating the gym for Spring Fling after the guys practice tonight, and *Grease!* opens Saturday and runs for a week. The Buccs will practice during last period next week, then the tarps get rolled out to cover the hardwood, and folding chairs are set up for the audience.

Ben says he hasn't heard from Dooney. Nobody has. And when none of the four guys shows up after lunch, the unofficial reports change: Dooney's dad has recommended that they should all "lay low until this blows over."

Something about that phrase *blows over* gives me a strange feeling in the pit of my stomach. It's the sense that this is a situation we can't fix with a pep rally.

The pyramid holds strong as it materializes three people high, on exactly the right beat of the driving dance tune that pounds from the gymnasium speakers. Then, an explosion happens in the music, and Phoebe Crane catapults over our heads. She does a full layout as she flies toward the metal rafters, her body arching and flipping almost in slow motion. She pops her arms up and out as she reaches the apex of her flight, an award-winning smile on her face that elicits a roar from the bleachers. Every single body in the gym rises with her. We are all on our feet now, whistling and screaming.

Christy and Rachel are standing up on our bench, whooping and shrieking, respectively. Lindsey is jumping up and down in time to the music. As quickly as it appeared, the pyramid disintegrates into a formation on the floor as the cheer squad back-handsprings out of the way. Most of them grab metallic pom-poms; two of them pick up a giant paper banner of a Buccaneer wielding a sword.

A new song begins as the cheerleaders form a tunnel for the players in front of the banner with their glistening poufs of blue and gold. Wyatt's voice booms over the speakers announcing the numbers and names of "Your Coral Sands Buccaneers!" Usually Dooney and Deacon are called first, but today it's Ben who comes tearing through the paper, running the cheerleaders' gauntlet. He is wearing his warm-up pants and his jersey. He bounces a ball between his legs, then pops it up behind his back. It flies in an arc over his broad shoulders. He catches it, then points out at us.

At me.

The crowd goes wild.

"Oh my god!" Rachel yells. "That's your boyfriend!" She jumps up and down, her enthusiasm making me blush and smile. I don't care who sees. That *is* my boyfriend. He pointed right at me. He wants everyone to know.

Wyatt announces Kyle, the center, who makes a run at Ben. They jump into each other and bump chests in midair, then high-five as the roll call continues.

The drill team floods in as the players are announced, arranging themselves on either side of the shredded banner and cheerleader welcome line. They are all sequins and glitz, one arm and the opposite leg missing from their spangled unitards, but there's something off about the lineup. There's an odd number. Usually, there are six girls on both sides, but today, the right side only has five.

Deacon and Dooney aren't the only ones missing.

I stare at the space where Stacey should be pulsing along with the rest of the drill team, all of them flashy and fun and moving to the music. Down at the corner of the bleachers, next to the door, someone else is watching the drill team, too.

Stacey isn't here today, but Sloane Keating is. I nudge Lindsey, who stops bouncing up and down next to me, and glances over when I point at the journalist. She's standing in the far corner near the doors by the main entrance. Mr. Johnston, our geology teacher, is smiling and clapping along with the beat of the crowd, oblivious to the reporter taking it all in over his shoulder.

Lindsey looks back at me with her eyebrows raised, and at that moment, Coach Sanders emerges from the cheerleader tunnel and joins the team. They stack their hands, plunging them down and up again to a shout of "GO, BIG BLUE." Ben leads the guys into a lineup behind Coach, where they take a knee as he grabs the mic.

Sloane Keating appears to be tapping something into her phone. Is she taking notes?

"Ladies and gentlemen," he shouts, "I need your attention." A hush slowly falls over the gym. Finally, it's quiet. The smell of the polished wood floor and ancient sweat floats through air that's filled with anticipation. "We were gonna wait and have this pep rally next Friday before we headed out for the tournament, but I was walking through the halls yesterday, and I realized we were in need of some school spirit!" Another round of cheers crests and falls. "I know it's been a tough week. There have been some vicious rumors, and a lot of stupid stuff said on the news." A chorus of boos fills the air. I see Mr. Johnston glance up at the stands, a frown on his face, but he doesn't look behind him.

Coach Sanders holds up his hands for silence again. "I want to ask you all to send some good thoughts to the players who aren't here with us this afternoon." The boos turn to polite applause here and there across the gym. Coach nods and says, "We are strong. We are a team—all of us—and we're going to get through this. We're gonna hang Buccaneer tough, and our boys will be home on this court where they belong, real soon!"

The applause ratchets up a notch, and Christy yells, "Yeah! Tough as BUCC!" in her deepest shout. Rachel whistles in the piercing way she does, two fingers wedged between her lips like she's in a black-and-white movie hailing a cab.

A couple other people pick up Christy's cheer, and a chant

starts up around the gym: *Tough as BUCC! Tough as BUCC! Tough as BUCC!* Kyle, LeRon, and Reggie join in behind Coach Sanders, pumping their fists.

"That's right!" Coach Sanders says, as the chant grows stronger:

Tough as BUCC! Tough as BUCC! Tough as BUCC!

"What happens to losers when they run up against the Buccaneers?" Coach Sanders shouts into the mic. "We BUCC 'em!"

This blows the roof off the gym again. Ben and the guys are all on their feet behind Coach Sanders, arms pumping in solidarity. Will and a bunch of the JV guys storm the floor to join them, all of them wearing the black tube socks Will dragged home last night from the back of Adele's Explorer. They have the socks pulled up over their jeans. They look ridiculous, but when the varsity guys see the show of support, there are high fives and chest bumps all around. Somebody cranks up the music as the drill team, minus Stacey, fills the floor with a dance routine.

As Coach hands Wyatt the wireless mic, he freezes, and I follow his gaze across the gym. He's staring directly at Sloane Keating, who is holding her phone out at arm's length, panning across the crowd.

"Holy crap." I yell this at Lindsey and point. "She's shooting video."

Coach Sanders pushes directly through the drill team, mid-dance routine, and makes a beeline for the reporter. Everyone is spilling out of the bleachers, an ocean of chanting, fist-pumping students in his way now.

Tough as BUCC! Tough as BUCC! Tough as BUCC!

He pushes and elbows his way through the crowd, his face twisted and dark, his eyes grim. Even over the music and the noise, I can hear him yelling, pointing a finger at Sloane's phone, the veins in his neck visible from a distance. *Get the hell out!*

Mr. Johnston turns around and sees the reporter as Coach Sanders yells again, words I can't make out over the roar. The reporter cocks her head, then taps at her screen once. As she tucks her phone away, I could almost swear she gives the coach a little smile, before she slips through the door behind her, into the hallway, and out into the parking lot beyond.

Coach Sanders is red-faced, sputtering at Mr. Johnston, who has his hands spread I-had-no-idea! style. Principal Hargrove finally makes it over to the two of them and puts a hand on Coach's shoulder. Coach shakes it off and stalks away, slamming the flat of his hand against the pads hanging on the wall under the backboard.

The drill team ends their number and runs off the court in formation. Ben starts a layup rotation with the varsity guys as the tone sounds to end classes for the day. The Buccs have practice now, and in a general flood of mayhem, the bleachers empty. Rachel shouts that she'll call me later, and she and Christy follow the others out. Finally, it's just Lindsey and me left on the bare metal benches as Coach returns to bark encouragement and corrections.

"Wonder why there wasn't a moment for everyone to send

good thoughts to Stacey?" Even as the words leave my lips, I know the answer.

It's because Lindsey knows, too, that I have the courage to say this out loud.

"Stacey who?" she answers. "It's like they all just wish she'd disappear."

We sit there, side by side, watching an intricate passing drill in silence for a few more minutes. Ben turns and sees me as he starts a shooting drill. He raises his hand and smiles, then catches a ball from Kyle and dribbles to the passer spot under the basket. He feeds the ball to Reggie and starts grabbing rebounds.

Ben barely has to jump to reach the balls as they drop through the net or ping off the rim. His face is pure concentration, his tongue pressed against his lower lip as he anticipates which way the ball will move. He makes sure his body follows.

Control. Stamina. Dexterity.

The power behind his passes makes them lasers—direct hits to their intended targets. As Kyle and Reggie circle the top of the key, Ben passes to exactly where he knows they'll be when the ball gets there—not to where they are when it leaves his fingers. From the bleachers, it looks like he's passing to an empty space in front of them.

Nothing is exactly as it appears.

By the time the pass reaches that empty space, Kyle or Reggie is there, hands snap open, the satisfying *pop* of leather on palms. The step back, the square up, the shot.

That promise of the consummate athlete I've watched a hundred times in our old soccer video has come to fruition. Perfect connection every time.

The closer you look, the more you see.

It dawns on me in this moment that the whole school is so focused on Dooney and Deacon, that no one has actually talked to Stacey. It isn't that she's disappeared. It's just that no one is focused on her. We're too busy looking at the stars.

When I turn to say this to my friend, I see Lindsey has disappeared, too.

eighteen

THIS VIDEO DOESN'T show you everything.

For instance, you can't see the whole drill team, so even if you know that Stacey Stallard is a member, you won't notice that she's missing from the formation. You can't see that every student is standing as Coach Sanders takes the mic from Wyatt, but even though the audio is terrible, you can hear the chorus of boos when he says the words *vicious rumors.*

Sloane was shooting this over Mr. Johnston's shoulder so you can't see the frown on his face when the chant begins.

Tough as BUCC! Tough as BUCC! Tough as BUCC!

You can't see that the blurry figures on the opposite side of the gym are Principal Hargrove and Ms. Speck. You can't make out Ms. Speck's charcoal tailored suit or her black high heels with the red soles. You also can't see her mouth drop open slightly when Coach asks, *What happens to losers when they run up against the Buccaneers?*

But you can see the anger cloud Coach Sanders's face when he spots Sloane Keating in the corner. You can see him shouldering through the drill team and a crush of chanting students as he makes a beeline for her. You can see Mr. Johnston's groovy glasses as he glances over his shoulder, then back at Coach—a look of comprehension, then apprehension, spreading across his face.

You can see Coach Sanders jabbing his finger and shouting above the din at Sloane Keating. But more importantly, you can hear what he's shouting at her.

Get the hell out of here.

You filthy liar.

I've got your number.

You better watch your back.

Mom gasps and sinks down on the arm of the couch. She has just walked through the door from work as Dad turns up the volume.

"Shocking footage from a Channel Thirteen reporter who was threatened this afternoon by Coral Sands High School basketball coach, Raymond Sanders. I'm Jeremy Gordon in Des Moines bringing you breaking developments in this case. As always, Channel Thirteen is on the scene, and we go now, live, to our very own Sloane Keating, who shot this incendiary footage—on your cell phone, Sloane, as I understand?

The screen splits, and Sloane's face fills half. Her blond hair is pulled back at the base of her neck tonight. She wears a dark wool trench over a black sweater that shows no cleavage. The effect is conservative, both somber and studious, stylish with a subtle hint of glamour. *I am not a model. I am a serious journalist.* She smiles grimly into the camera, then uses those words again:

Coral Sands Rape Case.

"As I reported this morning, last night, local authorities released all four of the young men taken into custody on Tuesday. Two are minors whose names have been withheld, but they are both eleventh-graders here at Coral Sands High. Seniors John Doone and Deacon Mills were also released on bail after pleading not guilty."

"And do we know if these young men have been cooperating with the investegation?" asks Jeremy.

"It's been extremely difficult to get any further information," says Sloane. "This town is a team—just like their coach says—and as you can see from this video, they don't take kindly to outsiders asking questions."

"That's not fair," Mom says. "Makes us sound like a bunch of stupid hicks."

Onscreen, Jeremy Gordon presses forward. "Sloane, have there been any statements from the alleged victim in this case?"

"Not a word," says Sloane. "As you know it's the policy of our organization and the media at large not to report the name or identifying details of the victim in situations such as these. But I have to say, Jeremy, with this video as evidence of the prevailing sentiment here in Coral Sands, it can't be easy for her. I imagine the young woman must be feeling intimidated, and quite alone."

Sloane says these words with a quiet determination that telegraphs a simple message: *I will get to the bottom of this.* As she says them, the screen cuts away from the two-shot and back to the grainy cell-phone video, Sloane's long pan of what appears to be the whole school, yelling in defiant solidarity with Coach Sanders. The basketball team and entire student body chanting a slogan only one consonant away from an expletive:

Tough as BUCC! Tough as BUCC! Tough as BUCC!

"Truly a chilling scene." Jeremy Gordon's voice brings us back to the two-shot, and Sloane promises she's staying right here until she has more answers. Jeremy tells us where we can follow along with the case on Sloane's *Thirteen's on the Scene!* blog. Then they play out to a commercial with a shot of the chanting student body. This time we seem even more rabid looking than we did before. It's the same footage, but now Sloane Keating and Jeremy Gordon have decided that this is *a chilling scene.*

Because of their pronouncement, this video now shows you more than you thought you saw when you watched it the first time. Two people with perfect skin and straight, white teeth have just explained that there's more here than a simple pep rally. Their eyes seem to be staring through the screen directly at me. Accusing me. Blaming me. Lumping me in with all of the other kids in that gym. According to them, we aren't individual students. We aren't people with our own thoughts and opinions. We're a mob and we are circling the wagons to protect our own.

Dad clicks pause just before the broadcast cuts to a commercial and wordlessly walks to the kitchen to get another beer. Mom shakes her head and follows him. I hear her pulling food out of the fridge and putting a pan on the stove. I stare at the frozen screen, and just when I realize what I'm looking at, Will sees it, too.

"No *way*!" he crows. "I'm on TV!"

Mom and Dad both come back to the living room. Coach's face is a blur in the foreground, but there in the center of the screen is Will, his arm raised next to Ben's, chanting along, black tube socks pulled up to his knees over his jeans. Will races out of the room. "I have to text Tyler! Don't delete this, Dad."

I wait for Dad to say something, but he only grunts and hits play, filling the living room with another few seconds of the chant. Mom sighs and goes back to the kitchen. I keep waiting for someone to say something. When no one does, I know what I have to do after dinner, because this video doesn't give you the whole story. It doesn't even try to.

There's more to what's happening in this footage than two news anchors can discuss in a ninety-second live report. It doesn't show you that some of the students standing in those bleachers would like to know what really happened Saturday night. It can't explain that some of us used to call Stacey Stallard a friend. It can't assure you that not everyone has decided who's guilty or picked a side or even understands where the battle lines are drawn. It can't show you that a girl was missing from the drill team on the court, or that I want to know what she has to say.

And in that sense, this video doesn't show you anything at all.

nineteen

AFTER DINNER, I tell Mom I need some new lipstick for the Spring Fling tomorrow night, which is true. I also need a bracelet. I know that Buccs Buy Local! and all that, but at eight thirty on a weeknight, there's not much open in this town, and I won't have time after school tomorrow. Besides, the Walmart Supercenter has decent makeup, and sometimes their jewelry isn't bad. You just have to know where to look. Plus, I'm on a budget.

Mom asks if I want her to come with me, but I tell her no. I have one more stop to make after I shop.

The turnoff for the Coral Creek Mobile Village is just a quarter mile past the Walmart. I've only been here a few times.

Back in seventh grade I rode along when Mom would drop off Stacey after LeeAnne got home from her double shift. A lot has changed in the years since. The trees used to hide the trailers from the service road, but when the Supercenter went in, they bulldozed everything right up to the creek and built a wall to block noise and light. Now, instead of oaks and maples, the back row of mobile homes is bordered by cinder blocks, and the creek is on the Walmart side.

The darkness is punctuated by random porch lights. Cats scamper beneath parked cars, eyes glowing like sentinels. Several times I hit the brake as two boys and a girl on bicycles weave on and off the main drive through hard-packed dirt yards. The girl is six years old at most and wears a camouflage tank top. The boys might be a couple years older, but one of them is wearing flip-flops, and the idea of having bare feet makes me shiver a little right now. The three of them look like they're racing to the beach even though it's been overcast and in the fifties again the past few days. I wonder where their parents are. I never saw the backside of eight thirty p.m. until I was in junior high. Don't these kids have a bedtime?

I slow down as I approach the row where Stacey's place sits one in from the corner, against the wall that now skirts the whole trailer park.

Park.

That word generally makes me think of wide-open spaces, filled with green: grass, trees, life in general. It is clear that in this park the term refers to a vehicle that has come to a stop.

There are scores of them here, trailers anchored beneath the alien glow of the Supercenter parking lot. The light spills over the high wall and casts a weird lavender haze into the sky over Coral Creek.

I pull Dad's truck over on the side of the main drag, turning off the engine and the lights. Stacey's trailer looks exactly as I remember it, only it may be painted a different color. The whole place is tidy—standing in stark contrast to the neighbors on both sides. At the trailer to the left, a broken screen door flaps in the breeze, banging against the paneling every few seconds. At the place on the right, there are several giant stacks of tires, overgrown with weeds that obscure the steps leading up to the door.

I slip out of the truck, close the door, and lean against it for a moment. A little white picket fence rings Stacey's front yard. As I click open the gate, a Doberman in the trailer next door appears at the window, snarling and barking, jaws snapping, claws against glass. I jump what feels like a foot in the air, then remind myself to breathe.

Relax.

You're just stopping by to say hi to Stacey.

To check on her.

To see how she is.

I tell myself this as if it weren't crazy, as if I did this every day. As if I have ever done this even once since seventh grade.

There's a covered porch that stretches along the front of Stacey's place, and a flag on a pole is bracketed to one of the upright supports that holds up the roof. It's not an American flag, but one of those seasonal flags. It's got spring flowers and a bunny on it. Hopeful. It won't be Easter for another month or so, but it did feel like spring last weekend. There are lights shining through the curtains in the front windows, and I can hear someone talking. As I reach the door I make out the sounds of a competition reality show.

A plaque next to the lit doorbell button reads LORD, BLESS THIS MESS! and I smile. Whether it's the Lord or Stacey's mom, it's working. This is the nicest place in the neighborhood.

Pressing the glowing orange button yields a classic *ding-dong*. I hear new voices over the sound of a pop star telling a contestant that she's "got what it takes!" then everything goes quiet.

The door swings open a few inches, and LeeAnne Stallard peers out through the glass and screen of the closed storm door. Her hair is wet, and her tired eyes become bare flint the moment she sees me.

"Yes?"

"Hi!" I say it too brightly, like I'm selling something. "It's Kate. Kate Weston?"

LeeAnne nods her head, slowly. "I know who you are, Kate."

I blink at her, trapped in the high beams of her derision. She waits, daring me to speak again. I swallow hard.

"Is . . . Stacey . . . home?"

A short, sarcastic laugh escapes her lips. "Where else would she be?"

The children on bikes I saw earlier go clattering by behind me, shrieking and laughing. The Doberman next door sounds the alarm.

LeeAnne doesn't move. She doesn't open the screen door.

"Just wanted to come by and . . . check on her," I say.

"Oh, did you?" It's almost a sneer. I search for more words, LeeAnne's steely eyes making my insides twist and squirm. Is she enjoying this?

"Do you think I could see her?"

"Stacey isn't really taking visitors right now," she says.

I nod, too quickly, too agreeably. *Oh! Oh yes. Yes, of course. How silly of me.* "Well, if she ever needs to . . ." My voice is shaking now, and I can't finish the sentence.

"Needs to what?" LeeAnne is determined to make this painful.

"If she ever needs to . . . talk or anything, I just wanted her to know that I'm . . . around."

LeeAnne shakes her head as her gaze sweeps up toward the ceiling of her trailer. *Dear god, deliver us from these idiots.* Then she swings the door closed with a thump. I hear the click of a deadbolt, the scratch of a chain.

Standing on the porch, afraid to move, I wish I could beam myself back to my bedroom. It feels as if moving even an inch on this redwood deck would open up a deep cavern beneath the Coral Creek Mobile Village and swallow us whole, pressing us into fossils, the wreckage of this moment left petrified for a future generation of Iowans to puzzle over. Then, I hear Stacey's voice muffled through the wafer-thin walls of the trailer.

"Why did you even open the door?"

"I got rid of her."

"She's one of them, Mom." Stacey sounds frantic, a thunder-head just before cloudburst. My feet move on their own, trying to outrun a storm. I race down the stairs as Stacey starts to sob. "She's one of them."

There are tears in my own eyes now, as I struggle to open the latch on the front gate. A light flashes on across the hard-packed gravel drive, and I can see the lever more clearly for a moment. I swing the gate open and closed before I hear a familiar voice.

"Are you a friend of the victim? Do you have time for a few questions?"

Sloane Keating strides toward me, the brightness I'd assumed was a neighbor's motion sensor hovers behind her, a floodlight mounted to a camera, the glare hiding the face of the man operating it as both of them quickly close the distance between us.

My first instinct is to freeze. On TV or across a crowded gymnasium, Sloane Keating seems small, mostly hair and shoulder pads—somehow inconsequential.

In person, she is different altogether.

She is taller than I realized, and confident. She powers across the gravel in high heels without the slightest wobble, her blond hair free and flowing behind. She seems to float toward me surrounded by harsh white light, a trailer park Galadriel, her piercing eyes discerning the truth. There is something physical about the force of her presence, and I now understand a term I often see on those *Entertainment!* blogs with the pink logos.

This is star power.

I'm terrified she'll pin me against Mrs. Stallard's white plastic pickets if I don't go now, but as I make a lateral move toward Dad's truck, Sloane grunts a throaty "three o'clock" to her cameraman. Both of them pivot, and somehow he's out in front of me now, Sloane coming in from behind, pelting me with questions:

Are you a friend of the victim's?

Did you attend the party on Saturday night?

I curse myself for wearing my bright blue Buccaneer zip-up. I pull the sweatshirt tightly around me, my fists jammed in the pockets, my arms wrapping around my stomach. A fleece strait-jacket somehow fits the crazed feeling of panic knotted in my chest, but offers no protection from the rapid fire of Sloane's inquisition. The words LADY BUCCS emblazoned over the canary yellow soccer ball on my back burn like a brand. Sloane may be stabbing in the dark here, but I'm clearly a good guess.

Do you know who was there?

I stare at my feet as I walk, trying to avoid looking at the camera.

Did you see what happened?

I have to glance up to see if I am even headed in the right direction. I shield my face with my hand for a quick peek, but the camera is two feet away, practically up my nose, and anyone watching in Coral Sands will recognize me. If Sloane can run iPhone video on the air, god only knows what she'll do with this. Now everyone will know I was here. How will I explain this?

As I get to the truck, I fumble through my pockets for the keys. The cameraman is shooting my profile as the key ring spills from my fingers and falls to the ground. Sloane's hand is on my arm now, a warm, firm current. I jerk away, grab the keys from the ground, and turn on her.

"Leave me alone!"

Even as I say the words, I realize it's too late. I've handed her a victory. I see it flash across the whites of her eyes: *contact.*

"I just want to get the whole story from someone who was there."

The sincerity in her voice startles me as I scramble to find the button on the key fob to click open the locks. I stare back at her for a split second, and Sloane holds a hand up to her cameraman. The light clicks off. He slides the evidence of my visit off his shoulder. Black holes float in front of my eyes, and I wish for a moment they would suck me into a different dimension.

"You were there, weren't you?"

My father's voice rings in my ears: *As far as this family is concerned, you don't even know where that Doone boy lives.*

I give my head a single shake, but Sloane doesn't buy it. My thumb hovers over the button to pop the locks. She reaches out again, tentative, with the gentle stealth of an expert defusing a bomb. She senses that at any moment I might blow. Her glossy manicure flashes across my sleeve, and once more her hand is on my arm.

There is no trace of the tough-as-nails reporter on Sloane's face now, no hint of the pleased-as-punch smile she gave Coach Sanders earlier today as she fled the gym. Here, in the shadows, Sloane appears oddly human. Without the harsh light from the cameras filling in every contour, her eyes look puffy underneath, and there are dark circles seeping through her concealer. Her lipstick has worn off. Her smile is sad. I can tell she's tired. For the first time ever, she looks like a real person. Even her voice is different, now. When she speaks to me, she's friendly, not official. "I'm only trying to find out what really happened that night."

That's why I'm here, too. I was there when Deputy Jennings read Dooney the charges: *sexual assault*. I've heard Sloane say the word *rape* over and over this week.

But what do those words mean? What really happened?

I came here to ask Stacey face-to-face. The only information I have is secondhand: Sloane's news reports and gossip at school. No hard evidence at all. Sure, there are formal charges, but right now, it's Stacey's word against Dooney's. Is Sloane as confused as I am? Or does she have more information than I do? If she does, do I really want to know what it is?

My thumb plunges down on the button. The locks on the truck slide and click like the bolt of a shotgun. In a flash, I slip out of Sloane's reach and into the cab, one fluid motion that causes her shoulders to slump in failure, and her voice to rise over the roar of the engine as it growls to life.

"She was raped. At least three different basketball players assaulted her that night. She was unconscious. She spent all day Sunday at the hospital."

I flip on the headlights and see Sloane make a move to race around the front of the truck. I spin the wheel to cut her off, then hit the gas and take Dad's advice:

Steer clear.

twenty

"PERMISSION SLIPS TODAY for the big field trip in a couple weeks!"

Mr. Johnston passes a stack of canary-yellow pages to the person at the first desk in each row. Hand over hand, they flutter toward the back of the room until everybody has one.

I hereby give my consent . . .

It's the second time this word has pinged against my brain today. It filtered up to my bedroom this morning from the TV in the kitchen while Mom and Dad had coffee. *Today in Iowa* was on Channel Thirteen. I wondered briefly if Sloane might air the footage of me at the trailer park, but there was no gasp of recognition from Mom, so I hit snooze and rolled over to grab another ten minutes.

Instead, all I could hear was that word, over and over:

. . . an ongoing conversation about consent. Whether the alleged sexual contact was consensual. Whether the victim was lucid enough to give her consent . . .

Mr. Johnston is stoked about this field trip. "The Devonian Flood Plain is about an hour and a half from here. We'll leave during first period and get back about the time school ends for the day."

Excitement buzzes around the room. The general consensus appears to be that a bus ride to look at fossils and fast food on the way back is more desirable than a full day of regular classes.

Rachel raises her hand. "Mr. Johnston, what if my mom won't let me go?"

"Why wouldn't she let you go?"

Rachel smirks. "Because she doesn't trust TV stars like you?"

Mr. Johnston smiles and shakes his head. "Not a star," he says. "More like collateral damage."

"No way, you were on all three newscasts last night," Christy says.

There are hoots and whistles of affirmation. One of the guys behind me shouts, "Lookin' good, Mr. J."

Phoebe's voice cuts through the noise. "How come you let

that reporter film for so long?" Her question hangs in the air like a heavy fog.

Mr. Johnston waves it away. "Didn't know she was standing there," he says. "She wasn't authorized to be in the building."

"Shoulda gotten a permission slip," Ben says.

"Exactly." Mr. Johnston frowns. "That's the trick about permission. You don't have it unless it's been given."

"You and Coach still wound up on the news," says Rachel, "even without your permission."

He pauses for a moment, thinking. "You're right. Ms. Keating took what she wanted without asking. Does that make people around here trust her? Think anybody's gonna want to talk to her now?"

"No."

The word slips out louder than I intend it to. Everybody turns to stare at me. Mr. Johnston nods. "Acting first and worrying about consequences later is a dangerous way to do things." He holds up the stack of leftover yellow. "Get 'em signed, you guys. One week. Due back to me next Friday."

At lunch, the Tracies announce that they've decided not to attend Spring Fling tonight.

"Too much of a downer," Tracy says.

Tracie agrees with a shudder. "Have you noticed? There are even more cameras around today. They creep me out."

Phoebe's calls to Dooney's house and texts to his cell phone have gone unreturned. The radio silence has her terrified. She may be dateless, but she is bound and determined that she will not be abandoned.

"You have to be there." Her voice leaves no room for denial. "If you don't come, Stacey Stallard wins." She spits Stacey's name from the tip of her tongue like spoiled milk. There is hemming and hawing. The Tracies waver and whine. As much as Phoebe would like to, there's no denying it: Something is missing.

Usually, on the day of a dance, there's a sort of zing in the air—a current humming beneath our feet, a hallway that nearly pitches and rolls with excitement.

Tiny seismic shifts.

But, today, no one seems to care about the dance. Our brains are too full of the one thing no one can mention.

So much is so different.

Tomorrow will only be one week since the party. It seems like a hundred years have passed since then—and also no time at all. It's as if the Devonian Era flashed by only yesterday, and we are now gulping air into newly formed lungs that used to be gills, taking first steps on our flippers-turned-feet.

In one short week, we have become different creatures.

When Ben rings the doorbell on Friday evening, I walk down the stairs in recycled silk, a light breeze of sauce-free organza fluttering around me. Mom has tears in her eyes, as if I am leaving forever instead of attending a two-hour dance in a thrift-store dress.

The shaky video of Coach Sanders threatening Sloane Keating ricocheted across the cable news channels again today, and as Ben steps through the front door with a plastic shell of red roses for my wrist, a graphic the color of bruises flies in beneath the cleft chin of a national evening anchor: CRISIS IN CORAL SANDS.

Dad turns off the TV while Mom snaps several pictures on the digital point-and-shoot she still insists on using. It's another one of the single-function gadgets my parents refuse to retire. Will tries to explain that his smartphone camera has more megapixels, but Mom says that he can take *his* pictures and she'll take *hers*.

Ben jokes with my dad. Will stands on the back of the couch to "get a cool angle." As Mom clicks and clucks and coos, I know that one of these shots will wind up in a gallery frame on the wall upstairs. Long after the continuing saga of Kate and Ben reaches its next chapter, I will find her in the hallway, gazing at the glass with shiny eyes and a full heart. These will be her fossils in bedrock, her coral clues to a bygone era. A strange lump forms in my throat as Mom gently tucks a strand of my loose updo behind my ear.

I was once your little girl.

Iowa was once an ocean.

Will tries to follow us outside. I think he'd have climbed into Ben's truck and come with us if I hadn't grabbed him by the shoulders and given him my *get lost* look.

He may have a bigger crush on Ben than I do.

The number of news vans in the parking lot has doubled to six, with affiliates from as far away as Kansas City, St. Louis, and Chicago. Sloane Keating is still front and center, but joined now by three women and two men, lined up with their camera guys at the front entrance. Sloane's blond hair is up in a tight French twist like Grace Kelly's in an old movie. It appears she had her hair done for the dance.

"Gotta be kidding me," Ben says as we park.

I stare at the gauntlet of cameras and hairdos, lips poised to question, microphones at the ready, bronzer so thick it glows orange. "Can you believe it was only a week ago Saturday?"

Ben frowns. "You mean a week ago Sunday."

I smile. "The party was Saturday, remember?"

"Oh. That."

"Wait, what are you talking about?"

He smiles a little shyly. "Sunday afternoon. When you walked over all brave and cute and hungover as hell."

"I wasn't that bad."

"Uh, you were green."

We both laugh for a second, then he reaches over and grabs my hand. He does it quickly as if he might lose his nerve, as if I might escape into the woods along the parking lot. He gently runs a finger along the roses on my wrist, then looks into my eyes. "When you tried to shoot over my head? I was a goner."

We kiss for a long time. I have to reapply my lipstick.

I don't care.

When I close my purse and announce my readiness, Ben looks over at Sloane and her minions crowding the front doors.

"Last chance," he says. "We can just go drive around. Get some tequila. Go back to my place."

"And waste the plaid jacket from Mars?" I ask. "Connie Bonine would never forgive us."

As he opens my door and helps me out of his truck, he flashes me that extra-juice-box grin. "Hang on tight."

I'm glad Ben is so tall. As I take his arm, I feel like nothing can touch me. I keep my head down and match his long, sure steps. As we approach the entrance, the reporters crowd our way, shouting over one another, just like they do on TV shows.

I've never understood that. As if the reason we're not answering is that we can't hear them. Even if I wanted to stop and answer a question, who wants to be yelled at? Where would I begin? How could I get a word in edgewise?

Ben pulls me closer, leaning forward with his shoulder, his arm around me, shielding me from the crowd, the lights, the noise.

The one thing he cannot block are the words.

Were you at the party?

Do you know the victim?

Is Coach Sanders trying to cover up what really happened?

Were you in the room that night?

Have you read the hospital report?

Did you see the alleged assault?

Have you heard about the rape kit results?

Do you know who else was involved?

I know we are close to the front entrance. When I glance up to check our progress, Sloane Keating is staring directly into my eyes. Silent as a statue, she's letting all the other reporters shout questions. She only smiles in greeting as we walk past her. Ben swings the front door open. I can see the check-in table by the gym entrance, and just when I think we're home free, Sloane speaks.

"Ben Cody, have you spoken with John Doone since he was released from police custody Wednesday?"

Ben jerks to a stop beside me. I can feel him turn when Sloane calls him by name. I know it's a reflex. I also know it's a trap.

"What?"

The other reporters rush to greet a group of students arriving in our wake. Sloane Keating holds the mic up near Ben's mouth. "Are you glad your friend is home?"

"Of course . . . yeah. I just—" Ben struggles to finish his sentence. "I haven't talked to him. I don't . . ." His voice trails off, and I see Sloane Keating's face soften as she waits for him to finish.

"You don't what?" she asks.

I grab her arm, pulling the microphone to my mouth. "Have any further comment."

I take Ben's hand and somehow manage to propel all six feet four inches of him into the hallway. The door swings closed behind us, but not before Sloane calls out one last thing:

"Great seeing you last night, Kate."

twenty-one

THE TROPHY CASE just inside the school's front doors is jammed with brass statues, plaques, and pictures. The "spirit stick" our cheer squad brought home from regionals last year catches my eye, and I imagine knocking it over Sloane Keating's head as Ben and I catch our breath.

"How does she know our names?" he asks me. "And what the hell did she mean? 'Great seeing you last night'?"

I have no way to explain this except the truth, but the words are slow to form on my tongue, and before I can say them, the doors swing open again. Rachel, Lindsey, and Christy stumble inside, the latest victors to make it past the reporters.

"Holy *hell.*" Christy flips her wild curls out of her face.

Rachel tugs at the triangular top of her shiny dress. "Now I know how Taylor Swift feels." She grabs my shoulder for balance, and pulls off one of her towering heels, shaking it upside down. "Got a rock in my shoe." Her hair has been hot-rolled into a giant fluffy pile on top of her head.

Once her shoe is back on, Rachel turns to face the group. "Okay. Let's go dance," she commands. Instead, we all stand there, sort of shell-shocked. "Oh, c'mon!"

There's a spark in Rachel's eye. It's one of those things no one else sees, but I know her. I know what's coming. Sure enough, she revs up her favorite dog and pony show.

"Am I going to have to do Rachel's Ray of Sunshine to get this party started?"

Assuming her Sunday-School-teacher smile, Rachel turns to face me and speaks in a cheery, breathless tone, often reserved for the elderly and children under the age of three. It's silly, but somehow completely sincere.

"Boys and girls, I want you to know that each one of you is special and beautiful! Kate Weston, your dress is magnificent. You are just a glamorous angel straight from heaven. And you, Mr. Cody, are the luckiest man in the kingdom."

Christy groans and rolls her eyes. Lindsey lets out a laugh, and even Ben cracks a smile.

"Miss Lindsey, your dress has such pretty feathers! And it's the color of my favorite ice cream bar. You're quite simply a Creamsicle swan of loveliness."

By this point, even Christy is laughing, and Rachel drops her wide-eyed act. "Are we good?" she asks.

"What?" purrs Christy. "I don't get a ray of sunshine?"

"I'll tell you what you get," Rachel says flatly. "You get us to the front of that check-in line." She smacks Christy on the rear. Christy whoops her assent, tugging at the knotted belt of her polyester pantsuit and herding us all to the check-in station at the other end of the front hallway.

Deputy Jennings stands on one side of the table, chatting with Principal Hargrove. Ms. Speck and Mr. Johnston are ticking people off a master list. There are a couple of sophomores ahead of us and as we reach the table, Coach Sanders barrels through the gym doors with a red bullhorn.

"Ready?" He tosses this over his shoulder at Principal Hargrove and Mr. Jennings, who nod and follow him to the front doors of the school. "Let's do this."

Coach Sanders throws his shoulder into the door, and instantly the lights and questions erupt into the front hallway. He raises the bullhorn to his mouth and shouts through a squeal from the speaker:

"All non-school personnel are considered trespassers and are hereby compelled to maintain a distance of at least fifty feet by order of the county sheriff. I repeat: All journalists must immediately retreat to a minimum of fifty feet from the front door of this property or you will be arrested for trespassing."

"Can they do that?" Lindsey stands at my elbow watching as

Coach shouts down Sloane Keating's protests.

"Whether they can or not, they just did." Christy is smiling. "Good riddance."

One by one the lights on the cameras begin to bob across the parking lot. Eventually, even Sloane Keating hoofs it toward the Channel 13 van. I realize now how far away fifty feet actually is.

Coach Sanders struts back through the hallway, a satisfied smile on his face. When he sees Ben his face lights up. "You kids look terrific," he says with a wink. "For god's sake, everybody stay off the Twitter tonight."

"Uh . . . It's just 'Twitter,' Coach." Ben grins and shakes his head.

"And you stay off the evening news," Rachel tells him.

Coach throws his head back and belly laughs at the ceiling. "It's a deal."

Mr. Johnston checks Ben's ID and his name off a list. "Excellent, Mister Cody. Have fun at the Fling."

Ms. Speck makes a big fuss over my dress, insisting that I turn around so she can see the streamer down the back. "Vintage *perfection*," she says, squeezing my hand as she hands back my ID.

As we wait for the rest of the group to make their way through the line, Principal Hargrove comes back in shaking his head. "Can you believe the nerve of those people? Asking our kids about *rape kits* on their way to a dance?"

Lindsey and Ben both hear this, and Coach sees them turn

to look. He shushes Principal Hargrove and smiles our way as Christy and Rachel get through the line and join us.

"Ignore all that crap, kids." Coach smiles grimly. "The cops are just doing their jobs. A little overzealous maybe, but we'll get this all ironed out."

Principal Hargrove swings open the door to the gym, and music pours out.

"I want you to go in there and dance your butts off," Coach says. "Just forget all about this for a little while and have a good time."

"We'll try," Rachel says.

And for a good hour or so, we succeed.

The sophomores are in charge of Spring Fling, and they hired a DJ from Iowa City. The music is infectious and drives away the weirdness I felt all day at school. Apparently, the thing missing in the air today was the rhythm of three hundred kids in hilarious party clothes and remixes that just won't stop.

As one song bleeds into the next, Phoebe tells us that this DJ plays all the big University of Iowa parties and flies all over the country to spin at clubs in New York, Miami, and Los Angeles. She's in mid-sentence when the Tracies (who decided to show up after Phoebe's cafeteria call-to-arms) shriek in unison because they recognize the beat. Both of them are wearing old tutus and ballet slippers courtesy of Connie Bonine's "dance rack" and they run for the center of the crush. Rachel throws an invisible lasso over Christy, who pretends to be dragged onto the floor with us, one lurching step at a time, and the music whips us together, pounding a clear path through my chest:

Do what you want, what you want with my body . . .

Ben is a great dancer. He knows how to move and, more importantly, what to do with his hands. He doesn't look like he's miserable or counting or trying too hard. He's the best dancer here next to Wyatt, who is getting down with his *Grease!* costars. He's sandwiched between Sandy and Rizzo. Both of them are all over him and each other. As I try to point them out to Ben, the music changes again, the swell of a female voice filling the air.

Baby, baby, are you listening?

Ben's hand finds the small of my back. As he pulls me in, he bends down a little, bringing him closer to my level. I clasp my hands behind his neck, and our bodies fit together in a way that makes everything else fade away. His lips find mine, and the packed dance floor disappears. I feel myself falling into him as the music soars above us.

Wondering where you've been all my life

My knees go a little shaky, and I list off-kilter in my heels. Ben pulls me back to center with a smile. "Easy there," he says. "You okay?"

I nod, but Ben takes my hand and says, "Let's get you something to drink."

"You don't mind?"

He shakes his head.

"What if they play something really great and we miss it?" I ask.

"I'm with you. I'm not missing a thing."

Several volunteer moms from the booster club are running the drink table in the back hallway, pouring pop into plastic cups. They are chatty, armed with grins and grenadine, garnishing drinks with limes and maraschino cherries. As we stand in line, I lean against Ben, his arms wrapped around my waist, but the spell from inside the gym seems broken by the fluorescent lights. He's quiet, and I can tell his brain is elsewhere.

I order a Shirley Temple, and he gets a cherry Coke, then we slip out the back door. The patio behind the cafeteria is a different planet, light-years away from the crush of the gym. The air is cool on my skin, and a breeze catches the sheer fabric of my dress, making it flutter as we walk toward one of the benches at a nearby table.

"You okay?" I ask him.

"I guess," he says. "Little weirded out."

"The reporters?"

"Them, too." He crunches on a piece of ice and stares out across the back patio to toward the ditch where we hunted fossils together last fall. "Mainly my mom."

"More Powerade?"

He closes his eyes and rolls his head back in a circle, trying to relax. "Toilet paper," he says wearily. "The half bath off the rec room? Stacked to the ceiling with twelve-packs."

I've seen plenty of weird people on cable shows. I've seen a woman addicted to eating Ajax and a man who sleeps in the garage because there are thirty years of newspapers filling up every inch in his house. It's easy to laugh at when it isn't happening to you.

Or to someone you love.

The thought comes out of nowhere, and I bite my tongue to keep it from slipping through my lips. I reach out and touch Ben's hand. He laces his fingers through mine and squeezes. For a while, we sit silently in the shadows, staring into the night, music and laughter and people drifting in and out of the gym.

"She was on her way back to the store when I left," Ben says.

"For more toilet paper?"

"Paper towels. I told her not to. We don't have any more room in the garage. I'm afraid she's going to fill up the rec room next."

It would be easier if I had some sort of advice—some surefire, short-term cure. Ben's dad found one at a bar in Nebraska. Adele found hers at the gym and the big box stores. Adults have the luxury of making their own decisions, but they don't stop there. They end up making our decisions, too. I know Ben can't just jump in his truck and drive away. It's why he has his sights set on the long game: college.

"If I can just get a verbal agreement for a scholarship this season . . ." He's lost in thought for a moment, then he turns and looks at me. "What's your plan, Weston?"

"What do you mean?"

He considers me for a second. "Coach says Duke is interested in me, too."

"Duke?"

"How far away you want to go for college?" he asks. "They've got a soccer team."

I'm not sure how to answer. When I'm silent, he turns to me with a smile. "They've got a kickass science department, too," he says, then hastens to add, "from what I understand. You know. If you were . . . interested in that sort of thing."

"Are you asking me to go to the same college as you?"

"Maybe . . ." He pauses. "Okay, yeah. I guess that's what I'm asking."

Watching him tongue-tied may be the cutest thing I've ever seen.

"I've got to see how the soccer season goes. Don't know if I'm good enough to be ranked."

"Sure you are," he says. "But your PSAT scores were huge, right?"

A sheepish smile gives me away.

"You're a National Merit Finalist, right?"

"Semifinalist," I say, "just like you. But it's nice to know you're paying attention."

He winks at me. "I've been paying attention to you for a long time, Weston. You're one of those girls who can do anything she wants to."

"Oh, am I?"

"There aren't many of you running around this one-horse town."

When he says this, I blush and am glad we're outside in the dark. Ben is the first guy I've ever been out with who's complimented my brains before making a grab at my boobs.

"So what about it?" he asks. "If I got an offer from Duke, would you consid—"

I lean over and stop his mouth with a kiss. He drops his red Solo cup to the ground and wraps an arm around my waist, pulling me closer on the bench.

When we finally come up for air, he taps a finger on my nose. "I'll take that as a yes."

"What about your mom?" I ask him.

"What about her?"

"When we talked before, you said you were afraid of leaving her alone. Afraid she'd fill up the house with crap."

Ben nods. "This week—finally being with you, like this—it's made me realize how fast things can change. There are some things I can control—like asking you out. There are some things I can't—like whether Mom will ever stop with the coupons. It's like ever since Dad took off she doesn't want to see me—really *see* me. Maybe when she looks at me, her heart breaks all over again. So she puts all this stuff between us."

My eyes well up. Hearing Ben talk like this I realize there's so much about him—so much going on beneath the surface that no one ever sees. I may be the luckiest girl alive—not only to know this, but to have him share it with me.

"You're a good guy, Ben." When I say it there's a catch in my throat. He hears it and squeezes my hand.

"I just don't think I can stick around and be worried about my mom for my whole life. If I had the opportunity to go play and didn't take it, I'd wind up hating myself and probably her. Then what good would I be to anybody?"

He takes a deep breath and leans back against the table attached to our bench. He stretches out his impossibly long legs, and lets go of my hand, wrapping his arm around my shoulders.

We sit there in silence for a little while, until Rachel comes looking for us and drags us back to the gym. We thread our way across the floor to Christy and Lindsey, and in a relatively low-volume moment, as the DJ mixes one track into the next, Ben pulls me close and whispers in my ear. "You're a knockout. You know that?"

I can't hide the smile that spreads across my face, but I roll my eyes. "Dork."

He laughs and in one easy move lifts his arm, spinning me away from him beneath it. He pulls me in close again, and just as I think this evening may be the most perfect of the known high school dances in all of recorded time, I see the doors to the gym swing open, and Coach Sanders steps inside with his arm around John Doone.

twenty-two

THE GENERAL MAYHEM that greets Dooney's entrance is the kind usually reserved for international recording sensations and movie stars. There are shouts and screams and a general rush toward him. Dooney is mobbed by most of the varsity team and anyone else who can get close enough. Amid the fist bumps and high fives, Phoebe and the Tracies follow the path that Christy clears, the four of them dancing toward Dooney through the crush.

Ben doesn't make a move, just stands there staring. By virtue of height, he's got an unobstructed view.

"He's here!" Rachel is flushed from dancing, and tugs on Ben's jacket. "Isn't that great?" She looks so relieved that I smile.

"See?" she says. "It was all a big misunderstanding."

Ben nods, but I see a hesitance in his eyes, something guarded about Dooney's being here. The music gets fast and loud again in answer to the energy that has surged through the crowd. The focus has shifted to John Doone at center court, and the look on his face says that this is his rightful place.

"Let's go say hi!" Rachel says.

"Looks like he's coming to us." Lindsey jerks her chin in Dooney's direction, and I see him making his way over. The crowd clamors, then falls away, and in a moment he's in front of us, reaching toward Ben in that way guys do, the first move of a secret handshake, thumbs hooked, hands clasped. They pull each other in for a thump on the back, a *brah* hug with their fists and forearms sandwiched between their chests.

Dooney is lit up like a Christmas tree. "Dude! I'm back. Can you believe this shit?"

Lindsey goes tense beside me. Ben smiles at him, but there is something in his eyes—wariness, or weariness. I can't tell which in the floating beams of the disco ball hanging over our heads.

"Didn't think I'd see you here," Ben manages. If Dooney notices how checked out Ben seems he doesn't let it bother him.

"Pops finally convinced mom it was time to let me out of lockdown for a couple hours." Dooney is crowing, vodka on his breath. He holds a hand up toward Ben and waits a second for Ben's halfhearted high five.

Phoebe reappeares at Dooney's elbow. "Hey!" she shouts.

Dooney swings around. She beams at him and gives him a hug. "Why didn't you text me?"

Dooney smirks at Ben. "Fucking chicks. More trouble than they're worth."

Phoebe smacks his shoulder and Dooney apes repentance. "Babe! I'm sorry. The cops still have my phone."

"Well, you coulda answered the phone at your house. Or messaged me online and let me know you were coming." Phoebe is pissed and no good at pretending. "You were supposed to be my date, you know."

Dooney shrugs. "Probably easier that we didn't come together," he says, winking. "I'm a star now. The press is all over me! Coach had to run interference so I could get in past the news vans. Couple of 'em have been following me around since lockup. They're camped out at my house, too." He pulls a flask out of his jacket pocket and waggles it in front of him at waist height to avoid detection. "Now that I'm here, anybody wanna get this party started?"

Ben frowns and shakes his head. "Driving," he says, throwing a glance over his shoulder. "Besides, shouldn't you be laying low?"

Dooney ducks and takes a quick gulp, then grimaces, not at the booze, but at Ben's question. "Hell no. Go big or go home, dude." He laughs as Ben tries again.

"If you get caught with that, won't they take you back in?"

Dooney slides the flask back into his pocket. "I'm never going back to jail," he says. There's a smug look of satisfaction on his face. "Dad's got a buddy in from St. Louis. Best defense attorney in the Midwest. He's gonna shut this shit down."

"What about Deacon?" The music is thumping so loudly that Ben has to yell this almost directly into Dooney's ear.

Dooney shrugs. "What about him?" he yells back.

Rachel touches my elbow. "Gonna grab a Coke with Lindsey." She has her church smile on, trying to distract from the fear in her eyes.

"Want anything?" Lindsey asks.

I tell them I'm good, and Lindsey promises to circle back. "I just can't with him right now," she tells me as Dooney takes another swig from the flask and steps on Phoebe's toe.

I give her a little wave as they head off to the bar in the corner.

"Where we partying after this?" Dooney slurs.

Ben takes my hand and says he's hanging out with me afterward. For the first time, Dooney notices me standing there, and I feel his eyes travel down my shoulders, across my chest all the way to my feet, and back up again. "Damn, dude." He whistles, still looking at me. "I wouldn't wanna hang out with me either."

Phoebe rolls her eyes. Dooney grabs her elbow and steers her in front of him. "C'mon, babe. Let's get our groove on." He pauses as he passes Ben. "Text me later, dude."

I see Mr. Jessup clapping Dooney on the back and laughing with him. There is heat and sweat and madness in the air. A group of Buccaneers thumps along with a new song.

First-class seat on my lap, girl, riding comfortable . . .

A dance circle forms around Phoebe and Dooney, LeRon slides in on his knees, then jumps up. He and Dooney leap into the air and bump chests.

Coach is hooting along as the guys chant and bark like Dooney's just been drafted to the NBA. The whole gym is crowding around them when Ben leans in behind me. "Let's get outta here."

The last thing I see as we leave is Phoebe, holding her high heels in her hand and plopping down against the wall of folded-up bleachers. For a moment, I think she might be crying, or about to. She looks up as we make our break for the doors, and in that split second she plasters on her top-of-the-pyramid smile. It's a smile I have seen a thousand times before, a smile that says *Everything is perfect.*

Only this time, I don't think she believes it.

And I don't believe it either.

twenty-three

WE ARE QUIET on the drive home, but it's not the comfortable kind of quiet I've shared with Ben before—the silence of *all is well.* This is the quiet of a duck floating on a pond: peaceful and serene up top, paddling like mad below the surface.

Ben is so distracted he doesn't turn on any music, and I can't turn off the questions in my head. I keep seeing Phoebe's face as Ben and I left the dance, and thinking of Ben's cool response to Dooney. Why didn't Ben seem more excited that Dooney is out on bail? What is Phoebe covering up with her smile?

The closer you look, the more you see.

I'm desperate to fill the quiet cracks in our evening with laughter or music or chatter about anything at all. I search for a sound to fill the air between us, words to drown out the tiny voice I can hear too well in this silence. It's a whisper that grows a little louder every day, and even now I can hear it turned up one decibel more. Over and over it asks a single question of one person.

That person is Ben, and the question is, *Do you know what really went on that night?*

The garage door is open at Ben's house when we pull into the drive. Adele Cody is almost hidden by Bounty eight-packs in a stack nearly as tall as she is. She flits in and out of the shelving racks wearing yellow yoga pants and a black sports bra. Her abs are clearly defined, the muscles in her arms ropy and straining like an aging pop star's, with too little fat on her body and too much Pilates on her schedule. She's making room for the paper towels, moving boxes of Band-Aids to the shelves above and Brillo Pads to the shelves below, displacing display flats of Carmex and Altoids in either direction.

Ben bumps his head slowly against the steering wheel three times then he rests it there. "Perfect."

My hand finds the back of his neck, and I run my fingers through his hair in a gentle massage. "Should we go say hi?"

"No. We should have her committed."

I laugh, but I'm pretty sure he isn't joking. "C'mon," I say, and unclick my seat belt.

As I turn to open the door, Ben tells me to wait, and when I look back at him he leans across the seat and kisses me. There is a depth of need in this kiss to which I am unaccustomed. I can feel it in the way he leans, the way he reaches, the manner in which his mouth draws on mine, the grasp of his hands. There's something fierce in this kiss, something raw and unguarded. Something that says, *Please catch me. I'm falling.*

After a minute my hands find his face, and I pull back, looking him in the eyes. Six days later, we are forehead to forehead again, but I *know* him now—not as an old friend with a shared history, but as something much more.

"Let's go inside," I whisper.

He glances out the windshield at the garage, where his mom teeters on a step stool, pushing a package of paper towels onto a top shelf. "Can we sneak in the front door?"

I smile. "It'll just take a second."

Adele wants to hear all about my dress while Ben hefts the Bounty rolls onto the top shelf, then quickly fills in the rest on the rack below.

"There isn't much to tell," I say. "Just found it at Second Sands."

"Can you imagine somebody letting go of that?" she says. "So glad you put it to good use. Didn't expect you home so early, Benny." She pats Ben's arm, but he ignores the question and continues putting stuff away.

"John Doone showed up," I say, trying to fill the silence, but Ben shoots me a look, eyes wide. *Why are you talking to her about this?*

"It's all anybody's talked about at work this week," Adele

says, shaking her head. "His daddy's been on the phone with the door closed for hours talking to lawyers. Margie's been in and out all week, too, crying buckets every time I see her."

Ben hefts the last pack of paper towels into place. "Well, tell her to come here if she needs a tissue. We're prepared for a flood. Won't need an ark. We can just mop up the whole planet with these."

"Thanks, hon." Adele tries to peck his cheek, but he squirms away. "Now we won't have to worry about running out for a while."

"Were we worried about running out of paper towels before? Was there some worldwide shortage I didn't hear about?" There's an edge of scorn in Ben's voice.

"It was just . . . such a good deal." Adele blinks, her eyes smudged with the liner she wore to the gym tonight. "I actually made twenty dollars when I picked these up." She looks over at me and smiles in hopes of a friendlier audience. "I had a coup—"

"A *coo*-pon," Ben cuts her off, mimicking his mom's pronunciation. "You and your *coo*-pons. Jesus, Mom. When's it gonna be enough? The stores aren't shutting down. We can go buy freaking toilet paper whenever we need some."

Ben's anger chokes Adele, and her eyes water. She glances at me, then blushes at the floor. "Just . . . like saving money, I guess . . ." She busies herself folding up the step stool. She leans it against the wall, then reaches the door that leads into the downstairs rec room. She pauses with her hand on the knob, trying to salvage this ruined moment. "What do you have planned for the rest of the evening?"

Ben shrugs. "Watch a movie or something."

She searches Ben's face, but he won't make eye contact. It's excruciating to witness. "That sounds nice." She turns and gives me a shy smile. "Good night, Katie. You look beautiful."

I say thank you as she slips through the door, closing it behind her. I am seized by the urge to chase after her and give her a hug, but I don't. Ben won't look at me for a minute either. He jams a stray case of Altoids back onto a shelf. I hear water flowing through pipes and imagine Adele, stepping into a hot shower upstairs.

Ben punches the button to close the garage, then opens the door to the rec room. "Coming?"

As I follow him down the hall, I feel a frown folding around the words that form in my mouth. *What the hell was that? Why did you yell at your mom?* As we reach the den I turn to say this. Ben kisses me. I kiss him back, and he wraps his arms around me. He slips an arm under my thighs as he bends, and lifts, gently laying me back on the sectional that outlines half the room.

"Wait," I whisper between kisses. I want to talk to him about what is happening. He is kneeling on the floor, his upper body slowly settling on top of me, his arm around my lower back pulling me close, every part of him pressed up against me. The same desperate kisses from out in the driveway fill my mouth, the heat of his body against mine steals my breath, and fogs all the things I want to say, words written on a mirror in a steamed-up bathroom.

He reaches for the zipper at the back of my dress and draws me up with the arm underneath me as he unzips it. I feel his bicep bulge and remember again how powerful he is. I say, "Wait," once more, but it's as if he doesn't hear me. His fingers are warm on my bare back, his tongue adamant against my own as he pulls the dress loose from my shoulders, one hand sliding down, down, down my back, cupping my hip in his hand. He pulls me more tightly beneath him, throwing one leg up onto the sectional with me, rolling his full weight onto the couch, while his fingers continue searching beneath me.

My pulse is racing now as fast as my mind. I press my palms flat against his shoulders, pushing back and up. I roll my mouth away from his and thrust my whole body against him, bucking him sideways, back off the couch and onto the floor.

"Jesus! *Ben.*"

He stares back at me, dazed. "What?"

"What is with you tonight?"

He blinks at me, then scowls. "You're the one who wanted to come inside."

"Yeah, I did, before you decided to make your mom cry. And I just told you to wait. Twice. What the hell?" I pull my dress up and sit back on the couch, huffing out a long slow breath.

He is kneeling on the carpet, his face red. He peers up at me, ashamed. "I'm sorry," he says. "Really. I wouldn't—"

"That was some bullshit out there with your mom."

His eyes darken and he looks away, pulling off his jacket

and tossing it onto the couch. "Don't tell me about my mom. She's crazy."

"You know what else is crazy?" I snap. "That you're way more upset about a stack of paper towels than you are about what's going on with Dooney and Deacon."

His eyes flash up to mine. "What do you mean?"

I can't hold the question in any longer. "Were you there when it happened, Ben?"

He gapes at me. "When what happened? I was dropping you off at home."

"After that." I drill down. "When you went back for your truck. What was going on?"

"I went in to tell Dooney bye. That's it."

"So, what Stacey says happened . . . you're saying it didn't?"

"I don't even know for sure what she's saying."

A response forms in my mouth but is pulled back by a jolt in my chest. It's the first time this phrase has entered my mind. Ben looks at me, expectantly. Finally I force out the words in a rush. "That she was raped, Ben. More than once. By different guys on your team."

Ben groans and rolls his eyes, but I keep going.

"Sloane Keating said Stacey was in the hospital all day on Sunday—"

"Wait." Ben holds up a hand. "That reporter? She said this on the news?"

"No. Last night. She told me."

Ben frowns. "Where were you talking to a reporter?"

I take a deep breath, then blurt it out. *Quick, like a Band-Aid.* "At Coral Creek. I went to see Stacey. Sloane Keating was hanging out in a news van."

I see Ben blink twice when I say this. Even in the dim light of a single lamp the color seems to drain from his face. "Kate. What the hell are you doing?" He hisses this in a loud whisper, as if he's afraid the walls are listening in or the whole house is bugged. "Why did you go talk to Stacey?"

"I didn't talk to her," I tell him. "Her mom shut the door in my face, and then I got ambushed by a reporter."

"We weren't there," Ben says. "Nothing happened. And even if it did, you and I were already gone."

"When 'nothing' happens at a party, charges aren't filed, and reporters don't show up." These words slice through the air between us, and Ben rocks back on his heels as they find their mark.

"Coach told us that we shouldn't talk to anyone about this. Why are you talking to reporters?"

"He's not my coach. And I didn't talk to her."

"She sure as hell knew our names tonight."

I sigh. "We're both all over the Buccaneers Facebook page. It's not hard to figure out. She's a reporter."

"Exactly," he says. "A reporter. She doesn't care about Stacey. Or any of us. She just wants to make a name for herself. That's why we should stay as far away from this whole thing as we can."

"Dooney isn't staying away from it. You saw him tonight. He's loving this."

Ben closes his eyes and rubs his temples like he has a headache. His expression is the same one he has when he sees his mom hauling stuff into the garage—like he wishes he could snap his fingers and make all of it disappear, me included.

Something about this makes me furious.

"Oh yeah. It's such a pain in the ass, isn't it? The fact that someone else had something terrible happen to her." It comes out more sarcastically than I mean it to, but I don't stop. "And what if Dooney did do this? So now he's got a hotshot lawyer, right? What if he gets off the hook? Won't he just think he can go on acting this way forever? Did you see how Coach and Mr. Jessup were smacking him on the back tonight? It made me sick."

Ben places his hands on my shoulders and looks right into my eyes. "Kate. We are not the police. This is not our problem."

I wonder if he's lost his mind. "Not our problem? Your two best friends might've raped someone."

"Why would Deacon and Dooney rape anybody?" he asks. "They can both have any girl they want. You saw Stacey hanging all over them at the party."

"That doesn't mean she wanted them to fuck her."

Ben jerks like I've slapped him in the face. "We don't know that," he says quietly. "We weren't there."

"Exactly," I say. "For all we know, it's just as likely that Dooney and Deacon are the ones lying. Don't we owe it to Stacey to believe she might be telling the truth?"

"I don't owe her anything."

Something about these words cracks me open. I try to choke back a sob, but start crying despite my best intentions.

Ben reaches for my hand. "Kate, no—please, I didn't mean—"

"What about me?" I choke. "Do you owe me something? I was just as wasted as she was. Why do I get driven home and kept safe but not her? Why not just leave me to Dooney and Deacon and the boys in the basement?"

"Because I love you."

He fires this back at me, then smacks a hand over his mouth. The words roll through my chest like a thunderclap. More tears stream down my cheeks and I try to wipe them away, but they won't stop coming. How many times did I imagine hearing *I love you* from Ben? How many times will I wish I had kept my mouth shut so I didn't have to hear it like this?

Ben collapses onto the floor, turning around to sit with his back against the couch, his arm against my leg. We stay like this for a long time staring at the dark TV screen on the opposite wall, watching different movies in our minds.

Mine is the image of Ben, walking back to Dooney's that night, pausing on the stairs to tell Rachel and Christy good-bye as they leave. He finds John and Deacon in the kitchen, finishing the Cabo Wabo with Stacey. Ben waves away the shot they offer. He bumps fists with Greg. He hears Randy call up the stairs from the den. He stops at the top of the stairwell and yells a *later* back down.

Then he leaves.

In my mind's eye, I see him closing Dooney's front door and walking to his truck. He climbs in, he turns on some music, and he drives home. I see the Ben I have always known, being the person he has always been: honest and kind.

I see the guy who loves me.

Of course he's angry and confused. Of course he doesn't know who to believe. Isn't that exactly how I feel?

Finally, Ben reaches over and slides his hand around my ankle. He runs his fingers up and down on my calf, hesitant, searching out some common ground between us. "You have such great soccer legs."

"The better to kick your ass with."

He turns toward me with a sheepish grin and I roll my eyes. "Where the hell did you learn to unzip a dress with one hand? Was there a clinic on that at basketball camp?"

"I've been the man of the house for a few years now," he says quietly. "I'm good at zipping them up, too. Here, lemme show you."

He stands and takes both my hands, pulling me to my feet. He turns me around and pulls the zipper up my back, adjusting the fabric on my shoulders. Then he places a tender kiss on my neck.

I turn around. He leans in and kisses my lips once. "Can I have a do-over?"

I nod.

"I love you, Kate Weston."

"I love you, too, Ben Cody." The words tumble out in a whisper.

He drives me home and walks me to the front door. Beneath the porch light, he gives me one last kiss. He wraps both arms around me, pats me on the back, and whispers in my ear the words he said that first time he hugged me when we were five years old.

"It's okay. It's going to be fine."

twenty-four

I WAKE UP to the sound of laughter.

It's early still, but I know it's only me and Will in the house. When his crew is on a project, Dad always puts in at least half a day on Saturday, and most of the time, he doesn't get home until five. Weekends, Mom meets her friend Mindy from work to speed-walk in the park. She talks about all the calories they burn when she gets home and makes sure to mention that afterward she had her omelet made from Egg Beaters, that yellow stuff that comes in a carton and looks like liquid eggs, but isn't quite.

I smile as I think about Mom and Mindy, pumping their arms and swinging their hips from side to side in the funny way that speed walking requires. All that movement, but they don't cover much ground. I know she'll switch to Sundays with Mindy once soccer starts. Hopefully, Dad will finish up this project soon and be able to make some games as well.

Will is glued to the screen of his laptop when I poke my head in the door of his room. He's sitting at his desk, his back to me and his earbuds in, giggling like a crazy person while he clicks through Facebook pictures. I can see he's on a video chat with Tyler, who must be cracking him up. I smile and tiptoe sideways around his bed so I can stay out of the camera frame. It is my general rule that I refuse to appear on any camera in any way until I have looked at myself in a mirror. I also want to spook the crap out of my brother. Will likes to sneak up and scare the bejesus out of me. This is payback.

I am stretching out my hands to squeeze his shoulders and shout *Boo!* when he says something that makes me freeze.

"No *way*, dude. She's a six, *tops*."

I frown and slowly lower myself onto my knees so I'm below the sight line of the camera, but can still see the screen if I crane my head sideways. Will clicks back and forth between two pictures of a girl named Emily from his class.

"She's got a mustache, Ty. I swear. That picture has more filters on it than Dooney's hot tub."

I see Tyler's head pop back with a hoot of laughter in the square at the corner of Will's screen. Will giggles like he used to when we were little and spent Saturday mornings watching SpongeBob in our PJs instead of . . . doing whatever this is.

Tyler says something I can't hear, and Will acquiesces. "Fine!" he shouts. "I'll give her a seven, but she is *not* in the top three." Will clicks to comment on the picture. He types a *7* then *#JVbuccs*, then *#r&p*.

As he moves to post this, I jump up and grab his wrist. "No!"

Will leaps to his feet, screaming. I would say that he yelled, but it was higher pitched than that. Definitely a scream. His headphones rip from his ears, but not fast enough, and the wire pulls his laptop across the desk. It hits his leg, and the padded seat of his rolling chair before bouncing onto the carpet.

"What the hell are you doing?" He's panting like he just ran a fast mile.

"I might ask the same of you," I say calmly. "You're not really about to post a rank on that girl's Facebook picture are you?"

Will's gaze darts to his laptop on the floor. He dives for it, but I smack my bare foot on top of it, and slide it toward me. His gangly ninth-grade limbs are longer than mine, but he's not in full control of them yet—no match for my fast feet and twelve years of soccer drills.

"Watch it!" he yells. "You're gonna break my computer."

"I'm gonna break your face if you don't knock it off."

"Why do you care?" he huffs. "It's just a game."

I cross my arms as my eyes go wide. "Just a game? Putting that number on her Facebook wall so everybody can see it? Are you kidding me?"

"It's a joke." Will is pleading now, his eyes downcast.

"No, it's not. It's somebody's feelings."

I flip open his laptop, and the screen blinks to life. The chat window is blank now. Tyler has disappeared back into the ether. He'll stay there if he knows what's good for him.

I put the laptop back on his desk. "Look at her," I command.

Will rolls his eyes and sinks into his chair, his lips a locked vault.

"How would you feel if I ranked you? Or Tyler?" I ask. "What if I put numbers under your pictures and told the whole world that you two aren't very attractive? Would you like that?"

His silent shrug makes me want to smack him in the back of the head. "Jesus, Will. She's a human being, not a hashtag. There's a person involved." As the word *hashtag* leaves my lips, the blinking cursor in the comment box catches my eye. I point at *#r&p.* "What is this? What does it mean?"

Will leans in and looks where I am pointing. "I dunno."

"Then why are you typing it under this girl's picture? If you don't even know what it means?"

He shrugs again. It's an epidemic with the guys in my world, this shrugging. None of them know. Or want to know. Or maybe they do know and just want me off their backs. "I just saw it on a bunch of tweets about . . ." He doesn't finish.

"Dooney's party?" I ask.

"Yeah."

"But you don't know what it means?"

He shakes his head. "No. A bunch of the varsity guys have been using it."

"Which ones?"

He huffs a huge breath and rubs his hands on his face. "Why do you care so much?"

"Why don't you care at all?"

He chews his cheek and drops his head. "Dooney, Deacon, Greg, Randy—"

"So basically, everyone who was arrested this week."

He nods, miserably. "But more, like LeRon and Reggie. Kyle, too."

I lean over him and delete the words he almost posted. "You do know you're not the only person who can see what you comment online, right? You may recall that whole thing about the police collecting people's phones?"

He groans. "Jeez. Fine. Okay, *Mom.*"

"If you want, we can certainly talk to Mom about it." This gets his attention. "Those pictures that girl posted? What's her name? Emily? They're not for you. They're not your property. You aren't entitled to use them however you please. How many other pictures did you rank?"

He grunts and plugs his earbuds back into the computer. "Why are you so hysterical about this?"

Something in me snaps. I grab the neck of his T-shirt and yank it toward me, almost pulling him out of his chair. My voice is a low, steady whisper. "I am not hysterical about anything. I am concerned that my brother is turning into an asshole." I push him back into the chair. "Delete every rank you posted on a picture this morning."

"Or what?" he counters. "You'll tell Mom?"

"Nope." I walk across his room and step over a pair of boxer shorts into the hallway. "You'll deal directly with Dad on this one."

As I close the door to my own room I hear what sounds like a shoe hitting the wall. I grab my phone and text Rachel.

I need to move my legs before I start using my fists.

twenty-five

BY THE TIME Lindsey joins me on the soccer field at school, I'm already in the middle of my first full line drill. Rachel and Christy are stretching and waiting by the goal nearest to the parking lot. I push buttons to clear and start the stopwatch on my wrist, then put my hands on top of my head to keep from folding in half.

Deep breaths.

Walking in circles.

Christy, bitching.

"Line drills? On a Saturday? How the hell did you let her talk you into this?" she asks Rachel.

"You'll be glad we did it come Monday." Rachel jumps up and

grabs her own ankle, pulling it from behind to stretch her quads.

"Might as well get the puking out of the way while Coach Lewis isn't watching," teases Lindsey. Christy doesn't even retort, just leans over in a hurdler's stretch and moans softly into her own kneecap.

"Forty-five seconds, ladies, then we go again." My breathing slows, but my pulse is still racing. I can't get the image of Will typing hashtags out of my head.

Line drills consist of running the length of the field from one end to the other in increasing distances: from the goal line to the penalty box and back, then out to the middle of the field and back, and so on, bending down to touch each line with a hand as the trips across the field grow successively longer. By the time Christy touches the goal line at the far end of the field the first time, she is doubled over with cramps and drops to her knees. Rachel, Lindsey, and I tap the near goal line as this happens, and Rachel yells *no* as loudly as she can. If Coach Lewis sees anyone stop, she adds another drill.

I am already exhausted from two full rounds, but I turn and follow Rachel and Lindsey down to where Christy is kneeling and heaving. Lindsey and I both take an arm and pull her to her feet, dragging her toward the goal while Rachel shouts threats and encouragements, alternating stick and carrot:

You're almost finished!

Can't do that Monday, or Coach will make you run it again!

Don't give up! Go, go, GO!

Christy collapses on her back, and I clear my stopwatch

again. "Four more to go. We've got forty-five seconds on the clock."

"I . . . can't . . . ," Christy says, panting.

"You can," I say, offering her a hand. "Get up. Walk. Breathe. You're the best goalie in our conference, but not if you can't turn on the speed."

Reluctantly, she gives me her hand, and I pull her up. "We're running in twenty," I say.

"I hate you," gasps Christy.

"You'll love her on Monday," Rachel says grimly. "We all will."

Then I count down from ten and we go again.

Miraculously, we all finish another four complete drills without seeing what Christy ate for breakfast, then collapse next to the goal breathing hard.

Christy pulls a handful of grass and tosses it in my hair. "What brought this on, Weston?"

I take a deep breath and blow it out through puffed cheeks at the sky above us. "My brother was driving me crazy."

Rachel laughs. "Send your brother to my house. He can deal with my sisters and I'll move in with you."

"Deal. He can be such a moron."

"He'll fit right in," she says.

"What'd he do?" Christy wants to know. "Don't you two usually get along?"

The breeze is chilly, but it feels good blowing across the sweat on my forehead. I can smell the dirt in the bare spots around the field. This poor grass. We'll rip it to shreds starting Monday, no matter how much they fertilize it.

I roll over on my side, propped up on an elbow, and run my fingers through the tufts of green. "He was posting stupid crap on Facebook."

"Like what?" asks Lindsey.

"He and his friend on the JV team were ranking the girls in their class."

Christy sits up fast, the gleam of nearby gossip in her eyes. "Who'd they say was the hottest?"

"Not the girl they were giving a seven to when I stopped him," I say.

Christy laughs, and I shoot her a look. "What?" she says. "Boys will be boys."

"That's bullshit." All three of us turn to look at Lindsey.

"Lighten up," says Rachel.

Lindsey isn't having it. "'Boys will be boys' is what people say to excuse guys when they do something awful."

"What are you so upset about?" Christy asks. "They didn't rank you."

Lindsey faces Christy full on, sitting up on her knees. "Can you honestly tell me you'd find it funny if someone posted a rank on your profile picture?"

Christy just looks away and picks another handful of grass. "Depends on my rank."

"Bring it," says Rachel. "I'd be a ten." She tries to make this a cute joke, flipping her ponytail.

Only Christy laughs. "C'mon. Don't you remember when Dooney was doing that last fall? He and Deacon would sit at lunch and scribble a score for every girl that picked up a tray in the cafeteria line?"

A small jolt of memory. It was the very first week of school. I was paying so much attention to Ben I'd barely noticed Dooney and Deacon scribbling big numbers with Sharpies in spiral notebooks, holding them up in the air. I hadn't even realized they were rating girls. *What did they rate me?* No wonder Ms. Speck marched over on her high heels and told them to knock it off. I'd forgotten all about it.

"That's just the way guys are," says Christy.

"Is it?" asks Rachel quietly. "Or is that just the way these guys are?"

"Yeah," says Lindsey. "I can't imagine my dad doing stuff like that with his buddies."

"Ben would never act like that." But as the words leave my lips, the tiny voice whispering questions clicks up one more notch on the volume dial.

Christy groans. "Yes, your knight in shining armor is practically perfect in every way." She lies on her back, both hands on her right calf, pulling her knee toward her chest. "Also, we're not talking about our dads. We're talking about a bunch of high school goofballs."

"Dooney and his gang aren't 'goofballs,'" Lindsey says. "They're creeps."

I frown. "Ben isn't a creep." It comes out defensive.

"Sorry." Lindsey means it. "I just think you should tell Will to be careful. He clearly thinks Ben and Dooney are the bee's knees."

Christy and Rachel giggle when she says this. I can't help but laugh myself. "The what?" I ask.

Lindsey laughs with us. "The bee's knees?"

"Oh my god," chortles Christy. "Who are you right now? My grandpa?"

Rachel stands up. "Well, thanks for the memories, you guys. See you on Monday." She has to drop Christy off and pick up her sisters from a birthday party. Lindsey and I watch them pull out of the parking lot, driving past the news vans that still linger by the front entrance.

"Will acted like I was a huge wet blanket because I didn't want him ranking the girls in his class. It was like I was this big . . ." I search for the right word.

"Bitch?" Lindsey asks.

It stings even coming from her mouth. "Yeah," I say. "I just want him to be a good guy, you know?"

Lindsey nods, but doesn't say anything. Sometimes, I think most of friendship is knowing when to keep your mouth shut and your ears open. Lindsey is an expert where this is concerned. She flips onto her back and stretches her hamstring, waiting for me to continue.

"What bothered me most was how Will didn't get it. He didn't understand why I was upset that he was telling these girls they don't measure up. He acts like he has some natural right to tell them they should look a certain way. Why? Because he's a dude?"

"It's not just your brother." Lindsey stands up and stretches her arms above her head. "Seen a Hardee's commercial lately? The whole planet is wired that way."

We walk to our cars, and when I tell Lindsey I'll see her on Monday, she hugs me. She's not much of a hugger.

I smile. "What was that for?"

"For being somebody who cares about this stuff," she says. "Not many people around here do." She gives me a little wave, then gets in her navy-blue hatchback and drives away.

There are only two news vans here right now, which leaves me wondering where the other three are. Off getting coffee? On the curb at the courthouse, waiting for word on whether Greg and Randy will be tried as adults? The trailer park, staking out Stacey's place again?

After I start the truck, I sit there for a second before I throw it in reverse. I'm not even sure where I'm headed, really, until I make the turn toward Walmart.

twenty-six

I DON'T MEAN to break in, exactly.

It's just that when I reach out to ring the bell, I notice the door to Stacey's trailer isn't latched all the way. There's no car parked out front. LeeAnne must be at work.

The Coral Creek Mobile Village looks shabbier without the benefit of an ethereal nighttime glow. In the stark light of a Saturday afternoon, Stacey's trailer is still the tidiest, but it looks tired, too—as if it takes a tremendous amount of energy just to stay upright; that it might, at any moment, give up altogether and collapse in a great wheeze of dust and fiberglass.

An elderly black man sits by a stack of the tires in the yard next door, leaning back in a green plastic lawn chair. He's reading a book while the Doberman snoozes, draped over his feet. When I walk up to the little white gate, the man smiles and waves a howdy in my direction. The dog stays silent and still, but I see his eyes open and follow me, like a painting in a haunted castle. *The closer you look, the more you see.* I smile back at him, then quickly open the white picket gate and close it again, as if these flimsy slats could protect me from a motivated Doberman.

I can hear a shower running as I climb the stairs of the redwood deck. Whatever possessed me to come here again must still have me firmly in hand. When I see the unlatched door, I push it open without hesitation, then walk in like I own the place, my hand held back to keep the storm door from banging behind me.

I find myself standing on a linoleum island right inside the door, surrounded by sculpted shag carpet the color of Mom's two-alarm chili. I don't know what I expected the inside of a trailer home to look like, but this one is as well kept on the inside as it is on the outside. It isn't covered in old take-out containers and doesn't reek of cigarette smoke. No one is standing in the kitchen to my right cooking meth.

I hear music coming from down the hall where the water is running. It must be Stacey in the shower. I make a decision then and there. I will wait for her. I will convince her that I'm not *one of them.* I just want to find out what really happened. I don't need her to be my best friend. I don't even need her to believe me.

I only need the truth.

Emboldened by my plan, a strange urgency takes hold. I walk around the living room like a detective in search of evidence. I quietly pull open the drawer of an oak end table next to an overstuffed couch, covered in a quilt. Remote controls. Loose change. A pack of peppermint chewing gum. I slide the drawer closed. It sends up a loud squeak, and I freeze for a moment, my heart pounding. I glance at the bathroom door. Still closed. Water still running. Music still playing.

I take a deep breath and let it out slowly, silently.

What are you doing?

What am I looking for? A filing cabinet with folders full of secret documents? A handwritten account of events labeled, "Dooney's Party: One Week Ago"? I take a moment to imagine Stacey, fresh from a shower, finding me in her living room, unannounced. I picture her wrapped in a towel, hair wet, screaming, the friendly old man next door and his Doberman racing to her aid. Me, on a gurney, explaining to the police, my parents, and Ben how I came to be mauled by a dog outside Stacey Stallard's trailer, and Sloane Keating's smug little smirk, floating above us all as her cameraman captures every moment.

This is crazy.

I turn to go.

As I do, I glance through a door on the other side of the living room and come to a dead stop. This is a bedroom—Stacey's it seems. There's a purple comforter she must have gotten when she was just a little girl, covered in stars and clouds. But it isn't the bed that catches my eye. It's the walls. The afternoon sun streams through sheer white curtains, bathing the room in a soft glow. I walk to the door and step inside.

Every vertical surface is covered with birds. Each one is a pencil sketch in the center of a page. Delicate, detailed, every one of them seems to be in motion. A beak digs into down or carries a twig, wings spread, tail feathers flutter. Not a single one of them is still. The very walls seem to ripple with the pulse of a thousand tiny heartbeats, as if at any moment, the entire flock might startle and take to the skies, carrying the whole room—this perfect aviary of art—and me away with it.

My mouth hangs slightly open. Turning slowly, I take in owls and orioles, jaspers and jays, sparrows and starlings. Hundreds of intricate, finely hatched feathers, dappled wings, and shining eyes somehow lit from within.

My gaze settles on one drawing centered over the bed. This is the sketch I saw from the living room. It's larger than the others and I recognize the subject immediately. This is the hawk from the trees behind the school. The details are so deftly rendered it looks like a black-and-white snapshot of the bird I saw through the geology classroom window. I can almost feel the rush of the air from her wings.

Stacey has captured it perfectly.

This drawing is more than painstaking precision. Her pencil strokes somehow show the raw power of the wings. It holds something else, too: the longing I heard in her voice all those years ago when I asked her why she liked birds so much.

Because they can fly.

"What the hell are you doing?"

Stacey has found me exactly as I'd feared she would. I turn to see her in the doorway, holding a dusty-blue towel around herself, her hair dripping onto her shoulders. There was something dreamy about the Stacey who watched birds out my window when we were kids, her head in the clouds. This Stacey has both feet rooted in trailer park carpet. No clouds. All spikes.

"I'm sorry. I just—the door—it was open, and I—" I sputter, flailing for an explanation.

"Get out!" She steps backward into the living room, making space for me to pass.

"Stacey, please. I just want to know about the party."

She gives a short, bitter laugh. "Know what, Kate? You were there."

"But I don't—I wasn't—there the whole time."

Her eyes flash fire. "Oh really?" She scoffs and shakes her head.

"Yes." I choke. "I was . . . I was too drunk to stay."

"Ben sure wasn't." She flings these words like acid, and every inch of me is singed.

"You're wrong." My heart pounds. Stacey gives her head a quick shake. She leans against the doorway. Her arms are so thin, reeds crossed against her chest, pinning the towel in place.

"I was too drunk to stay, too," she sneers. "Didn't even know what happened when I woke up. Saw it all online. Sure you can find it, too."

My stomach lurches. "What do you mean?"

"I mean you're an idiot." She points at the front door again. "Get out."

twenty-seven

MY EYES FLOOD as I roar away from Stacey's trailer. I can barely see the gravel road that leads out of Coral Creek. When I reach the Walmart blacktop, I pull in beside a leafless sapling sticking out of a planter that separates parking lanes. It is wired to stakes that are thicker than its own trunk—a stunned captive, surrounded by asphalt, doomed to struggle for breath in the haze of a thousand tailpipes.

I scramble for my phone. I've seen Ben's tweets in my feed, but maybe I missed something? Tapping to his Twitter account, I scroll through the posts. There are just a few from this past week, and I get to last Saturday's tweets faster than I expect to.

The first one is a selfie. He's just gotten dressed for the party. His hair is perfect. One hand holds the phone, the other points into the mirror. His face is a flirty smirk, lips closed, eyes full of mischief:

@BCody17: Getting turnt w/my #buccs.

A little later:

@BCody17: Headed to #doonestown. #buccs

Another picture—this one, a shot of Dooney's kitchen, early on. All the bottles lined up, the red Solo cups neatly stacked, the bottle of Cabo Wabo still full.

@BCody17: It's going down . . . #timber #doonestown #buccs

The next two make my stomach roll.

@BCody17: You guys. She's here. #doonestown #dying

@BCody17: She don't know she's beautiful.
#doonestown

Is he talking about . . . *me*? He invited me as an afterthought—didn't he? Maybe he was playing it cool? I remember now what he said in the hallway on Monday about wanting to ask me out at Dooney's party, but not being sure if I really felt that way about him—if it was just the tequila talking.

There's only one more tweet from Saturday night. It was posted at 11:17 p.m. and has no hashtags.

@BCody17: Long walk with the perfect girl. Best way to end the night.

His next tweet was on Sunday night—late, after he'd gotten home from dinner at our house. He'd tagged a fantasy show on

HBO. Something about the mother of dragons? I scroll back through to check again. Nothing about Stacey from Saturday night, or even Dooney for that matter.

Maybe he deleted some tweets?

His Facebook page shows no posts on Saturday, and his Instagram account only has the selfie and the booze. He's friends with his mom on Facebook, so I assume that's why he didn't put up the picture of the bar at Dooney's.

The thought of Dooney makes me feel sick. I remember him on Tuesday, checking Ben's phone at my locker.

You sure it's gone?

What was gone? Ben must've deleted something. How could I not have asked? How could I not have noticed? Why wasn't I paying attention?

I tap back to Twitter and scroll through Ben's tweets one more time. There's a new one at the top now:

@BCody17: Surprising my girl tonight.

I hate myself a little bit for feeling pleased. I am tempted to tap the star to favorite this, but the memory of Stacey's scorn stops my thumb on its way to the screen.

As I stare at the phone, trying to make sense of what Stacey said, it begins to ring. The caller ID flashes a name on the screen: BEN CODY.

I take a deep breath, and swipe to answer.

"Hello?"

"There you are."

"Hey," I say. Cool. Distant. Busy. Not entirely interested.

He catches it. "You okay?" he asks.

"Just saw your tweet."

"Dang. Knew I shoulda called you first." I can hear the Irresistible Grin in his voice. *Some things never change.* "Whatcha doing tonight?" he asks.

"Depends."

"On what?"

This can't wait a moment longer. "On what you deleted from your phone."

Thick silence hangs in the air between us. It lasts 300 million years. Is this the beginning of the ice age?

"Huh?"

"Dooney," I say. "Tuesday at lunch, when I walked up to my locker he was looking at your phone. He asked you if you were sure something was gone." This sentence takes every bit of breath I have. I am winded like I ran a line drill. I gulp for air and forge ahead. "You said it was."

More silence. If only I'd driven to his house to ask him in person. I need to see his face. I don't know what he's thinking. Is this a stony silence? A refusal? Is this how our era ends?

Given enough time, everything changes.

"Oooh, yeah." A realization. A memory. "I deleted the Facebook pic I posted of the booze. Dooney's dad was flipping out about all the underage drinking. Yelling at him about getting disbarred and crap."

I consider this. "That picture is still up on your Twitter and Instagram."

"Crap. Thanks. I gotta delete those, too," he says. "Dooney was worried about Facebook 'cause his dad is on there. But good call. Better safe than sorry." Affable. Not defensive. Easy going. My lungs expand a little. Then he says my name. "Kate?"

"Yeah?"

"Were you worried that I'd posted that pic of Stacey or something?"

I close my eyes and lean my head back against the seat. He told me the truth. Now it's my turn. I want to explain. I want to tell him about Stacey and what she said about him—get it all out in the open. He was so upset the last time I mentioned Stacey. He's trying to keep his head down and do what Coach tells him to.

Dad's voice echoes in my brain: *Steer clear.*

The look on Ben's face when he blurted, *Because I love you,* flashes in my mind. His surprise as the words flew out, frustrated and fierce and forthright. He's been patient and up-front with me all week.

Stacey was so drunk she doesn't even remember what happened. She just told me this herself.

"Maybe a little," I admit.

"Yeah, I get it."

A thick, dark shame oozes down my throat and puddles in my stomach. "You do?"

"Sure," he says. "You're smart. Don't wanna date a jerk."

Tears well up again. This time, they spring from relief, cool and clear. Every time I doubt him, Ben turns out to be better than I expect him to be.

The closer you look, the more you see.

"Sorry for being so . . . weird about it. Wish I could get my mind off this."

"I've got just the ticket," he says. The grin is back in his voice. "Two tickets actually."

"What?" I ask, his smile spreading to me, winging its way across the wireless connection.

"*Grease!* Tonight. Just you, me, and the T-Birds. Maybe pizza afterward?"

"That's perfect." *You're perfect.*

"Need to ask your mom or anything?"

"Yeah, but she'll say yes."

"Cool," he says. "Pick you up at six thirty."

As I hang up with Ben, the afternoon sun glints off the creek that runs along the wall at the back of the Supercenter. It winds its way along the smooth, sand-colored bricks—a gleaming snake of water, a serpent of light. It disappears into a culvert at the far end of the loading docks. A round mouth of corrugated steel set deeply in the cement of a man-made spillway swallows up the stream and directs the water elsewhere. A finite answer engineered for an infinite flow. The unpredictable, harnessed and channeled to make way for Everyday Discount Prices.

I am seized by the sudden urge to pull up the strangled

sapling staked here near the curb and plant it down by the wall at the edge of the stream. I imagine the dirt beneath my nails and the strange looks from half the town.

Is that the Weston girl?

What the hell is she doing?

"Sorry, little tree." I whisper these words at the wretched bare branches, then start the engine and head toward home.

twenty-eight

ACCUSED TEENS PLEAD "NOT GUILTY"; HACKER COLLECTIVE THREATENS ACTION AS POLICE INVESTIGATION STALLS

By Sloane Keating
Published: March 21

CORAL SANDS, Iowa—Ramsey Swain, legal counsel for John Doone, one of the Coral Sands High basketball players accused of assaulting a female student during a party at his home last week, held a press conference this afternoon, declaring his client's innocence.

Mr. Swain pointed to the lack of witnesses who have come forward to aid police in their investigation as proof that Doone, fellow senior Deacon Mills, and two unnamed minors also accused had done nothing wrong.

He spoke to reporters on the steps of the county courthouse. "Did these kids have a wild party? Sure they did. Did a young woman decide to have a little fun with these boys? Certainly. Was it an attack of any kind? Absolutely not."

Deputy Barry Jennings and Detective Flora Hughes have reported difficulty in finding students who will speak to them about what went on during the party one week ago.

County prosecutor Barbara Richter, who held her own press conference today, plans to proceed with the case aided by still pictures that were captured from social media and the cell phones of several of the accused. When asked about a rumored video of the crime itself, Ms. Richter said she could not confirm its existence as of yet. "Video of the crime was made and circulated," she said. "So far we have been unable to locate it."

Reports have surfaced in recent days that Coach Raymond Sanders led an effort to have the video deleted by threatening to remove any player who was found in possession of it from the top-ranked Buccaneer athletic program. Coach Sanders received unwanted national media attention this week after threatening this reporter on camera during a pep rally at Coral Sands High and could not be reached for comment.

Meanwhile, amid increased national scrutiny, self-described

hacker collective, UltraFEM (identified on their website as "the anonymous hacker protest collective dedicated to full prosecution of crimes against women") has posted a statement on its website that they are in possession of the video in question and demand those charged in the Coral Sands rape case change their pleas to guilty. If this demand is not met, the group promises to release the video to the media and public at large one week from Monday. Their requirements also extend to those involved in what they refer to as the "pervasive rape culture of the Coral Sands Buccaneers basketball team," and any who witnessed the alleged crime of Saturday, March 14.

twenty-nine

SLOANE KEATING IS reporting live from the steps of the courthouse, and we are all glued to the screen when Dad walks in from his Saturday shift, gone long. He's covered in sawdust and sweat, and as Sloane ends the special report, he cracks open a beer and asks what the hell a hacker collective is.

Will fills him in as I dip baby carrots in a tub of hummus and check the clock on my phone. Have to leave time to brush my teeth before Ben comes to get me.

"So, they've broken into somebody's computer and lifted this video?" Dad asks. He shakes his head. "That sounds like the crime to me."

"Who would make a video of something like that?" Mom asks.

"Tyler's brother thinks they're bluffing," says Will. "Just a bunch of feminists trying to stick their noses in where they don't belong—causing problems when they don't even know what they're talking about."

"I hope there's no video." Mom sighs, unconvinced. "I hope there was nothing to record."

Dad raises his eyebrows at me as I put the lid on the hummus and the carrots back into the crisper. "Pretty fancy outfit for mowing the yard," he says.

"Oh, *Carl*," Mom says, smiling. "She has a date."

"Besides," I say, "mowing the grass is Will's job."

"How about I go on a date, and you mow the grass?" Will asks.

"For that to happen, someone would have to want to go on a date with you," I say.

Mom and Dad laugh. Will tries to hit me with a throw pillow as I dart upstairs to the bathroom.

Wyatt Jennings is a knockout.

By the end of "Summer Lovin'" he and Shauna Waring have us all on our feet screaming like sixth-graders at a boy-band concert. Even Ben is cheering. *Cheering.* Fist pumping, yelling, whooping.

Offstage, Wyatt's just this tall, skinny kid. Handsome

enough. Sort of a big forehead and a horsey jaw. He seemed so scared of LeRon and Kyle on Tuesday when they pinned him against the lockers. He could barely look Ben in the eye.

But onstage?

He's a star.

His hair is sprayed up in a perfect pompadour. His black leather jacket clings to his broad shoulders like he was born wearing it. When he sings, he struts. He owns the stage like Dooney owns center court. But unlike Dooney, Wyatt wants you to join him, not worship him. His presence invites you in, instead of keeping you out. When he swivels his hips and hits those high notes, he's not showing you he's better than you. Wyatt is doing it *for* you. He lets you know that there's room for you here, too, his voice soaring above Sandy's in a gorgeous falsetto that makes you smile and clap in the middle of a song. You know you'll have this tune stuck in your head for the next month.

And that's the problem with *Grease!*

The music is so catchy.

When the lights went down tonight, I was amazed at how many of the songs I still knew by heart. I haven't watched the movie for a long time. It used to be on cable a lot when I was little, and I remember Mom sitting down with Will and me one night to watch it.

This was my favorite when I was your age.

Back then, I understood why right away. I felt so special that my mom was sharing this with me. I'd never seen a musical movie that wasn't animated—one where it was actual *people* singing, not cartoon characters. For a couple years after that, every time Will and I saw *Grease!* on TV, we'd dance around the living room for hours afterward singing "You're the One that I Want" and "We Go Together."

The stage version is a little different from the movie. For starters, Sandy's not from Australia, and she doesn't sing "Hopelessly Devoted." They took out all the cigarette smoking and curse words for our high school production, but most everything else is the same—especially the way this music still excites me. It makes me want to get up and dance with my arms in the air.

Which is why I say the music is a problem:

It's so good that you forget the plot.

You forget that "Summer Lovin'" is the story of how hot and heavy Sandy and Danny got before school started. You forget that after exaggerating to the T-Birds how far they went "under the dock," Danny basically blows Sandy off. You forget that later, he tries to get her to have sex in his car when she doesn't want to.

You forget that at the end of the show, Sandy gives in.

Sure, Danny makes that half-assed attempt to join the track team, but you can tell he doesn't really mean it. Nobody at Rydell High expects him to change. For that matter, no one in the audience expects him to either. It's a funny part that we all laugh at. *How ridiculous! Boys don't change for girls.*

We all expect Sandy to do the changing.

And after she flees the drive-in movie when Danny pressures her to go farther than she wants to? Twenty minutes later, she shows up at the Burger Palace in skintight pants and a low-cut shirt. Her hair is huge, and she's wearing tons of makeup. She becomes *exactly* the person Danny Zuko wants her to be. She makes herself into the version of the girls that *he's* decided are attractive.

She doesn't ask him *why* he has the power to decide what she should look like. She doesn't say, "Okay. Yes, I'll go have sex with you now." She doesn't have to.

A lot of this musical went way over my head when I was a kid.

But then? Just as you're about to feel annoyed about it, the music kicks in.

It's this big feel-good number. Now that Sandy has completely changed, Danny sings to her: *You're the one that I want.* Then everybody else joins them onstage and sings "We Go Together."

By the end of that number, we're all on our feet, clapping and stomping and singing along with this rambunctious, infectious, life-affirming music. And it's so bright and so shiny and so happy and so perfect that by the time Wyatt takes his final bow?

You lose track of the lie.

By curtain call, this music has made you completely forget the whole point of the plot—the takeaway of this entire story—which is that Sandy decides that what Danny wants is more important than what she wants.

Even with all the cheerful music, I find my brain wandering toward Stacey and Dooney. The truth is, I've done so much thinking this week about what it means to say no that I haven't done any thinking at all about what it means to say yes.

What if I want to say yes?

I am thinking about this during the musical, sneaking quiet glances at Ben as he watches the show. His eyes light up, and his perfect lips erupt in laughter. He reaches over to squeeze my hand during "Beauty School Dropout" without taking his eyes off the stage. He simply runs his hand down my arm and laces his fingers through mine as if it were the most normal, perfect thing in the world.

As he does it, I think, *Yes.*

I am thinking about this in the car on the way back to Ben's place, when I bring up what a lame message *Grease!* has, and how surprised I am that people let their little girls watch it without even talking to them about it. He laughs—not at me, but in a way that tells me how much he likes me. He asks me questions about my opinion. We talk about it all the way to his house, and he nods, like he's never thought about it that way before.

He says, "Guess it's sorta like porn."

I say, "What?" perhaps louder than I mean to, because I feel like I might fly out the window of his truck at that moment. "How is *Grease!* like porn? And how do you know what porn looks like?"

He smirks at me. "I just mean that you know it isn't real life. You know what's happening on-screen is way different from what would happen when you actually have sex. It's the same thing as watching a car chase in a movie. You'd never try to drive like that on your way to school."

It's such a weird, wonderful moment when I realize that this guy I am talking to has opinions. Smart ones. I feel so lucky that we have known each other for so long, and still feel comfortable talking like this. It's so frank and so honest and so . . . easy.

It makes me want to say *yes*.

I am thinking about this when Ben orders pizza, when he tells me that Adele is gone for the weekend at a Zumba competition in Chicago, when he asks me if I want a rum and Coke.

I say, "Yes."

I eat pizza, but not too much.

I drink Bacardi, but not too much.

I kiss Ben for a while on the couch in the rec room, but not too much, because after a little while, he pulls me close, wraps his legs through mine, and lays his head against my chest.

He tells me he means it when he says, "I love you." He tells me he's loved me ever since the day I kicked him in the head.

I run a hand through his hair, messing it up a little. He closes his eyes and leans into my touch. I tell him that I want a future beyond the county line, too. Someplace where I don't "know" anyone, but where I *know* him.

"Think we can make it through college together?" he asks.

I don't know if it's the rum or Ben's body pressed into mine, but I can hear the blood pounding in my ears. I pull his face toward mine and have time for a single word before our lips touch:

"Yes."

What does it mean to say yes? To consent to a kiss? To a touch? To more than that? When we finally move to his bedroom, he takes my hand, and I know exactly where we are going. I follow him because I want to. I haven't said the words *yes, I would like to have sex with you*, but I can feel myself telling him in so many other ways that this is okay, that I want this.

I pull off his shirt as we climb onto his bed. I can feel the power coiled in his shoulders and arms, the strength beneath his skin, but I'm not afraid. He is listening to every word I haven't said. We are communicating, but in a quiet give-and-take that doesn't use our voices

He's so tall, and yet somehow, wound up in the sheets on his bed, our bodies are a perfect fit. One shirt and one sock at a time, our clothing falls away, and when there is nothing more between us, he speaks:

"Kate, is this okay?"

One more time, I say, "Yes."

And if this were a movie, there would be no more words. There would only be a magical fade-to-black moment where our simultaneous first times were the stuff of legend. There would be no discussion that Ben has done this once before with someone else. Or that he is worried about hurting me. Or that I am a little worried about that, too. There would be no ten-minute break while he digs through his mom's nightstands (yes, both of them) until he finds the condoms. There would be no giggling about how, after the Great Condom Hunt, I have to pee and abscond to the bathroom momentarily.

But this is not a big-screen car chase.

This is driving in real life.

So, we talk to each other. We go under the speed limit. We keep it cautious and safe, buckled in by all of the trust between us.

At first there is laughter. Then there is fumbling.

But finally . . .

An ocean of *yes*.

thirty

"DO YOU REALLY think there's a video?"

Rachel has been quiet all afternoon, both of us sprawled across my bedroom carpet with our laptops. She came over after church so we could write our poet papers for AP English. Mine is on Robert Browning, and hers is on his wife, Elizabeth Barrett Browning.

I almost told her that I needed to study alone today. Sometimes our Sunday study sessions become an excuse to stream Netflix or for her to talk about the guy she flirted with at the coffee-and-doughnuts table after services.

But today, I had news to report. I gave her the whole story about last night—stopping just short of the sex part. I want to keep that to myself for now. I don't know if she'll be weird about it.

I feel great about it.

There's this little bubble of happiness floating around in my chest. I sense that telling anybody else about having sex with Ben would be letting some of the air out of this beautiful thing that happened—like somehow I'd be leaking away a part of my own joy. I'd probably tell Rachel if I didn't have to risk her judgment. I don't want to have to deal with anyone else's feelings about it for now. I only want to enjoy my own.

If I think about it too much, a goofy grin appears on my face. I'm glad I have a paper to write and a friend to distract me. Otherwise, I'd be tempted to text Ben every twelve seconds and I think, technically, that is the opposite of playing it cool.

We work on our laptops, mainly in silence, for about an hour. Rachel asks about the video, and I'm not sure what to say. I see the fear on her face again, and she sees my hesitation, so she keeps talking.

"I mean, if there was a video, we'd know, right? There's no way a bunch of feminist hackers would have it and we wouldn't."

She says the word *feminist* like Will did last night—with scorn and derision—as if she's spitting something out.

"Why does everybody say 'feminist' that way?"

"What way?"

"The way Dooney kept saying 'herpes' after health class last year. Like it's this terrible, unspeakable thing."

Rachel blinks at me, blankly. "Feminists are women who

believe in evolution and just don't want anybody to tell them what to do. They want to be able to abort their unborn babies."

She says this as if everyone else on the planet knows these facts to be true, and I have clearly missed the memo. I frown and search "feminism" on my laptop, turning it around so Rachel can see the screen when the definition pops up. I read it aloud: "The advocacy of women's rights on the ground of political, social, and economic equality to men."

Rachel sighs. "All I know is that you can't be a feminist and believe the Bible."

"The Bible talks about feminism?"

"It talks about *families*," Rachel clarifies. She sounds more and more like her mom now. "God created women to be good helpers for men. It's just better for families that way."

"Not for Elizabeth Barrett Browning."

"Huh?"

"Her dad disinherited her for marrying the man she was in love with. They were broke for years because back then a father could just decide who his daughter married and take away her money if she did otherwise."

Rachel shakes her head. "It was a different time then. It doesn't really affect us now."

I want to tell her that this issue affects everything. Even our friendship. I want to be able to tell my best friend about my first time having sex with the guy I love, but I can't risk it because I don't want her to get all snooty about me losing my virginity— as if somehow she and her mom and the youth pastor at her church should have a say about that. I want to tell her that I don't think a book from the Bronze Age is a good enough reason to relegate women to the role of "helpers" for all time.

But I don't know how.

We go back to our papers, but something between us is strained. I can feel us slipping away from each other. After a minute, I can't stand it any longer, and put down my computer. I reach over, and pull Rachel into a hug.

"Get off me," she huffs.

I hug her harder, and she squirms. I squeeze her until we're basically wrestling on the floor. She tries to get away, and I try to hold her closer until both of us start laughing so hard we can't struggle anymore.

We lie on my carpet for a minute, staring up at the ceiling fan.

"Whatever you think of UltraFEM," I tell her, "there must be a video of something."

"I know," she says. Her voice sounds tiny and far away. "But I wish I didn't."

When I wake up on Monday morning, it's still dark outside, and there's a single thought on repeat in my brain:

Will something be different when I see Ben at school today?

I can't seem to lower the volume on this idea, which makes catching another hour of sleep impossible. I can hear Dad downstairs making coffee. I get up and take my laptop to the little desk in the corner of the kitchen to print out my report.

"Mornin', early bird." Dad smiles, pouring coffee into his big travel mug and thermos. "Fresh outta worms today, but I can offer you a cuppa joe."

"Sure." I smile and cover my yawn as I wait for the printer to spit out my pages. Dad pours coffee into a mug that reads WORLD'S GREATEST DAD and places it in front of me on the counter. He points at the words and I laugh as he goes back to spreading peanut butter on bread. When Mom went back to work after the factory flood, her only stipulation was that everyone was on their own for lunch.

As the printer delivers page number five, Dad pauses behind me and plants a kiss on the top of my head. "First practice today?"

I nod, impressed he still keeps track of little things like this.

"Bring me home some Happy Joe's."

It's a tradition we started in junior high. After the first practice of the season, Rachel, Christy, Lindsey, and I go get pizza. Our parents used to come along, but last year, we started driving ourselves.

I tell Dad I will as he latches his thermos into his gray lunch box. As he passes me on the way to the garage, he slides a crisp twenty-dollar bill onto the desk next to my computer. When I turn to tell him thank you, he just nods and closes the door behind him. I hear the automatic door open and his year-old Dodge Ram purrs to life.

I take the twenty back upstairs with my laptop and paper.

Not a bad start for a Monday.

My fear about things being different with Ben ends when I park behind the gym and see him waiting for me. He is leaning against his truck, his backpack slung casually across one shoulder, early man armed with provisions.

He bumps fists with Will, who struts off to class like he's Captain America. As he goes, Ben turns to me.

"There you are."

"Waiting for the T-Birds?" I ask.

"Nah. You're the one that I want."

I laugh, and he kisses me. We skirt the news vans, walking in the side doors at the end of the hallway hand-in-hand.

Dooney, Deacon, Randy, and Greg aren't coming back to classes yet. The school board doesn't want any more media attention, and the guys are all studying at home this week. Stacey isn't back either, and I'm secretly relieved. I don't want to have to explain to Ben what happened Saturday afternoon.

Dooney is absent and everywhere at once. His presence looms large even though his seat is empty. A bunch of guys from the basketball team have started wearing his jersey number, 12, emblazoned on armbands with Sharpies. Some of the cheerleaders have made buttons—royal blue with a yellow twelve—and are handing them out before school. I see them everywhere on the way to class, pinned to hoodies, T-shirts, and backpacks.

By the time Mr. Johnston dismisses first period on Monday

morning, there is more to the story that surges through the hallways:

Phoebe broke up with Dooney yesterday.

Ben hasn't heard from Dooney to confirm, but Christy swears up and down that it's true. As Lindsey, Christy, Rachel, and I wade through the halls toward history, I see Phoebe close her locker with an armload of books as the Tracies approach.

Tracy bumps into Phoebe. Hard. Her books explode in all directions.

Tracie scowls and rolls her eyes, stepping over a binder. The rings have popped open, and its insides spill across the linoleum. Neither one of them stop.

Tracie doesn't say sorry.

Tracy just yells, "Whoops!"

Then they both laugh and keep walking.

Phoebe is scrambling on her hands and knees to gather her notes and books, but no one is stopping to help her. In fact, no one is stopping at all.

I grab Rachel's arm. "What the hell?"

Christy shrugs. "That's what happens."

I am about to ask her what she means when I see LeRon bump into Phoebe, still squatting to pick up her things. He knocks her sideways onto her hip as Kyle slides his size fourteen high-tops across the papers from her notebook, tearing them into pieces.

"Stop it, you asshole!" Phoebe is crying in frustration.

"You hear something?" LeRon asks Kyle.

"Nah, man. Don't hear nothing."

Reggie cocks his head to one side like he's listening. "Wait!—oh—no, me neither."

Phoebe pummels her fist against Kyle's leg, trying to pull a spiral notebook out from under his shoe. "God. You're such *dicks*."

"*We're* dicks?" Reggie says. "You're the one who dumped Dooney."

"Such a *bitch* move." Kyle spits the words at her, kicking the spiral under his foot a little farther out of her reach.

"Right?" Reggie tosses an arm around Kyle as they start down the hall with LeRon.

I've had enough. I thrust my book at Rachel, who grabs it and hisses my name in an attempt to stop me. I storm across the hall.

"Leave her alone," I tell Reggie, stooping down and sweeping a pile of Phoebe's stuff toward her.

Kyle turns around, zeroing in on me. "Whatcha gonna do about it?"

"She won't do a thing." I look up and see Ben towering over us. "But if you say one more word to her I'll rearrange your face."

Kyle wilts. "Bro—I didn't—"

"See me? Know?" Ben offers him options. "Well, now you have. And now you do."

The three stooges stutter apologies and *it's cool it's cool*, extricating themselves from the razor wire of Ben's steady gaze as quickly as they can. I hand Phoebe the last of her ruined papers. She scoops up the whole tangled pile and scrambles away without a word. Ben holds out his hand to help me up. I take it.

"Where'd you come from?" I ask.

He holds up his history text. "Grabbed the wrong book."

"What is going on?" I ask him.

"People choosing sides," he says. He checks his watch as Rachel hands me my book. We have to hurry.

Ben pecks me on the lips and winks. "Try not to get caught in the middle."

Coach Lewis is a drill sergeant with a stopwatch and a clipboard.

Christy is dragging by the end of the third line drill, but she doesn't stop. When she finally taps the last goal line, Coach clicks the button and nods. "Not bad, Miller." She pitches Christy a water bottle. Christy raises it in my direction and nods.

"We can do another couple of those, or we can scrimmage now." Coach tosses her clipboard onto the grass while half the team shouts *scrimmage*.

"Fine. We'll scrimmage until I see somebody walk. If you're standing still, you're running a drill."

Rachel and I are usually pitted against each other during practice. She's got speed and no fear. I've got fast feet and good instincts. Together we're unstoppable. Head to head, we push each other hard. Even in practice, Rachel plays for keeps. It's one more thing I love about her.

We face off at center field.

"Gonna smoke you, Weston."

"Don't get cocky," I warn her.

She grins. "Just telling the truth."

As soon as Coach drops the ball, Rachel lunges, but in a flash I snag it sideways, crossing it behind me for a pass to Risby, a junior with a slight overbite and a leg that might as well be the Hammer of Thor. She's still working on accuracy and speed, but on a wide-open field, she's the fastest way to get the ball deep toward the other side's goal in one swift kick.

Rachel and I are neck and neck as we watch the ball sail toward the penalty box. Lindsey comes charging at it with a wild yell and launches the ball to the midfield.

It's great to be back, all of us in action and united as a team again—even if we're practicing against each other. I've missed the feeling that Christy, Rachel, Lindsey, and I are on the same team. Ben's words from earlier have been ringing in my ears all day.

People choosing sides . . .

As I try to work the ball down the field, the tension slips away. Since the arrests last Tuesday, I've been white-knuckling things with my friends. Holding on tight, as we all lean toward different opinions of the truth.

And what is the truth?

Stacey's allegation? Did something happen to her that she didn't agree to? She says she can't even remember. Does that mean she was really passed out in that Instagram picture?

Risby tries to aim a cross-field kick in my direction. It is a rocket slightly off course. *Houston, we have a negative on that trajectory.* As I race toward the loose ball, the image of Stacey in her blue towel pops into my head. Were there any marks on her arms or legs? Cuts? Bruises?

I didn't see any, but does that really mean anything?

The ball bounces once, and I leap in for the header. Coach Lewis yells across the field, but her words are lost. Rachel has materialized from the opposite direction and jumped into a Hail Mary bicycle kick. Her cleat is a brick wall.

I'm flat on my back in the grass before I feel the pain. When it hits, I reach up and touch the bump that's already formed above my right ear. It's wet, and I know that I'm bleeding.

I don't cry, but Rachel does. The cut is small, easily stanched with a Band-Aid, the pain already subsiding. Coach makes sure I don't need professional medical attention, while Rachel apologizes over and over.

"I'm so sorry! Did you not hear me call it?" she asks. "I said, 'heads up'!"

That's the typical courtesy yell, but my brain was occupied elsewhere while my body was running around on the field.

Coach tells all of us to keep our heads in the game. "There's a lot of crap floating around this week. Eyes on the ball, ladies. Don't lose focus." She points to the sideline and says I should sit out for a bit, then she gets practice going again.

A cosmic rage wells up inside me as I watch. Not at Rachel

or at Coach. I'm angry with myself. *Why do you keep asking questions you don't want to know the answers to? Why can't you let this go?* Whatever happened or didn't happen to Stacey, I wasn't there. Ben wasn't there. My friends weren't there.

I finally have a boyfriend, and if I work hard this year, I might be able to get nationally ranked. Maybe even be in the running for a scholarship. My best friends in the world are on this team with me.

So why can't I just let myself be on their side?

Coach is right. It's time to get my head back in the game.

thirty-one

BEN IS COMING out of the gym as Rachel and I walk toward the parking lot after practice. He sees the cold pack I'm holding against my head and frowns, jogging across the grass to meet me. We explain what happened and when I show him my bump, Ben smiles and taps the scar behind his ear. "Now you finally know how it feels."

Rachel laughs as I protest. "It was an accident."

Ben takes my soccer duffel, adding it to his own gym bag and backpack. He doesn't seem to notice the extra weight. He slides his arm gently across my shoulders and we walk together. Will comes trotting over, a loyal hound dog sniffing for a hand-out.

"Can I come to Happy Joe's with you?"

My mouth opens to say *absolutely not*, but Ben says, "Pizza sounds good." Rachel tells him to meet us there, and just like that, our first day of practice tradition is expanded to brothers and boyfriends.

Given enough time, everything changes.

I realize I have forgotten my geology book and have to go back inside to get it. Lindsey and Christy are already on their way. I tell Ben and Rachel to go ahead.

"Wanna ride shotgun, Pistol?"

Will's face almost falls off when Ben says this. Ben, making it easy, surprising me one more time by being even better than I expect him to be. I smile and tell them I'll meet them there, then head back into the deserted hallways.

On the way back to my car, I follow Principal Hargrove through the side door to the parking lot. He is leaving for the day, a briefcase in hand. I realize he's started parking behind the school. The faculty spots in front are probably too close to the news vans. As I step outside, I see I'm not the only one who has figured this out.

Sloane Keating is dressed to the nines from the waist up: salmon-colored suit jacket, flat-ironed hair, and a full face of makeup. Anything the camera will see is perfect but she's wearing jeans and Nikes down below. She puts the sneakers to good use keeping up with Principal Hargrove's long strides toward his station wagon, shouting questions at him all the way.

How much do you know that you aren't saying?

How many kids were at the party?

Why aren't you insisting they come forward with any information they have?

Are you involved in the cover-up?

This final question makes Mr. Hargrove pull up short, halfway to his car. A flush of righteous indignation spreads from his cheeks in both directions, dribbling down his neck and scalding his bald spot.

"Ma'am, your questions are out of line."

"Your refusal to answer the questions makes people suspicious." Sloane says this pleasantly, like she's discussing the state basketball tournament this weekend or the fact that the weather warmed up again last night.

Principal Hargrove takes a deep breath. "The boys who have been dragged into this mess are good kids and—"

"Who've been accused of rape." Sloane is not backing down.

"They are innocent until proven guilty," he fires back.

"You've decided they're guilty already." The principal jabs a finger in the direction of the front parking lot. "You people are holding your own trial out there."

"Nothing can be proven at all until we have the facts." Sloane is firm and unwavering.

"The facts?" Principal Hargrove puffs. "The facts are that these guys come from good families. Their parents are good people, friends of mine. Their homes are stable. They are pillars of this community. All of that has been called into question by a young woman who has little supervision, and by most accounts has made some very questionable moral judgments."

"Can I quote you on that?" Sloane is speaking into her phone and holds it back toward the principal, recording every word.

"No, you may not," he thunders. Mr. Hargrove wipes his hand across his forehead. It's a fruitless attempt to settle the hair he no longer has and the nerves over which he has clearly lost control.

"I'm telling you," he says in a low voice, "stop chasing the narrative you want. Look at what's right in front of you, for Christ's sake. What do you gain by ruining these boys' futures?"

Sloane furrows her brow in concern and nods slowly, thoughtfully. "See, Wendall, the question I'm curious about is, what do you gain by protecting them?"

Principal Hargrove's eyes narrow. "You're gonna have a scoop even if you have to make it up. Is that the way it works now? We just invent the news?" His voice creeps up in volume. "Mark my words, young lady, you're not a hero. No washed-up movie star is gonna play you in the Lifetime movie version of this story."

Sloane lets out a musical laugh that surprises me, all tinkling bells and fairy dust. When she looks back at him, her smile is warm and endearing—like she's flirting over a beer at Applebee's—but when she speaks, her voice is a deep freeze.

"So tell me, have you seen the video?"

The question is ice water. I stand frozen on the sidewalk, three feet from the back door as Wendall Hargrove jerks his head in silent disgust. He opens his mouth, thinks better of it, then stalks to his car in double time. He tosses his briefcase onto the passenger seat, slams the door, and achieves the only station wagon peel out to which I have ever held witness.

Sloane Keating watches him go, arms crossed, her back to me. She shakes her head as his car disappears, then taps at the screen of her phone while she strides toward the satellite trucks. Her voice is strong enough that she doesn't have to turn around when she calls out, "Good to see you, Kate." She knows I can hear her, and she keeps on walking without a backward glance.

By the time I pull into the parking lot at Happy Joe's, Will is sandwiched between Rachel and Christy in one of the big round booths at the back. Lindsey is on one side about to fall off the edge, and Ben is on the other, saving what looks like just enough room for half of my rear end.

I slide in next to him, and he pulls me toward him. It's cozy.

"How's your head?" he whispers.

"Better now," I tell him, which is partially true. My head doesn't hurt so much anymore, but it's spinning after what I saw in the parking lot.

"Hey, Rachel," says Will in his cool-dude voice, "put your arm around me, so I'll look like a *playa*." Rachel laughs and complies while Christy moans. Ben grins and holds a fist for

Will to bump across the table.

"Don't encourage him," I tell Ben.

"Aw, c'mon. He's just getting the hang of it."

Lindsey catches my eye, and I know what she's thinking. *Boys will be boys.* I look away like I didn't notice. I plaster on a big smile and try to find the confidence I had while holding the cold pack to my head during practice.

This has nothing to do with you.

It isn't working.

After hearing Sloane in the parking lot and seeing Principal Hargrove's reaction, the voice whispering questions is back. The volume goes up a notch when Ben tweets a picture of Christy and Rachel kissing either side of Will's face. My brother's snapback is cocked sideways and he's making that duck-lips face, staring straight into the camera. Ben tags it #youngbucc, and it takes everything in me to ignore the whispers.

Is this how it started?

Innocent pictures of silly kisses?

When the pizzas arrive, there's barely room on the table. Lindsey makes a toast to the new season and we clink plastic glasses full of Coke and Sprite as David Sissler jockeys a BLT, a Combo Plus, and a Meatworks into the middle of the table.

David is another one of those people I "know" without *knowing.* He was a starting point guard a few years back, just like Ben. Nabbed a scholarship to Florida State, but blew out his knee during his first season and wound up sitting the bench. He stayed in Tallahassee over that summer, supposedly to get back in shape. Instead of running drills and lifting weights, he ran a lot of pot to Tampa and drank a lot of beer. He got cut that fall. Without a scholarship, he wound up back here, slinging pizza at Happy Joe's and reliving the glory days every time a current Buccaneer shows up.

"You guys ready for state?" he asks Ben.

"You bet." Ben smiles.

"Heard Doone got out on bail. He still playing?"

We all turn to look at Ben for the answer. The rules are that if you miss practice the week of the game, you can't suit up. Dooney and Deacon were both MIA today. Ben glances down at his plate. Just that tiny tell, and I already know what he's going to say. It's not good news.

When he tells David, Christy goes ballistic. "You're freaking kidding me!" Her voice is so loud that we get a glare from the mom in the booth next to ours.

"That's what happens when you miss practice." Lindsey takes a bite of Meatworks.

"God, that sucks." David looks like he's the one who has to play without two of the five starters this weekend.

Ben nods. "Yeah, it's too bad, but I liked what happened in practice today. We're all pulling together. Tough as bucc."

Another glare from the mom next door. I don't think she heard the *b* on *bucc* but she does hear David say, "Hells yeah, bro," as he bumps fists with Ben.

"Can't believe Stacey Stallard might cost us state," Christy moans.

"No way," Will pipes up. "They still got Ben and Reggie. Plus LeRon and Kyle." He turns to Ben. "You can still pull it off, right?"

"Not gonna lie," says Ben. "I'd feel better if Dooney was playing."

"I'll bet Stacey would feel better if she hadn't gone to his party." Lindsey says this quietly, but it's a lit match in a gas can.

Christy leans forward to face Lindsey across the round booth. "Whatever it is that Stacey says happened is her own damn fault. That girl is a hot mess."

"How can you say that?" I ask.

Before Christy can answer me, Rachel does. "Look at us, Kate. We're not like her. You're not like her."

Lindsey frowns. "So what?"

"Yeah," I agree. "You keep saying that, but what do you mean?"

"All I'm saying is there are rules." Rachel's face has gone chalky. Her voice is soft and quavers a little, as if she's desperate to convince us of something. She stares into her plate, afraid to look at me. "You don't get wasted. You don't take off your top. You don't flirt with raging drunks." She leans in and grips the edge of the table, lowering her voice. "You don't dress like a slut. You have to play by the rules. If you don't, this is what happens."

Even Christy is silent, all of us taking this in. Rachel glances up and realizes we're all looking at her. "Don't you guys get it?" Her eyes meet mine. If I were closer, I could fold her into a hug. If we were alone, I could tell her it's going to be okay. She looks to Christy, who is suddenly busy chasing a piece of ice around the bottom of her empty glass.

"Oh, what?" asks Rachel. "So, now you think I sound crazy?"

After a moment of silence, Lindsey reaches over and takes Rachel's hand. "No," she says. "Just scared."

Lindsey is right, but not only about Rachel. Fear is the reason I can't let this go, either. It's the reason Rachel needs to believe that whatever happened is Stacey's fault. It's why she insists that we're all very different from Stacey. Because the truth is that if it could happen to Stacey, it could happen to any of us.

By the time we pay and walk to our cars, it's dark outside. The air is humid and a light fog rolls through the parking lot, making everything vague, obscuring the details. We've all been wandering around in a haze about what really went on at Dooney's party: who was there, what happened, how it happened. There are two sides right now. Stacey claims she was raped. Dooney says she wasn't. Everyone says there's no way to know for sure.

But there is a way to know.

There's a video.

I glance at Ben, wondering if he might've been able to hear my thought, but he kisses me and helps me into the truck. He tells Will not to eat the leftovers before he gets home. He tells me he'll be right behind me so we can study for our geology quiz.

I'm extra cautious driving home. Visibility is limited and

my knuckles go white from squeezing the steering wheel, just like Rachel's did grasping the edge of the table. As Will talks about Tyler and the tournament this weekend, I wonder which is worse: the fear of the unknown? Or knowing for sure that something terrible is true?

thirty-two

"IMAGINE BEING SO dedicated to finding the truth about something that you're willing to go against the prevailing thought of everyone around you, and become an outcast."

Mr. Johnston is talking about a geologist named Alfred Wegener, but I'm sleepy and having a hard time focusing until he says this.

Last night, while Mom and Dad ate leftover Combo Plus, Will quizzed Ben and me on the differences between igneous, metamorphic, and sedimentary rocks. I lay awake for a long time after I went to bed, phone in hand, typing "Coral Sands rape video" into the search field of the browser, then deleting it. I'm still not sure if I'm more afraid of knowing what happened or not knowing. Last night, I couldn't bring myself to look.

"Sometimes inspiration requires looking at things from a different point of view." Mr. Johnston's voice snaps me back into the present.

A map of the world flashes onto the screen. "Wegener was looking at the same maps everybody else had, but he noticed something nobody else had seen and formed a hypothesis."

Mr. Johnston runs his pen along the eastern edge of the South American continent, pointing out its symmetry with the western edge of Africa. "Wegener hunted for clues on both sides of the Atlantic. He found the same dinosaur fossils in both places, the same plant species, too. For years everybody had explained this by saying that at one time, there must have been land bridges that crossed the Atlantic in a couple spots. But ol' Alfred wasn't satisfied with that answer, mainly because—well, look at it." Mr. Johnston laughs. "How could you not see the big picture when it all fits together so well?"

Mr. J is fired up, his eyes glowing in the light of the projector. "The thing that sealed the deal for Wegener was when he found the same formations in the rock on both coasts. Sure, a plant or an animal could cross a land bridge—but rocks? How'd they get from one side to the other? The answer seemed simple to him."

Mr. Johnston taps a button on his laptop and the map starts to move, the continents drifting slowly into one another. South America snuggling up to Africa. The world, assembling. This picture makes so much sense that when he returns to the previous image, it's impossible not to see the way the continental shelf used to fit together.

"In 1912, Wegener presented this theory at a major conference. He stood up and told them all, 'Hey, you guys. I think you're looking at this wrong. I think the continents moved and took the plants and rocks and dinosaurs along for the ride.' And guess what happened?"

Mr. Johnston waits. Lindsey raises her hand. "Miss Chen?"

"He was right?"

Mr. Johnston nods. "Yep. But that day? Nobody believed him. The whole scientific community was committed to seeing things one way: The continents were permanent; the land bridges had gotten washed away. Wegener spent years collecting evidence. He could demonstrate that continental drift was happening, but he couldn't explain how. He was pretty sure it had to do with the centrifugal force of the earth's rotation and the pull of other planets. His 'capital T' theory explained everything he observed, but he wound up becoming a pariah in the geology community."

"Like a fish that eats people?" Reggie asks from the back row.

"That's *piranha*, Reg. But nice try. A *pariah* is an outcast. Somebody who gets shunned and avoided."

Rachel pipes up. "What a miserable way to spend your life."

Mr. Johnston nods. "Maybe. But what he saw changed the way we look at the world. Alfred Wegener is a scientific superstar because he was right."

"How do we know?" Reggie asks.

"Yeah." Ben's voice comes from just behind me. "Did we ever figure out how this whole drift thing happens?"

"Sure did." Mr. Johnston smiles. "There have been tons of new advances, but guess what the easiest way is to observe the continents floating around on the earth's mantle today?" He reaches into his pocket and pulls out his cell phone.

"GPS," he says with a grin. "There's an app for that."

"Oh my god. Kate. Sit down. You're pacing like a caged animal."

I flop down on Lindsey's bed as she continues to click around on her laptop. She is typing the email addresses of different varsity players into the search field on Reddit. She has been pairing these with different hashtags for about an hour now, looking for a video neither of us want to see, but have to find.

"Are you sure Sloane wasn't just trying to get a rise out of Hargrove?" Lindsey asks.

"No," I say. "Okay, maybe, but if there was no video, why wouldn't he just say so?"

Lindsey nods, conceding the point. "Did you ask Ben about it?"

"Not really."

"Not even when UltraFEM threatened to release it next week?"

"No. I already stalked his Twitter feed and his Facebook.

I felt so guilty when I talked to him about it afterward. I don't want to be that girl."

She frowns. "How does asking about something this important make you 'that girl'? Don't you want to know for sure what kind of guy your boyfriend is?"

I pull a pillow over my face and groan into it, then throw it back at the head of her bed. "I *do* know for sure. I've known him since we were five. If Ben knew about this video, I just don't believe he'd keep it from me—or the police."

"He's way into you," Lindsey agrees, her fingers tapping on the keys. "Couldn't keep his arm off you last night at dinner."

"To be fair, he was also keeping me on the seat. There wasn't much room in that booth, and—"

"This might be it." Lindsey slides her laptop toward me so it balances on both our legs. The words leave my lips first, and then my brain. The video in the browser is titled simply *#R&P*. The frozen image is the arm of a couch. It's the signature white leather of Margie Doone's brand-new basement media room. I'm overcome with the certainty that I have asked to see too much.

"Whose account is this?" I ask. "What email did you use to search for it?"

"No one's," she says. "All you can see on Reddit are user-names. I finally found this buried in a sub-Reddit by searching a bunch of the hashtags people were using that night." She points at *#R&P*. "Almost forgot about this one."

We stare at the screen for what feels like a very long time. *Eons.*

Finally, Lindsey crosses her arms. "I found it," she whispers. "You have to push play."

My finger is trembling as I hold it over the silver track pad. I swallow hard, and click.

As the image springs to life, the person holding the camera jumps over the white leather sofa arm onto the couch. Stacey is lying on the chaise that sticks out from the opposite corner of the sectional. Her halter top is missing, but her bra is still on. Her eyes are closed.

Dooney is lying next to her, rubbing his hand up and down her stomach, cupping her breasts, laughing. Deacon pulls up her skirt as Kyle leans in and out of the frame over the back of the couch with a red plastic cup and shouts, "Buccaneers! R-and-P, *babeeey.*"

Dooney buries his face in Stacey's breasts, shaking his head side to side and making a motorboat noise with his lips. He slides a hand down into her underwear.

"Dude! She drunk or dead?" I recognize the squeak of Randy's voice, his words slurring from behind the camera. He must be filming this with his phone.

Greg is there, hooting and pushing Randy, the camera jerking and shaking. I gasp as it pans around the room.

There are so many people there.

I catch a glimpse of the Tracies, one of them making out with LeRon, the other sitting in an overstuffed chair with a glassy gaze. She looks stoned out of her mind.

Some areas are more well lit than others, but the footage is remarkably clear. As Randy swings the camera back to the couch, he gets closer. Dooney is pulling down Stacey's underwear with one hand, the fingers of his other hand already inside her. Randy shouts and giggles hysterically. "Oh my god, dude!"

Greg leans over the couch again, smacking lightly at Stacey's face. "Yo! Anybody home in there?"

She moans and twists away from his touch, a drowsy hand comes to her mouth like she's batting a fly away from her lips. She's barely conscious.

"I got something that'll wake her up!" roars Dooney.

Deacon and Greg collapse in laughter. Dooney is sloppy, flailing around, undoing his belt and his jeans. He pulls off his shirt, whooping. "Let's get our buzz on!"

"Dooney! Where's the tunes, man?" The camera spins again, as Reggie leans into Randy, then notices what's going on. "Oh, shit!"

We get a close-up of Reggie as he sees what is about to happen on the other end of the couch. "No way, dude!" He laughs like a seventh grader who has just heard a fart joke.

When Randy spins the camera back around, Dooney is already on top of Stacey, the belt of his jeans flopping against the side of the couch as he pushes his hips into her. She grunts and moans, eyes still closed.

She has no idea what is happening.

Acid rises in my throat. I want to run, but I'm paralyzed,

staring at the screen. My heart is beating out a command to flee, but I know I have to stay. I have to see this.

The voices and faces overlap. The sound and focus blurs and snaps.

Randy shouts, "Get a *roooooooom*," from behind the camera.

Reggie laughs and yells, "Timber!"

Greg high-fives Deacon over Dooney's back. "Your turn to wake her up next, man."

Reggie circles the couch and appears next to Greg, standing over Dooney for a closer look. "You taking a crack at that?"

"Hells yeah," says Greg. "Battin' cleanup."

Dooney rolls off Stacey, who isn't moving at all now. Deacon pulls at the front of his boxers, angling away from the camera, and takes Dooney's place.

Randy jerks the camera up to catch one of the senior cheerleaders—a friend of Phoebe's named Janelle. She walks by with Tracy, pointing and giggling, "Oh my god!" Tracy whispers something to her, and Janelle bursts out laughing. One of them—I can't tell who—shrieks, *"Trashy!"* before they wander out of frame.

Greg takes a turn, then Dooney again, holding his beer up to the camera before guzzling the last of it and getting into position.

"Buccs be *rapin' and pillaging!*" he yells. "R-and-P, *babeeey!*"

I bat at the keyboard, striking the space bar, freezing the scene. The counter flashes up at two minutes, seven seconds. The video is four minutes long, but I've seen enough. I dive toward Lindsey's desk in the nick of time, heaving into the wastebasket underneath. There are tears running down my face, as my mouth floods with more bile. I leap up and race toward the Chens' bathroom as Lindsey slams the laptop closed.

thirty-three

SOME THINGS ARE worse than an unanswered question.

Some answers make a situation less clear, not more so. Instead of putting my questions to rest, this video has only posed more.

"How could they just . . . mill around like that?" I ask Lindsey. She is lying on her bed, staring at the ceiling when I get back from the bathroom. "How can they walk around in the hallways at school like nothing happened? Like they didn't witness—" My voice dissolves into tears again.

"A crime?" Lindsey says without moving.

"Yeah."

"They don't think it was a crime," she says quietly. Her eyes never leave the ceiling.

"How?" I ask. "How could they walk right by Stacey and call her names while that was happening?"

Lindsey sits up and looks at me, her eyes are bright, but clear—quickened by the rage that fills her voice. "You heard Rachel's 'rules.' If you learn what we learn here—that Dooney and all those guys are entitled to tell you if you're pretty or not, that it's up to you to make sure you don't give boys a reason to hurt you? Then you don't think it was a crime. You think what happened to Stacey was fair game. It was boys being boys. Just a trashy girl learning the hard way what can happen when she drinks too much and wears a short skirt."

For what feels like a long time, I sit there in silence, taking it all in. "What do we do now?"

"I don't know."

"We have to go talk to Ms. Speck tomorrow, right? I mean, we have to at least do that. Go tell her what we've seen, that we know who else was there."

Lindsey is silent, but she shakes her head.

"Lindsey"—I jump up, pacing again—"we have to say something. If we don't, how will the prosecutor build a case? All four of those jerks pleaded 'not guilty.' If we don't say something, they'll get off. They'll get away with this, and then what's to stop them from doing it again?"

Lindsey reaches out and takes my hand, stopping my march

back and forth across the rug in her room. "Kate, look at me," she whispers. "Look at me."

The realization crushes me beneath an avalanche of cold, hard facts. Lindsey: one of three Korean kids in our high school. Lindsey: whose dad owns a janitorial service, whose mom works all night long vacuuming other people's offices.

"My parents' first client when we moved here was Dooney's dad," Lindsey says. "Where do you think all their other clients came from?"

"But Ms. Speck is the guidance counselor. She has to keep things confidential. She can help us." I'm pleading, but Lindsey's mind is made up.

"I'm as angry as you are," she says. "But I can't risk it. If Mom and Dad's work dries up here . . ."

She doesn't finish her thought. She doesn't have to.

"I have to go talk to Ms. Speck at least."

"I know," she says. "I wish I could go with you."

I give her a hug before I leave and tell her I will see her tomorrow. As I drive away from the Chens' house, I wonder how I will face Rachel and Christy. How can tomorrow be a normal Wednesday? How will I be able to walk down the hall past the Tracies or LeRon or anyone else who was there that night, and pretend I don't know? And has Ben seen this video? Has he been pretending it doesn't exist?

Every answer is another question, and the only answer I'm certain of is this: There's no going back. Once you know something for sure, the only path through it is forward.

* * *

Alfred Wegener had it easy.

He only had to show up at a conference and be surrounded by people who rejected his theory for a single day in 1912. On Wednesday morning, as I walk into geology, Ben and Reggie are laughing about something as Reggie takes his seat.

What are they talking about?

How can Reggie joke around after what he witnessed a week ago?

Ben sees me and smiles, tapping the back of the empty desk in front of him. *C'mon. Join me.*

I walk through the classroom toward the desk he always saves for me right next to Lindsey. She holds my gaze without smiling, then drops her eyes, like if we look at each other, everyone will know what we've seen.

I pass Janelle mid-monologue, railing on her cheerleader friend about the girl's nasty boyfriend, her hand waving back and forth like a diva at a microphone. I hear her say the word *trashy* and it rumbles through me like an earthquake.

A tiny seismic shift.

Everything looks different now, and it always will.

After class, Ben tells me he'll meet me at the cafeteria after fourth period. "Miss you already," he says, then kisses me on the lips. As he walks away, Kyle rounds the corner to join him with a smile and a fist bump.

I expect to feel disgust or rage when I see him, but instead my eyes fill up and my stomach lurches. I quickly turn and walk the other way.

I miss me already, too.

The thought is a whisper in my head that spurs me on to the French room. I make an appointment to talk to Ms. Speck at the end of the day.

You see your boyfriend—the guy you've known since you were five. He's leaning against your locker in the hallway, swiping through his phone, the muscles of his neck drop into a navy-blue V-neck. He stands head and shoulders above the stream of students around him, an island in the flow.

Waiting.

For you.

As you walk down the senior staircase toward him, more bodies flood through the hall. Phoebe, her eyes darting back and forth, her confidence shaken, scurries toward her locker, quickly twisting the combination, dropping her books, grabbing her purse and keys, ready to flee campus as soon as she can. *What is she running from? What does she know? Why did she break up with Dooney? Where was she when the video was made? Did she see it? When?*

The Tracies watch Phoebe leave, the metallic sound of their laughter as sharp as their fingernails against their lockers, their eyes rolling, their tongues slashing. *Were they ever her friends? Why did they stay that night, watching and laughing? Did they show Phoebe the video, only to turn on her when she broke up with Dooney?*

Kyle, Reggie, and LeRon surround your boyfriend. Layers of sediment. You think about trying to brush them away, but you freeze on the stairs, your knees trembling. This is not a tiny seismic shift. This is something deeper—a dark rift. A canyon has opened up inside you, and you feel yourself falling.

Christy and Rachel are laughing with the Tracies as Lindsey shoulders her purse and slips down the hall toward the parking lot. Ben starts to move with the guys, drifting away from your locker toward the gym for practice. With one last glance around, he is swept away, leaving you petrified on the stairs above, his voice ringing in your ears:

There you are.

Alone.

thirty-four

"I SWEAR IT was there last night."

I have been typing hashtags and usernames into the sub-Reddit for the past fifteen minutes in Ms. Speck's office. My voice sounds frantic and somehow far away as I continue to search for *#doonestown #r&p #rapeandpillage*. The link I emailed myself from Lindsey's laptop no longer works.

"Kate?" I feel her hand on my arm. "I believe you." She pulls her laptop away from me and closes the lid.

We are sitting at a small, round table jammed in the corner of her office. Ms. Speck sits back in her chair and crosses her legs. She's wearing a deep red lipstick and a black knit suit. Maybe she's fifty-something? She looks like a hip, young grandma on a soap opera.

"Do you want to talk about what you saw in the video?"

I open my mouth to answer, but I am crying again instead and the only word I can find is "No."

I bury my face in my hands. Ms. Speck picks up a Kleenex box and offers me a tissue. I take two and use them while she waits. She doesn't seem bored or annoyed or in a hurry. Her eyes are full of kindness.

"It seems that what you saw in this video was hard to look at." It's not an accusation. She's holding the door open for me.

I nod. "It was . . . awful."

"Did you mention it to anyone?" she asks.

"No." No one else but Lindsey know's I've seen it, and I'm sure she didn't tell anyone.

"Maybe it was blocked by the site or taken down by the person who posted it." She waits as I take another tissue and wipe my nose.

"Sorry," I say.

She waves away my concern. "Kate, I know it's hard to talk about something like this. We don't have to continue if you don't want to."

"Yes," I say. "I have to."

"Why do you have to?" she asks.

"Because I don't want it to happen again."

She nods and asks if it is all right for her to take a few notes while we talk. I tell her that would be fine, then start crying again as I explain what Lindsey and I saw in the video, shot by shot. I repeat every word I can remember. I list every name.

Who was there. What was said. What they did.

What we saw.

When I finish, Ms. Speck tells me that she is bound by state law to file a report. I knew that she would be. I want her to. That's why I came. She leans in to me and places a hand on the knee of my jeans. She tells me how very brave I am, and that I can come talk to her anytime.

As I stand to go, Ms. Speck asks one more question. "Kate, I wonder if you noticed how long this video was?"

I stop and picture the numbers flashing up on the screen of Lindsey's laptop as I hit the space bar to end the playback. "Four minutes," I say.

"And you watched the whole thing?"

I shake my head. "About half of it. Had to stop after that."

Ms. Speck nods. "I certainly understand," she says, scribbling a note on her legal pad. "My door is always open, Kate. A burden shared is a burden lifted."

I step into the hallway wondering why I don't feel any lighter.

Adele Cody is in the driveway with her own burden when I pull up to Ben's house that evening. She's hauling two brown paper grocery bags full of Tylenol PM from her Explorer into the garage. I grab a third that sits by her truck and follow her up the drive.

"Oh, thank you, Katie! What a lovely surprise. Ben said you had a good time at the musical."

For a moment, I wonder what else he's told her. Has she noticed her condoms are missing? I plaster a smile across my face. "It was great. How was Chicago?"

"So much fun! Zumba'd my buns off." She laughs and playfully slaps her own hip, clad in shiny black workout tights over neon running shoes. "Gotta get to the gym." She jogs down to her Explorer. "Go on in. He got home from practice a little bit ago."

I wave as she pulls out, then walk into the rec room as she punches the automatic door closed behind me.

Ben's playing a video game, kicked back on the couch in a pair of gray sweatpants and a T-shirt. His hair is wet from his post-practice shower, and his tongue is sticking out of his mouth in concentration as he mashes buttons. He glances up at me, then back to the screen with a smile.

"There you are," he says.

The character he's playing looks like Indiana Jones, hiding behind a low wall, shooting a gun at bad guys, aided by a buxom brunette, who throws explosives.

I don't wait another moment before I toss a grenade of my own.

"I saw the video."

Ben turns to look at me, his eyes wide. "What?"

"The video. Of Stacey . . . at Dooney's. It was online."

His character on screen dies in a hail of bullets, yelling in anguish.

Ben blinks at me. "How did—"

"Lindsey found it." I cut him off. "It was buried on Reddit." I feel like I'm floating above myself, detached from this room, these words. Ben sits, staring at me, silent, afraid to move.

"I couldn't even watch all of it," I tell him. I thought I was done crying about this, but I can't stem the current. "I had to turn it off after the first couple minutes, but I saw enough."

Ben sets down the controller and lets out a long sigh. He stands up and walks over to me, wrapping his arms around me. Every muscle in my body tenses. I'm a living fossil. Solid bone. All my soft parts eaten away.

"Did you know about it?"

"Yeah," he says. "I did."

I'm surprised by the roar of my own voice as I push him away. "Why didn't you tell me about it?" Every ounce of my frustration from the past two weeks is channeled into this moment.

"Are you glad you saw it?" he asks, short and clipped.

"No," I say, sobbing. "I wish I could burn out my eyes."

He hugs me again, his lips pressed against my hair. "That's why."

I collapse into him and cry against his chest. His arms feel massive, like they could crush the life from my lungs or shield me from anything.

Of course he knew about the video.

Of course he didn't want you to see it.

"Coach told us it existed at practice last week—the day Dooney was arrested. He told us copies had been posted online. He told us anybody who had posted it was off the team.

Thought that took care of it."

Ben leads me over to the sofa and we sit down as I wipe my nose and eyes with the heels of my hands. "So, you haven't seen it?" I ask.

"Didn't want to."

I let out a long deep breath. "Well, it's gone now, so you can't."

A look of relief softens his face, and he sinks back on the couch. "Good."

"It's not good," I tell him. "We could've helped Stacey. They asked us to come forward with any information about what happened that night."

"I don't know what happened that night," he says. "I didn't see the video. I didn't go looking for it. I'm sorry you put yourself through that."

"Ben, we can't just do nothing. Do you understand what they did to her?"

"No." He says this so firmly that the word almost pins me against the couch. "I don't want to know. Kate, I can't know." He stands up and runs a hand through his wet hair. "If I know, then I have to come forward, and if I come forward, I'll get messed up in this whole . . . thing."

He kneels on the floor in front of me, leaning across my lap, his arms sliding around my waist, pulling me into him. I bury my nose in his damp hair and breathe, inhaling his sporty boy-shampoo smell, one of those forcefully FRESH! fragrances they label with rock 'n' roll fonts in dark gray bottles: FOR MEN.

"I went to talk to Ms. Speck today." Ben sits up. Our eyes meet, but I can't tell what he's thinking. "I had to. I was going to show her the video."

"That's when you saw it was gone?"

I nod. "I can't do nothing. I can't let Dooney just . . . get away with this."

He takes both of my hands in his. "I get it, Kate."

"Do you?" I ask. "Why does it feels like I'm the only who cares about this?"

"I care. But I haven't seen that video," he says. "And I don't want to. I have to play on Friday and Saturday. I have to show the scouts what I can do." He brings my hand to his lips and kisses it. "I have to get out of here."

thirty-five

THE HAWK IN the trees at the edge of the back parking lot is standing guard on Thursday morning as I walk back to my truck after first period. I'm hoping my French workbook fell out of my bag behind the seat this morning and isn't still lying on my desk at home. My homework is folded up inside it.

The bird above me screeches in the direction of the news vans still clogging the drive. Sloane Keating has been reporting nightly, hounding the police and the prosecutor for details. Last night it was news about John Doone's text messages with Stacey the day after the party—no specifics, but apparently he was trying to get her to keep quiet.

The hawk takes off, and I wish I could follow her up into the blue. Is it just my imagination, or is everyone giving me side-eye in the hallways? Is there a monster behind that bush, or do I just *think* there's a monster behind that bush?

Either way, the answer to this question seems to be yes. Whether it's real or all in my head, I feel like everyone is looking at me differently. Ben and Lindsey are the only people who know I talked to Ms. Speck about the video. I'm sure neither of them would tell anyone else.

Would they?

I find my book wedged against the floor behind the seat. I close the door and turn to see Ms. Speck walking across the parking lot with a cardboard box. I wave when she sees me, and hold up my French book. "See you inside," I say.

"Not today, I'm afraid." She stops as she says this and waits as I walk over to her. I can see more clearly that her box is full of binders and folders. A couple of picture frames and a purple quartz from her desk are nestled on top.

"Oh . . . are we having a substitute?" I ask.

She smiles grimly. "I'm not sure," she replies. "I don't work here anymore."

The ground is shifting again. My insides start to slide in different directions. "But . . . why?"

"I filed a report with Principal Hargrove after we chatted yesterday. This morning, he was waiting in my office, and when I refused to give him your name as my source, he dismissed me."

"But . . . can he do that?"

She gives me a rueful smile and shifts the box onto her hip.

"Well, he did. Because I can't show him the video you saw, he's convinced the report is all hearsay."

"It was there. I saw it. It exists." I feel numb all over. *Is this really happening?*

Ms. Speck looks over my shoulder, and sighs. "As if on cue . . ."

I glance the same direction and see Sloane Keating marching toward us. "Walk with me," says Ms. Speck.

I follow her to a car as sleek and black as her high heels. She opens the trunk and deposits the box inside, then opens the driver-side door and turns to me. "Wendall Hargrove is an ass. What you did is important. You're the first student to come forward with actual names."

She slides behind the wheel and rolls down the window, swinging the door closed. "Don't back down, Kate."

"What about you?" I ask. "What will you do?"

She slides on dark sunglasses. "My mother is gone. It's high time I got back to New York. I'll be fine." She smiles and reaches through the window, laying a hand on my arm. "And so will you, Kate. I know it may not feel like it now, but you'll come through this. I promise."

"Leaving early today?" Sloane Keating's voice is right behind me. She steps up to the car just as Ms. Speck's hand comes back through the window, a thick white business card extended between two fingers.

"Not in the parking lot, Sloane. Happy to meet you for a drink later." Sloane takes the card as the grating tone sounds to start second period. Ms. Speck smiles at me. "Goddamn, I won't miss that stupid bell."

I smile in spite of the situation. "Guess I'm late."

"Guarantee no one will notice." Ms. Speck turns on the car and addresses Sloane Keating over my shoulder. "Call me. And leave Kate alone."

As the black sedan drives away, Sloane raises her hand to me in farewell and heads back across the parking lot. "See you around," she says.

I hear another screech from the hawk above our heads, and turn in time to see her soar out of sight. I stare up at the place where the green reaches the sky.

If Principal Hargrove can silence anyone who disagrees with him, how will the truth ever be seen? How will anyone get to the bottom of this?

There are no longer two sides to what is happening. The thought sends a tremor of fear down to my toes, and I remember what Ben said all those years ago in his monkey swim trunks when I asked him if you could see the other side of the ocean:

There's only one side. The waves go on forever.

thirty-six

**TEACHER FIRED IN WAKE OF REPORTING
ALLEGED RAPE VIDEO**

By Sloane Keating
Published: March 26

CORAL SANDS, Iowa—A teacher at Coral Sands High School was fired this morning in what appears to be a reprisal for speaking out about the ongoing rape investigation that has rocked this small town. Charlotte Speck was released from her position as a guidance counselor and French teacher by Principal Wendall Hargrove. Speck said that the firing was the result of a standard report she had filed in the role of guidance counselor after speaking with a student.

The unnamed student had reported to Speck the existence of a video of the alleged rape that took place at a party twelve days ago. "If evidence of a crime is made known, I am bound by state law to report that evidence to proper authorities," Speck said. "I am under no compunction to reveal the identity of the student source," she continued. "That information falls under client-privilege laws for the protection of those who come forward with information." Speck maintains she was terminated when she refused to reveal the name of the student who had come to see her.

Reached for comment at his office, Hargrove would say only that Ms. Speck's report was filled with "inaccuracies and speculation. She acted impulsively and irresponsibly, filing a public report based on hearsay."

The rumored video of the alleged rape was viewed on a sub-Reddit by the student who reported it, but subsequent searches for the video have yielded no result, leading authorities to believe that either the video or the account it was posted from has since been removed.

When asked whether she would pursue a wrongful termination suit, Speck said only that she was "keeping all options on the table."

UPDATE

Since this story was first posted earlier today, members of UltraFEM, the anonymous hacker protest collective dedicated to full prosecution of crimes against women, has reaffirmed its statement from last week. In a new post at their website, they confirm once more that they are in possession of the video in question, and demand those charged in the Coral Sands rape case change their pleas to guilty by Monday, or risk exposure online.

In part, the statement reads:

"Those of you who were present during this horrific act of violence against a defenseless female must become witnesses and give statements to investigating authorities. Otherwise, you will be identified and exposed as accessories to the crime."

Coach Raymond Sanders and high school Principal Wendall Hargrove are also named in the statement from UltraFEM. Both are called upon to "stop hindering the investigation, misleading police, and deleting evidence."

Sanders and Hargrove could not be reached for further comment.

thirty-seven

SAY WHAT YOU will about Sloane Keating, she works fast.

Her post went up on the Channel 13 website around four on Thursday afternoon. By five o'clock, she was on with Jeremy Gordon out of Des Moines, filling in all of Iowa. Thirty minutes later, she was talking on *NBC Nightly News*, explaining the situation to all of America. By six, I was curled into a ball on the couch trying not to hyperventilate.

"There's a video? Of what?" Mom shouts from the kitchen as she drains pasta into a colander. "I thought that girl made the whole thing up."

"Maybe Ms. Speck made it up," Will says, putting a bowl of shredded Parmesan on the table per Mom's direction. "Nobody knows if she's for real or not."

"Well, that girl-power computer group sounds pretty 'for real' to me," Mom says, and calls Dad and me to the table.

Will scoffs at this. "The feminazis? They're just bluffing."

"Enough! Where did you learn that word?" Dad shoots daggers at Will with his eyeballs, and my brother slides gingerly into his chair as if it were made of dynamite.

"This is what I was talking about last week when I told you both to stay out of it," Dad says. "It's national news now. No one even knew this town existed last week."

I can barely breathe as we pass around the pasta, making small talk as we eat. Will drones on about the tournament this weekend, and whether Ben and the guys can pull off a win without Dooney and Deacon. Mom is taking off work tomorrow afternoon to drive us up to Des Moines for the first game of the tournament. Coach Lewis is letting us out of practice early so we can get there on time. Dad will still be working tomorrow night, but he'll watch the game on TV.

"It won't matter who wins," says Dad, cutting through Will's chatter. "The only thing anyone will remember when the Buccs are mentioned now is the Coral Sands rape case." He shakes his head and carries his plate to the sink before grabbing a beer from the fridge and settling onto the couch in the living room.

I stay in the kitchen for as long as I can, helping Mom with the dishes and putting the leftovers away. When everything is finished, I stand by the little desk near the island pretending to fiddle with the printer, waiting until Dad has fast-forwarded through a commercial break on the buddy-cop drama he watches. One of the two is a robot. Or an alien? I can't remember. They have a problem understanding each other every week that leads to a life-or-death moment. They always survive by learning something new about the other one.

As soon as I hear a high-tech shootout happening, I slip through the living room as quickly and quietly as I can, dodging Dad's eyes.

When I get to my room I close the door behind me with a quiet click and lean against it for a few minutes. I wish there were a way I could explain to Dad why I had to go against his advice, why I had to steer directly toward the collision.

Sometimes, I think Dad and I are standing at the edge of different continents, so far apart that we can't even see each other. He felt so close on Monday morning. How does this happen?

How do we drift so far, so fast?

Ben is waiting for us in the parking lot on Friday morning. Will whoops and high-fives him about the big game tonight. The varsity team leaves right after lunch today to get to Des Moines, check into their hotel, and get warmed up at Wells Fargo Arena.

"Brought my rally socks." Will grins, pulling up his jeans to show the black tube socks he's wearing.

"You guys are coming up tonight?" Ben asks.

"This might be the last game of your junior year," I say. "Of course we'll be there."

"Shut up!" Will shouts, alarmed. "They're going to the championship tomorrow. Don't junk it up."

Ben laughs. "That's the spirit."

Will bumps his fist and bounds off to class.

"Do we have to go in there?" I ask.

"Any other day I'd say no"—Ben puts his arms around my waist and pulls me in to him—"but I can't miss class, or I can't play."

I put my arms around his neck. I needed this. I'm terrified of walking inside. Ben must sense this without my saying so. "Nobody knows," he whispers. "There's no way they could."

"What if somebody saw me in the parking lot yesterday," I ask, "talking to Ms. Speck?"

"Coincidence," he says.

I laugh nervously in an attempt to keep the fear at bay. He takes my hand and I walk inside with Ben, the honorable Buccaneer.

When I step into the geology room, Rachel is mid-screech, telling Reggie and Kyle to shut up. "You're both *freaking morons*," she hisses.

Christy jumps in, too. "Shut this crap down *now*."

Reggie winds up to pitch more of whatever he's slinging, but sees Ben coming toward him and leans back in his seat. Ben gives him and Kyle a chin flip and a 'sup, sliding into the desk behind me.

Reggie and Kyle glare at me, their eyes drilling into the back of my head. Hostile curiosity is heavy, and hot. I glance over at Lindsey. "What is going on?" I whisper.

She shakes her head. "Just forget it," she says. Her smile is sincere, but short.

As soon as the tone sounds, Mr. Johnston collects our permission slips for the field trip next week. Counting through the growing pile of crumpled yellow paper, he stops at Reggie's row and looks up.

"Missing one here," he says.

"Can't go." Reggie's arms are crossed.

"How come?" asks Mr. Johnston. "It's part of your grade for the class."

"Can't risk it."

"What?"

"Don't wanna get accused of *raping* somebody on the bus."

The air is sucked out of the room. Mr. Johnston stares Reggie down. "You're out of line."

"Am I?" Reggie says, all swagger. "Can't be too careful these days. Never know when some girl's gonna get wasted and throw herself at you. If I can't help myself, I don't wanna wind up arrested."

Mr. Johnston tosses the pile of permission slips on his desk, then whips off his glasses. "You done?" he asks Reggie.

"Just sayin.'" Reggie slouches in his seat, a smug bandit pleased with derailing the train.

"What exactly are you 'just saying,' Mr. Grant? That if a drunk girl approached you on a school bus, you'd take advantage of her?"

If the room was silent before, it's a sterile vacuum now. I dare a quick glance behind me. Reggie squirms, then shrugs. *I don't know. I don't wanna know. I want you off my back.*

"A shrug." Mr. Johnston's voice is an arrow making its mark. "Am I to interpret that as 'you don't know' or 'you don't care'?"

"Jeez. Let's just drop it," Reggie says quietly, buckling.

"No, no." Mr. Johnston doesn't drift an inch. "You brought it up. You decided geology class was the proper forum for this. So let's talk about it. It sounds like you're saying that if a drunk girl approaches you you'd be unable to 'help yourself.' Am I to understand this means you'd be unable to stop yourself from having sex with her, whether she consented or not?"

"That's . . . that's not what I said." Reggie's voice is shaky now.

"But in this scenario, the young woman is drunk, correct? I believe the word you used was 'wasted.'" Mr. Johnston reaches over and grabs the yellow wad of permission slips, holding them up and addressing the entire class. "If a female student is 'wasted,' is she capable of giving her consent?"

"No." Lindsey says this firmly and loudly. We all gasp for breath as if a hatch has been blown open and oxygen has once more flooded the room.

Mr. Johnston puts his glasses back on. He goes to the

whiteboard and picks up a marker. "I have a hypothesis that there may be other choices to make if you come into contact with a young woman who is 'wasted' and 'throwing herself at you,' Mr. Grant. What else might you do in that situation—besides have sex with her?"

"I dunno." Reggie mutters this, staring at his desk.

"Oh, c'mon. You're a bright kid. B average. Doing pretty well in my class. I'll bet you can think of one other option." Mr. Johnston waits at the whiteboard, his eyes locked on Reggie. After a moment, he says, "Okay, I'll open this up. Let's help Reggie out. What else could you do if you're at a party, or out somewhere, and you come across a wasted young woman? And for now, I just want to hear from the guys."

"Get her some water." Ben says this right behind my head, and his voice makes my whole body relax.

"Excellent." Mr. Johnston writes *1. Water* on the board. "What else?"

Wyatt's hand flies up across the room. "A ride home."

"Good thinking." Mr. Johnston's marker is squeaking away. "Other ideas?"

Guys all over the room start speaking up—some of whom I've never heard say a word during class before.

Find her friends.

Call her parents.

Get her a pillow.

Some Advil.

Make sure she has a safe place to sleep.

Don't let her drive.

A list soon fills the board. "Thank you, men. All excellent alternatives to rape. There's one other," Mr. Johnston says. "Not as kind as the others, perhaps, but at least not harmful." He adds the words *Just walk away* to the list, then turns back to face the class.

"Got the idea, Reggie?"

Another shrug.

"Sorry, didn't hear you," Mr. Johnston says.

"Yeah. Got it."

"Glad to hear it." Mr. Johnston puts the cap on the marker and places it back in the silver tray. "Words have *meanings*. When we call something a theory in science, it *means something*. Reggie, when you say that you 'can't help yourself' if a girl is wasted, that means something, too. You're saying that our natural state as men is 'rapist.'"

Mr. Johnston leans toward us on the lectern at the front of the room. "That's not okay with me, Reggie." He points at the list on the whiteboard. "That's not okay with the rest of this class, either."

Mr. Johnston walks over to his desk and pulls open a drawer. He takes out a new yellow permission slip and walks it down the aisle, placing it on Reggie's desk. "You have until Monday to get this back to me."

Just before the tone sounds to end fourth period, Coach Sanders announces over the intercom that the bus for the varsity players will be parked behind the school, out of view of the news vans.

In addition to the satellite trucks, there are now a handful of protestors standing fifty feet from the front doors of the school. Several of them are wearing pink masks. Most are holding signs:

COME FORWARD

YOU TELL OR WE WILL

SHE NEEDS YOUR HELP

When we get our food, Ben walks with me to a table in the back of the cafeteria. None of the senior players left campus for lunch today. They have to be on the bus for Des Moines in thirty minutes.

With everybody here, it's crowded. The cheerleaders are in uniform and keyed up. The drill team is doing the "cup thing" with their plastic water tumblers, beating out a rhythm that echoes across the room, adding to the general pandemonium. Christy and Rachel are already sitting with Lindsey at the end of the table. We're all wearing our blue BUCCANEER hoodies today. Even in the face of everything else going on, we want to show solidarity.

As Ben slides his tray across from LeRon and Kyle, he pulls out my chair. "You guys ready?" he asks.

There's no answer. Both of them continue shoveling in bites of cheeseburger. Finally, Kyle glances up at Ben and nods. "As we'll ever be."

The images of Kyle and LeRon pointing and laughing in the video play over and over in my head, but I try to smile and force myself to speak. "Are you nervous? I always get so nervous before a game."

LeRon looks at me, then shakes his head and goes back to his food.

Rachel sees this, and jumps in. "Yeah, me too. Crazy butter-flies."

"We'll be there cheering you on," says Christy.

LeRon looks up at me. "You coming, too?"

Big smile. Everything's fine. "You bet."

He glances at Ben, then back at me. "Take good notes."

"What?" I ask.

Kyle smirks. "So you can write your report about the whole thing."

My stomach drops and I see Ben's face turn to stone. "What the fuck is that supposed to mean?"

"Aw, c'mon, man." LeRon drops back in his chair, dragging a couple fries through ketchup. "Your girl can't let this go."

I glance down the table. Cheerleaders, drillers, benchwarm-ers, starters, Reggie slouched at the end, laughing into his tray. Every face straight ahead. Every eye turned toward me. Side-ways. Watching, without seeing me. Listening, without hearing me. They've already made up their minds. I realize I'm still holding a turkey sandwich I can't imagine ever bringing to my lips.

Ben, Rachel, and Christy all explode at the same time.

Shut the fuck up.

Leave her alone.

You don't know what the hell you're talking about.

There's an argument I can't hear, then a silence that is deafening. In the awkward moments that follow, I glance across the room and see Phoebe, looking over at our table. She's sitting with another cheerleader named Amy. Dooney always used to joke that Amy was only on the squad because they needed a "solid base." Phoebe gives me a shy smile. I nod once and look away, wondering if she's heard the rumors, too.

Before Ben gets on the bus he tells me not to worry. He gives Christy a high five, Rachel a fist bump, and Lindsey a smile, then pulls me aside and gives me a hug.

"You're finally getting out of here," I say. "At least for a night."

"Get packed," he says with a wink. "Pretty soon you're coming, too."

He kisses me, then climbs onto the bus. The trace of his lips lingers for a long time, even after the bus of Buccaneers has rolled away from the news vans and protestors toward the tournament, effectively trading one battle for another.

thirty-eight

I WAS WRONG about the satellite trucks.

When we pull into the parking lot at Wells Fargo Arena in Des Moines, there's a whole area for news vans, and it's packed. There must be thirty of them, lined up from all over.

Iowa basketball is a big deal—even if you're a high school team. I "knew" this, but I didn't really *know* this until we file inside the arena. It's massive. It could seat the population of my entire town, and still have room for another four thousand people.

With twenty thousand people in the same room, it's hard to stand out. For the first time in a couple weeks, it's nice to feel invisible. No one cares who I am. No one is looking at me—even sideways. As we fight toward our seats through the throngs of people, I'm almost giddy with relief that no one is staring after me. Lindsey notices this, too.

"So weird not to see Sloane Keating lurking somewhere," she says.

"Keep an eye open," I warn her. "She might jump out at any moment." Lindsey laughs, and suddenly it feels like the last two weeks are a bad dream. Rachel and Christy are as wound up as Will, each of them talking over the other. Will drapes his arm around Rachel's shoulder every now and then to see if he can get away with acting like "a baller." Rachel jabs her fingernail into his ribs every time he says that or refers to himself as "Pistol," and takes to calling him "Pipsqueak" instead.

When Mom leads us down toward the court, instead of up toward the cheap seats, Will almost has a coronary. "Wait, *what*?" he asks, grabbing Mom's arm.

"Surprise!" she shouts. "Adele got three extra court-side seats because she's a player's mom, and I bought two more so we can all sit close."

Will may have shed actual tears, but I can't be sure because he was screaming so loudly that we all had to turn away.

Adele waves us toward our seats in the second row, just behind our home bench. She's dressed head to toe in Buccaneer blue and gold. Her brassy auburn curls are piled on top of her head in a gold lamé ribbon. She has even painted her lips blue with some sort of lipstick so opaque that it makes me immediately concerned about the amount of chemical coloring she will ingest during the game.

Before long, Phoebe is flying over our heads, her perfect smile frozen in place. The Buccs are announced one by one, and pandemonium breaks loose.

From the very first moment at tip-off, the game is physical. The other team has a couple of burly forwards, and their defense is deadly. Even if Dooney had been present to nail jump shots over their heads, we'd have had to fight hard. LeRon gets into foul trouble early and Coach Sanders has to rotate several other guys in and out.

Through it all, Ben is unflappable, studying the court as he brings the ball down, slowing it up at the top of the key, pointing and directing, calling plays, setting picks. He sees the whole picture every time. When nerves cause a couple of the other guys to make bad passes or Kyle to miss a shot, he shouts encouragement.

Control. Stamina. Dexterity.

Some things never change.

At the half, we are down by only two, and as the guys head into the locker room, Ben turns and points directly at me and his mom. We all cheer our heads off, Adele leading the charge, then digging into her giant purse and passing fruit snacks and candy bars down the row.

"You think of everything," Mom tells her.

"Had a coupon," Adele says in a low voice. "But don't tell Ben."

A man with dark hair in a navy-blue suit sitting in front of us turns around, smiling at Adele. "That your son?" he asks.

"Sure is," she says.

He extends a hand to her. "David Langman," he says. "Duke basketball. We've had our eye on Ben for the past few weeks. Think he could make a great addition to our program."

Adele is speechless for a moment, then digs into her bag for more candy, offering David Langman a Twix bar. His laugh is knowing and kind. "I'm good," he says, declining.

"I'm sorry!" Adele drops the candy bar back into her purse. "It's just so exciting to think that he might be able to get a . . . scholarship?"

"You should be excited," David says with a smile. "We had our eye on another player, John Doone." His face turns somber. "Guess he got mixed up in this whole scandal at a party a couple weeks back? Anyway, we aren't looking to bring on anybody who would be a PR problem," he explains. "Want to keep the focus solely on basketball. Ben has great court sense and a solid handle on the ball. Glad to see he kept his nose clean."

He hands Adele his card. "I'm going to see if I can fight the lines at the bathroom. We'll be in touch."

Rachel and Christy go with Will to get Cokes, following the Duke scout into the stands. Adele sinks back down onto her seat, staring at the business card between her glossy blue fingernails. When she looks up, I see tears in her eyes.

"Are you okay?" I smile, and put an arm around her. She nods, glancing up toward the bright lights on the ceiling, trying to keep her eyes from spilling down her cheeks.

"It's just—" She fans her hand in front of her face. "He's

worked so hard for this. It's exactly what he's always wanted."

This last sentence reaches a cracked falsetto and releases tiny tears of joy. Mom hugs Adele from one side, and I lean in from the other. A dance mix booms over the loudspeakers and Adele springs up from between me and Mom, hooting, "Go, Big Blue!" as the drill team takes center court. They've adjusted the spacing for their routine, covering Stacey's absence completely.

"It's like she never even existed," says Lindsey.

I nod, but don't know what to say. Her comment is true, but it also reminds me that for the past hour, I haven't thought about Stacey, or the Crisis in Coral Sands even once.

For a little while, I was just a girl watching her boyfriend play basketball—excited and cheering—and wishing things could always be just that simple.

When the second half starts, Ben sinks two threes early, and we keep a lead of six points for a while. The other team is ferocious. They have desperation on their side, and finally, with five minutes to go, LeRon fouls out. Four minutes later, it's a tie ball game.

With twenty seconds winding down on the clock, Ben brings the ball down, passing out to Reggie, who tries to drive in for a layup but has to toss the ball back to Ben at the top of the key. Ben tries again, threading an expert pass to Kyle. Kyle can't get clear either and passes back up to him.

Five, four, three . . .

As the whole arena thunders with a countdown, I see Ben

square up and let fly with a jump shot that seems to sail in slow motion toward the basket, the *thwfft* of the net drowned out by the buzzer and the roar of twenty thousand people.

Almost single-handedly, my boyfriend wins the game.

As we leap from the bleachers and run onto the court, I see Adele spring forward into David Langman's arms, smearing blue lipstick across the shoulder of his suit. Ben is nearly tackled by the entire team in the middle of the court, but he somehow stays upright and fights his way over to me.

"There you are," he yells as he sweeps me up in the sweatiest, smelliest, most perfect embrace I have ever known. His lips find mine at center court, the strobes of a hundred photographers, flashing in purple bursts through my eyelids. Ben promises to text me as soon as he gets onto the bus, then is hustled toward the locker room on Kyle's and Reggie's shoulders.

The cameras are in full force outside the arena, too, but not all of the journalists are covering the game. As Mom and Adele push through the doors that lead into the parking lot, we are greeted by a line of anchors, using a huge crowd behind them as a backdrop for live reports. Police are roping off a walkway in the middle of what is now a full-on media circus. The handful of protestors from the school parking lot has quintupled in size, their faces covered in pink masks, their voices raised in a chant:

Not a victory for the victim!
Not a victory for the victim!

Lindsey catches my eye. "Guess not everyone has forgotten," she says.

Far from it.

Here in the parking lot, beneath the glare of the camera lights, Stacey Stallard is the main attraction.

thirty-nine

FRESH OUT OF the shower after the game, I open the bathroom door to air out the steam. I'm wrapping my wet hair in a towel when I hear the words drift down the hall.

"Get a rooooooooom!"

I have heard those words from that voice before. I never wanted to hear them again.

Almost before I realize what's happening, I'm throwing Will's bedroom door wide-open.

"How the hell did you find that?"

He jumps and slams the cover of his laptop, spinning around. I swing his door closed behind me as quietly as I can. I don't need Dad coming to investigate.

Will's eyes are wide and looking anywhere but at me. "What? I don't know! What are you talking about?"

I scramble across the piles on the floor of his room and flip the computer open again. There is the frozen image of the white couch, the blurred bodies of Dooney, Stacey, and the rest. My hand is trembling as I point to the screen.

"Where did you find this?"

He crosses his arms and sets his jaw. "I just . . . found it."

I turn around and head toward the door. "Fine. You can tell Mom where—"

"Wait!" His whisper is a hurricane, angry with a silent plea at the center.

I pause, hands on my hips. Will growls quietly under his breath. "Fine," he says. "Tyler sent it to me."

"Where'd he get—"

"I don't *know*. Jesus. He wouldn't tell me."

I shake my head, chewing on my front lip. "What site is it on?"

"It's not on a site," he says. "He emailed it to me."

"Delete it," I say. "Now."

"No way. *You* saw it."

I sputter, eyes wide. "What? How do you know that?"

"Oh, c'mon, I'm a freshman, not an idiot."

"Debatable. Explain."

"Everybody knows you were the one who went to Ms. Speck," he says.

"And why the hell would everybody know that?"

"It's not my fault that you were out in the parking lot talking to her and that reporter. The school has windows, you know."

"Fine," I say. "You want to watch it? Let's watch it. The whole thing."

He blinks at me, his cheeks flushed from the heat of my rage. Slowly, he turns around and taps the spacebar.

The video I never wanted to see again flickers to life once more. Will sits in his desk chair, and I sink down beside him on the corner of his bed.

Rape and pillage, babeeey.

Is she drunk or dead?

I got something that'll wake her up!

Trashy.

This time I watch the corners of the screen instead of the horrible thing happening at the center, and I realize there are more people in the room than I initially noticed. The recessed lighting in the ceiling has a spotlight effect. There are a lot more people walking in and out of those bright bursts than I saw the first time. They're laughing, drinking, making out, playing beer pong on the other side of the room.

The closer you look, the more you see.

Every now and then, a group wanders by the corner of the couch that Randy is filming. They shout or point or laugh.

Dooney. Then Deacon. Then Greg. Then Dooney again. Reggie laughing. Randy shouting.

Will gasps.

I glance at him as he watches the guys paw at Stacey,

climbing on and off her. Her head flops toward the camera, her eyes roll back in their sockets. Every now and then she grunts or groans. As Will watches, his face, set like stone only moments ago, is crumbling—first the contraction of disbelief, then the crinkle of discomfort, the wide smooth planes of shock, and now the heaviness of disgust.

"No more," he whispers. He reaches up to pause the playback only a few moments past the place where Lindsey and I called it quits.

For the second time in a week, I grab his arm, stopping his wrist over the keyboard. I push his chin back toward the screen.

"No. We have to watch, Will." My voice chokes with tears, and I see his eyes are shining and full in the glow of the laptop. "We have to look," I say. "We have to see what happened, so we can tell the truth about it. Stacey can barely remember. We have to help her. Not being able to say no isn't the same as saying yes." I look back at the screen as the video continues. "She didn't deserve this."

Will nods. He swipes at his eyes. "Nobody does," he whispers. "Nobody deserves this."

I ask him who he recognizes. I can't make out for sure who everybody is. We point at different people, trying to identify everyone we can see as the video ends. A split second before the playback freezes, someone steps in front of the camera. He's facing away from the lens, watching Greg and Dooney, who are still taking turns on top of Stacey. The guy stands under one of the recessed lights so close to Randy that you can't see anything but the back of his head. The iPhone tries to refocus, going completely blurry, then zeroing in on the closest point beneath the light.

The thing nearest to the camera happens to be this guy's left ear, glowing under the halogen bulb directly over his head. He's so tall, I can see he's ducking a little to avoid scraping the low basement ceiling, and as the focus snaps sharp I see something else, too: an inch-long scar that I'd recognize anywhere.

forty

THIS VIDEO DOESN'T show you everything.

For instance, you never see the face of the young man who has the scar behind his ear. You never hear his voice. You don't know how long he's been standing there, watching what is happening on the couch, or what he says after the camera is turned off. You don't know if he's walking downstairs to say good-bye and stumbling upon the scene at that moment, or if he's been there the entire time, looking on behind Randy, a silent witness.

This video can't show you the face of the young woman who *knows* that scar because she inflicted it. You can't hear the strangled cry that escapes my lips. There's no shot of me crumbling to the floor of Will's bedroom or of Will racing to get my mom. He does his best to explain to her about the video, but he doesn't notice the scar on the screen. Neither does Mom. Neither of them look closely enough to see more, and I cannot find the words to tell them.

No footage exists of me crying myself to sleep that night or of the tears that begin to flow again when I wake in the gray light of Saturday. I know I can't return to Des Moines for the championship game, and Mom is so concerned about me she decides we will all stay home. Will watches the Buccaneers lose by six points on television and comes to my room to tell me the news. He finds me holding a piece of coral from my nightstand, desperate to go back to that day in September when Ben was only a childhood memory in my mind and a wish in my heart.

This video can't explain to you how I cursed myself for falling in love. It could never show how much easier it would've been to simply keep nodding at Ben as we passed in the halls. It would've been easier to never have known the warmth of his love—the taste of his lips on mine, his body tangled up in my own—than to know all of those things, and then see him in the final frame on that screen.

The video doesn't show you the texts I get that afternoon from Ben as he rides home on the bus from Des Moines. It can't reveal all of the promises that are swept away, or the hope that is buried once more beneath layers of lies, lost in the sediment of deceit.

In that sense, this video doesn't really show you anything at all.

It *does* show you that my boyfriend was present in the room while his friends assaulted a girl he could've helped, but chose not to.

And in that sense, this video shows you everything you need to know.

forty-one

"THERE YOU ARE."

I drove to Ben's house the next day propelled by an iron-clad disbelief that melts into rage the moment I hear these words. The garage door is open, and he's standing in the driveway shooting baskets.

He walks toward me slowly, the ball tucked under his arm. He leans in to kiss me, but stops. My eyes are puffy and blood-shot, leaking tears again now that I see him. For a moment, I wonder if I can bury this deep inside me and act as if nothing is wrong—keep it forever hidden from view by the force of my will alone.

"I'm sorry you lost." These are the only words I can muster

before my voice cracks and I cover my face with my hands, sobbing.

I feel his arms wrap around me. His lips on my hair.

Is this the last time?

He walks me up to the garage and grabs a bottle of Smartwater off a shelf between Saran Wrap and Sticky Tack.

"Hey, it's cool," he whispers. "Don't cry."

He twists off the cap and hands me the water, smiling his Irresistible Grin. "Duke is still gonna make me an offer. Silver lining, right? We're gonna get outta here."

"I can't come with you."

He frowns. "What are you talking about?"

"The video. I saw it all. To the end."

His face goes slack. "What?"

"Will found it. It's . . . out there."

"So? What's that got to do with us?"

The tears start again, streaming quietly this time. A vise on my throat makes it difficult to speak, but I force myself to say the word: "Everything."

He tosses the basketball into a bin by the rec room door. "What are you talking about?"

"You're in the video."

He freezes for a split second, then reaches for me, trying to wrap his arms around me. "I promise," he says. "I was only there to say good-bye and I—"

"Don't." I am crying so hard I can barely speak. I push a hand into his chest, holding him back.

"It's no big deal. I just couldn't—"

"Stop! You couldn't what? Be honest? Tell me the truth? Couldn't help Stacey?"

He drops back like I've punched him in the stomach. "That's not fair. You know that's not fair."

"And what happened to Stacey, while you watched, was that fair? That I loved you while you lied to my face? Is that fair?"

"Listen to me. I'm sorry. I didn't want to lie—not to you, not to anyone—but we have to keep this quiet."

"No. We don't. We can't." I shake my head. "You know who was there."

"We'd had a lot to drink."

"You can tell the police what you remember. You can be a witness."

He laughs bitterly. "Witness? Against Dooney? And Deacon? I'd get run out of town."

"Isn't that what you want?" I snap. "To get out of here?"

"Not like that, Kate. I want you with me. Look! *We* can get out of here. Look at this. Look at me." He turns around sweeping his hands toward Adele's shelving, the garage packed to the rafters. "I can get away from this. Duke is happening. And you can come with me."

"But who would I be coming with?" I ask. "Who are you? A guy who lies? Who lets his buddies get away with this? A guy who just stood by and watched?"

"No!" Frantic he grabs both my hands in his. "You *know*

me. That's not who I am. I told Dooney it couldn't ever happen again. That it wasn't cool."

"And then you helped him delete the evidence?"

"I told you, that was just the pictures of the booze."

"Why should I believe you?" This slips out quickly and softly, more of a statement than a question.

He walks away from me in a fast circle, running his hand through his hair. When he turns back, his eyes are flashing. "Because it's me! Because I love you."

"Just not enough to tell me the truth?" I ask. "What if you'd come downstairs and it had been me on that couch?"

He yells when I say this, kicking a blue bin of paper grocery sacks, nested inside each other like Russian dolls. "How can you say that? That would never be you."

"Why not?"

"How can you even compare yourself to her? Stacey is so messed up. She's an alcoholic loser who's been a slut since seventh grade when she—"

"Was my friend," I yell, cutting him off; the tears are fresh and hot and endless. "When she was my friend."

Ben looks down at me, suddenly exhausted. In his eyes is a fear I've never seen before. "Please, Kate. If you tell the police I was there, they'll want to see that video, and if I get hauled in to witness at the trial Duke won't give me an offer. You heard what that scout told my mom yesterday. I have to keep my nose clean—stay away from this."

"That hacker group has the video already," I remind him. "If we don't come forward, they'll release it on Monday. Everyone will know anyway."

"Let 'em release it. It's the back of my head for a split second. Who's gonna tell them? Who's gonna know?"

"I will," I whisper. "I'll know."

I collapse onto a nearby step stool. Ben drops to his knees in front of me, one hand on both of my thighs, as if he can hold me here, hold us together, keep me from drifting away.

"What do you want me to do?" he asks.

"Come with me. Tell the police about the video. Help me identify who was there."

"I can't. Even if Coach didn't cut me from the team next year, how would I ever face the guys again?"

"How can you face them now?" I ask. "After what you saw them do?"

"Kate, I only want one thing. *Us.* Somewhere bigger. Somewhere better. We're so close. We can have it. Together. All we have to do is get through this."

"By lying?"

"By not saying anything. Please," he begs.

"I can't do that."

Ben's eyes fill up as I say this. "So what? I go with you to the police or you're gonna break up with me?"

I shake my head, and a sob escapes my lips. I reach out and place my hand on his cheek. "No, Ben. I'm breaking up with you now. If you come to the police with me, then maybe we can find a way to be friends."

He swipes at the tears rolling down his face. "But I love you, Kate."

"Not enough," I choke. "Not enough."

He calls after me as I struggle down the drive on shaking legs. Learning how to walk away uses a different set of muscles, new ones that I haven't yet developed. The task is slow and arduous. I force myself forward. I don't look back.

I keep hoping he'll run after me, but he doesn't, and I realize that everything is past tense now.

This is how an era ends.

Iowa was once an ocean.

I was once the girl you loved.

As I crank the key in my old truck, I hear a roar to equal the engine and turn in time to see Ben ram his shoulder full force into the first of Adele's shelving units. It teeters for a moment, then topples over onto the one behind it, sending a spray of bottles and cans, bags and blister packs in every direction. A domino effect levels the stockpile in a matter of seconds.

Sometimes, change happens over eons. Other times, in the blink of an eye.

I pull away from the curb. My final glimpse is of Ben, holding his head in his hands, weeping in the middle of the wreckage.

When I get home, Dad is out puttying and painting the trim around the front door. I'm crying so hard that I trip on one of the stairs that leads up to the porch from the driveway. Dad hurries to help me up, sitting next to me and pulling me against his shoulder.

"Hey there," he whispers. "What's the matter, Katie?"

I hold him tight and sob into his flannel work shirt. I want to tell him everything, to explain, somehow, that I will never be the same.

Instead, I sob the only words that I can find over and over:

I hurt my friend.

I hurt my friend.

I hurt my friend.

forty-two

THE DETECTIVE IS a woman.

I don't know why this surprises me, but it does. She asks us if we want some water while Will turns on his laptop. I nod, and she leaves the room for a moment, returning with two white Styrofoam cups filled from the drinking fountain in the hall.

She notices me eyeing the camera mounted on the ceiling in the corner of the room. "Just a procedural thing," she explains. "We tape all of our interviews."

Yesterday, when I got home from Ben's, I told Mom and Dad everything. We showed them the video. I told Dad that I knew he didn't want us to get involved and started to explain why I had to. He stopped me with a raised hand, closed Will's laptop, and picked up the phone to call Deputy Jennings.

I texted Ben this morning on the way to the station. I told him what time we'd be here and asked him to join us. Will and the detective start and stop their way through the video, pausing it every so often as he points out people, and she writes down their names. My phone vibrates in my hand, and I glance at the screen, swiping open the message with my thumb to reveal Ben's response:

> **I love you. Please don't go.**

My eyes fill up and I hear the video come to an end.

"Any idea who this guy is?" the detective asks Will, pointing at the screen. As my brother turns to look at me, she follows suit.

"His name is Ben Cody," I say.

"You sure?" she asks. "Just the back of his head."

"He has a scar behind his ear." I point it out on the screen.

The detective squints as she leans in. *The closer you look, the more you see.*

"Oh yeah," she says, writing down his name. "Must know him pretty well to catch that."

"We've been friends since the day I gave it to him."

"When was that?" she asks with a smile.

"We were five." I can't keep the tears out of my voice. The detective looks up at me, then pulls a tissue out of a box on the table and hands it over.

"You're doing the right thing," she says.

"Doesn't feel like it." I wipe my eyes. I am so tired of crying.

She nods, reading back over her list and flipping to a new page in her steno pad. "Sometimes, that's how you know," she says without looking up. "That's how you know."

forty-three

THERE IS A difference between rejection and betrayal.

To be turned down is a sting that fades away—a scratch that burns, but scabs. You can hypothesize why it didn't work out, gather evidence, and formulate a theory that explains all of the reasons it wasn't right—or simply chalk it up as "never meant to be." After some time, when the scratch heals, it disappears completely.

The thing about betrayal is that it cannot be explained. It would be easier if Ben were evil, I suppose, an angry guy who kicked dogs and sold drugs and hated all women everywhere.

But he isn't.

In the weeks that followed our visit to the detective, that's how almost everyone in town was painted. Adele and Ben, Stacey and Phoebe, Dooney and Deacon, me and Will—anyone who'd ever worn Buccaneer Blue—we were all reduced to a cautionary tale again and again, on CNN and Facebook, on thousands of blogs and talk shows, our humanity siphoned off, drained away 140 characters at a time. In the end, you might have forgotten there were any people besides John Doone and Deacon Mills who lived in Coral Sands at all.

By Sunday evening, all four pleas were changed to guilty, and a list of new subpoenas had been issued with Ben Cody's name at the top. On Monday morning, UltraFEM released a statement instead of the video, thanking those "brave enough to come forward." The world at large never had to see those four minutes that changed everything.

Those of us who did tried to make sense of it any way we could. Some wrote it off as boys being boys. People who'd never even been to Coral Sands decided our whole town was evil. Others chalked it up to a mix of hormones and alcohol. They said that this is what happens when teenagers drink. Maybe they're right about some teenagers. Still there were plenty of us at that party who were just as drunk as our friends in the basement, who could never have imagined the things that happened that night.

I was one of them.

I can't understand being drunk enough to see that go on and ignore it. How Ben could be in that room and not speak up, I will never know. What I do know is that Ben loved me, but it didn't keep him from lying to me. One day, I hope to forgive him, but I'll never be able to be with him again.

The hardest part about betrayal is that as bad as it hurts, it doesn't stop you from loving the one who lied. In the days and weeks that followed, I was constantly surprised to find that no one had told my heart to cut it out. I kept remembering Ben's touch and missing his Irresistible Grin. Just as I hadn't been able to choose who I fell in love with, I couldn't choose when to stop caring for him, either. The heart is a muscle, it would seem, both literally and figuratively. It does some things like beating and loving from memory, completely on its own.

By lunch on Monday, I had become persona non grata, as invisible as Phoebe and despised as Stacey—a pariah, just like Alfred Wegener. Christy and Rachel were polite and smiled from a distance, but drifted as far away as possible. I kept forgetting that Ben would no longer be sitting behind me in geology and not to look for him on the senior staircase. When he saw me, he would nod, then look away, which was even worse than if he had ignored me completely. Lindsey sat with me at lunch, and on the bus en route to the class field trip the next Friday. To her credit, she really tried, but it's hard to talk to someone who is always on the verge of tears, and that afternoon I found myself standing alone in the Devonian Fossil Gorge at the edge of the spillway.

I knelt down and ran my fingers along those ancient shapes in the limestone. I tried to imagine these sea lilies and brachiopods, teaming with life in the shallow soup 375 million years ago, but I found that both observation and imagination have their limits. Iowa was once an ocean, yes, but I will never know it any other way than landlocked hills that end too soon and waves of windswept cornfields, rolling out in all directions, as far as my eyes can see.

Even when presented with the evidence itself, there are some phenomena that I will never grasp completely.

To catch the one who loves you in a lie leaves a wound that never fully goes away. I will never understand how the Ben I knew so well could deceive me so completely. I can only say that his feet were in the wrong place at the wrong time, and he went down hard.

That day, in the warm sun, surrounded by the solid proof of an ancient realm, I let go of forming theories, I only know that, given enough time, this wound will scar over. The layers of my life will slowly cover and fill the gulf cleft through my heart. But deep in the bedrock of who I am is a record of these things that I will carry with me, a new map whose boundaries have forever altered the way I view the world.

forty-four

ABOUT A MONTH after the geology field trip, I am changing out of my plaid skirt and navy vest in the Saint Mary's locker
room when it happens:

I catch sight of the deodorant at the bottom of my gym bag.
Stuffing the duffel into my locker, I think about Adele rushing
off to stock up on Right Guard.

And I think about the look on Ben's face.

And I smile.

It doesn't last long. A split second later, Olivia Jaynes comes
bounding in with her crazy Afro in a sweatband. She is a disco
dance party looking for a place to happen and, for reasons yet
to be revealed, calls me "Sweet Pea." In the month since Will

and I changed schools, Olivia has been my welcome wagon, tour guide, and activity director.

"Move it, Sweet Pea," she barks.

I pinch her at the waist and she yelps, chasing me onto the field.

At this school, our coach is a guy, and our colors are burgundy and navy, but the line drills are the same. Coach Orson likes to see what he calls "go-getter initiative," and by that he means people who are on the field and running drills before practice officially begins. For the past few weeks, Olivia has made it her mission to ensure we're the first ones out of the gate.

Tomorrow we have our final game. It's been an okay season: six wins, four losses, one to Coral Sands. It was weird playing my old team, but I survived, and Lindsey came out to dinner with us afterward.

That was the night I found Dad in the kitchen. I had come down to get some water before I went to bed, and he was standing at the counter making his sandwiches for lunch the next day. He's been going in even earlier lately. The developer he works for let him take on a second crew so he could cover the tuition at Saint Mary's. We've cut back a lot, but he and Mom agreed that if we wanted to switch schools we could. Will wasn't thrilled about the uniforms, but the classes are smaller, and he likes his chances of making varsity as a sophomore next fall.

I slid my arms around Dad's waist and murmured "thank you" into his back. He turned around and put his hands on my shoulders.

"I love you," he said. "You're all right, Katie. You're all right."

For my dad, that's as close to "I'm proud of you" as we get, and even though so much has changed, I realized then that he was correct:

I *am* all right.

Sometimes, when change happens, you can't stop it or control it or direct it. You can only hang on for the ride.

Stacey's ride took her south. Mom ran into LeeAnne in the Walmart parking lot the week after we met with the detective. She was collecting empty boxes from the Dumpsters behind the store so she could pack up. Lawyers from as far away as New York tried to convince her to bring a civil suit for damages on Stacey's behalf, but she said she couldn't put her daughter through any more. What she could do was move to her sister's house in Nashville and put her daughter in a nearby charter school for visual arts. "I can wait tables anywhere," she told Mom. "There's nothing left for us here but heartache."

I never talked to Stacey after I went to the police. But the day she moved, Will got the mail and found a folded piece of paper with my name on it. There were no other words, only a pencil sketch of a beautiful mockingbird, the state bird of Tennessee, its feathers spread and majestic, head held high, flying toward a new horizon.

I watch as little news as possible these days, but sometimes it's hard to avoid. Sloan Keating is a regular analyst on CNN now, and just the other day, I saw her on a screen while I was in line at the dry cleaner. The judge went easy on Dooney, Deacon,

Randy, and Greg. Dooney's dad helped the prosecutor out of a messy divorce a few years back, and when the guys changed their pleas to guilty, he bargained down the charges. All four were sentenced to just under one year each. With good behavior, they might be out as early as September, and Coach Sanders is already talking about "second chances."

I haven't heard from Ben.

I don't expect to.

Every now and then I see him—down the aisle at Walmart or driving by on Oaklawn Avenue; in a town the size of Coral Sands, it's unavoidable.

Sometimes, I look at his Facebook page and wonder if we will ever speak again. Lindsey says that Duke is waiting until next season to give him a scholarship offer. I wonder if he blames me for the delay, and whether he ever thinks of me and smiles.

The topography of who I am is different now, but the continent of my heart will always bear a jagged edge, where once I knew the perfect fit of true connection. I used to wonder if I would ever fall in love and if the person who I loved would love me back.

Now I try my best not to consider the *if* and the *when*, but to stay focused on the here and now.

The crust of our earth is in constant motion. Scientists say that at some point in the next 250 million years, the continents will have fused back together again. There will be drift and disturbance—old oceans squeezed closed, and new ones

created. All of this tectonic upheaval will happen with no con-
sideration for the people on the surface of our world—supposing
our species is still around by then. Our planet is indifferent to
the life that it supports. The natural forces take their course
regardless of who is standing over the fault line or lying in the
path of the torrent. We feel a rumble now and then—a tiny seismic shift—a whispered reminder from the universe:

Given enough time, everything changes.

Maybe this sense of how fragile our connections are is what
makes us obsessed with saving them—writing them down, taking pictures, recording them in tweets, documenting them with
status updates and videos. It is clear to me now that when the
earth does move beneath our feet—when our hearts slam and
scrape and break apart—when we barely survive the flood, we
take precautions.

We try to hold on to the things we think will keep us safe
and maintain that place we can point to and say, *This is normal.*
Adele and her stockpile of provisions, Connie Bonine and her
storefront full of all that Willie left behind, Mom and her gallery wall, Dad and his antique flip-screen camera, the coral on
my nightstand: all of these are records of an era past; the sym-
bols we cling to that we might explain our present and chart
our changes; the fossils of a secret history we carry deep within
us, etched into the bedrock of our beings.

As I bend to touch the far goal line, I hear Olivia whoop for
me to hurry up, and I turn on every ounce of speed that I can
muster. By the center of the field, I've caught up with her, and as

the afternoon sun warms the crust of our slowly drifting continent, I push past my newfound friend.

Our teammates are all gathered now, cheering us on as we race the final fifty meters in a full-out sprint. I cross the goal line one hairsbreadth ahead of her. As we collapse onto the grass panting and laughing, I see a hawk soar high above us and feel a rush of gratitude for the knowledge that just this once we have escaped the gaze of a camera lens or a status update.

Some moments should only be recorded in our hearts.

acknowledgments

Thank you to Michael Bourret, the best agent there is, for steering this ship with a steady hand.

Thanks also to the incredible team at HarperTeen: Kristen Pettit, whose unwavering commitment to excellence makes me work harder; Jen Klonsky, for believing I'm up to the challenge; Elizabeth Lynch, for making shit happen; and Gina Rizzo, publicist extraordinaire. Michelle Taormina, your cover design is exquisite, and, Ulla Puggaard, your handlettering turns the whole thing up to eleven. Anne Heausler, this is the first time I've ever fallen in love with a copy editor. Thank you for your eyes, and your heart.

To the writer pals who text me back and keep me sane—especially Grant Sloss, Andrew Smith, A.S. King, John Corey Whaley, Francesco Sedita, Deb Caletti, and my West Coast YA/middle grade crew: Margaret Stohl, Melissa de la Cruz, Pseudonymous Bosch, Rachel Cohn, and Tom & Laura McNeal—I'd have never survived the last year without you.

Finally, there's family: Holly Goldberg Sloan and Alice Pope, your expertise on writing is certain and sure, but it's your wisdom about life that has changed mine forever. Jenny Janisko, you are always by my side, even a thousand miles away. Jason Press, you are a true brother. Caleb Hartzler, you show me how it's done every day with style and grace—my role model, through thick and (hopefully) thin.